THE RED BARN

L M WEST

Read more about the books at
www.lmwestwriter.co.uk

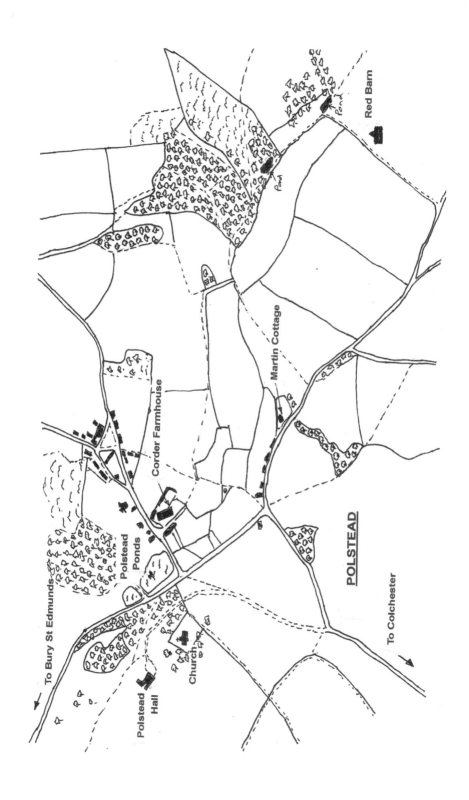

Red Barn

Pond

Pond

Martin Cottage

Corder Farmhouse

To Bury St Edmunds

Polstead
Ponds

Polstead
Hall

Church

POLSTEAD

To Colchester

PROLOGUE

This I remember. The earthiness of his fingertips as he holds the cherries, one after the other, to my lips. They are black, shining in the afternoon sun, like dark gems suspended on narrow green stems the colour of new shoots. I open my mouth and feel the weight of them as he places them, one by one, on my tongue. I close my eyes and bite. A slight pressure, the skin breaks, sweet salt, a tingling burst of sharpness, then the hard surface of the stone. Juice runs down my chin and, laughing, he puts up his neckerchief to wipe me clean. He offers me another, then another; I cannot have enough.

'*Oh, Maria.*' The way he says my name, soft and low, makes such sensations rise in me. I open my eyes. His face is close now, the corners of his blue eyes creased in a smile and his look is kind, loving, and full of desire.

'*Maria, my love.*'

At that moment I reach for him. He stretches his hand to me then his face seems to shimmer and fade.

'*William?*'

My fingers meet cold air. I cannot touch him anymore, I am gone from him.

I am Maria.

I am dead.

CHAPTER
ONE

They say a girl should be good and obedient, that she should first serve her father and then, later, her husband. So I was doomed from the start. For I was born to a better life and knew it from an early age.

My father caught moles for a living, did farm work to supplement our income, and we grew vegetables and fruit in our cottage garden to sell when money was short. Our cottage was simple, a hallway with rooms on either side, the same upstairs. My mother took in mending to earn a little money but Thomas Martin was the man who everyone called upon if they needed labouring done, for they knew he could always use a few extra coins and, though wiry, was strong and reliable. But he was not the father you see in picture books. He never dandled me on his bony knees or spoke soft words to me. It was he who rebuked and disciplined me and his narrow face never seemed soft but always hard and remote. He seemed to house a bitterness that all my childish sweetness could not change and I often wondered if he really wanted me or even loved me, his oldest daughter. Because of his distance, it was my mother whom I clung to. She was my shining light. She did not

3

raise her voice to me as Father did, merely spoke to me firmly when I lost my way or did not do as I was told. But if I fell, she held me, if I was hurt she consoled me and if I did wrong she protected me from Father's ire and, even then, I saw nothing but love in her eyes. She always wore a soft smile whenever she looked at her children; my older brother Thomas, named for our father, and the sisters who came in close succession after me. Then there was me, Maria, the changeling. My brother and sisters all had my father's pale hair, his long face, and his thin build. I was different, moulded in the image of my mother, all dark curls and flashing green eyes, my small body sturdy, my nature wilful.

BUT SO MANY children in quick succession took its toll and soon our cottage, like many, became weighed down by sorrow and loss. My brother Thomas, whom I followed around from the day I could walk unaided, died of consumption when I was only four. Little Hannah, birthed and buried within three short months, a sickly babe from the start. And then Jemima, born the year after Thomas died, her sunny smiles and inquisitive nature wiped out after only eleven short months. My mother spoke of them sometimes, when my father was not around, and I would watch her face become creased and pale with grief, her mind distant, as I tried in my childish way to comfort her. In truth, I remember little of my lost brothers and sisters. I was her only remaining child and she fixed all her love and attention on me. She would take me on her knee, tell me I was her best girl and that she would never leave me, and I believed her. The loss of the children came hard to Father and he turned in on himself even more, becoming so morose and silent that even my mother could not raise his spirits. Then, after many months of tiptoeing around him, his mood seemed to lift and he was brighter, occasionally smiling at me or ruffling my hair. It was at the same time that I began to hear my mother retching into the outside privy in the mornings, as she grew thin and pale, and her stomach began to bulge. I was only six years old, I did not understand why she was ill and the not-knowing hung heavy on my small shoulders. But one day she drew me to her side and held me tightly.

'Maria, I am to have another babe. A brother or sister for you to love. Is that not happy news?'

I nodded as I knew she wished me to but I could only watch as the weeks progressed and the life seemed to drain from her. I tried to be as good as I could for her, to help her as much as I was able, but she began to change. She no longer had time for me and would push me away when I tried to hold her, rubbing her brow with her hand, her eyes looking into the distance at something only she could see. She no longer felt like my mother, and I began to wonder what I had done to stop her loving me.

SHE WAS SWEEPING the floor when it began. She cried out and gripped her side and I looked up from where I was playing, frightened by the expression on her face. Her stomach was huge now, round and tight as a ball and it seemed to heave before my eyes as the broom fell from her hands, hitting the floor with a clatter. She clung to the back of the settle and looked at me.

'Maria, get your father, quick!'

I ran from the room and sped down the lane to where Father was working in the fields.

'Father, Father, you must come quick. It is Mother.' He looked up from his tilling and dropped his hoe.

'Maria, go to Mrs Stow, tell her your mother's time has come.' He pushed me from him and strode back the way I had come, as I turned and made for our neighbour's cottage. Phoebe Stow was draping wet white sheets over the hedge to dry. When she saw me running towards her she wiped her hands on her apron.

'It is time?' I nodded, bending forward, trying to calm my breathing. 'Wait in here Maria, I shall go to your mother.' I started to cry, the shock suddenly overcoming me. Mrs Stow bent down and brushed my hair from my eyes, wiping my face on the corner of her apron. 'You must not mind, Maria, you will have a little brother or sister very soon. Sit here, play with the cat – look, see, she has had kittens. Are they not sweet?' She grasped a bag from the hook behind the door. 'I will come for you soon, I promise, and then you may return home. Here.' She passed me an apple. 'I should not be long.' The door slammed behind her and I was left, staring at a cloak which swayed from side to side on its hook.

I looked around at the little cottage, neat as a pin, as I bit into the crisp apple, then I knelt down to see the kittens, smoothing my apron under my knees. The cat lay watchful, her narrowed eyes intent as I lifted them gently onto my lap. I could not take my eyes from them and my mother's travail was forgotten in that moment, for I had never seen such tiny, fluffy creatures. When they began to mew I put them back with their mother and watched them latch on to her, saw her eyes closing in pleasure as she suckled them. She washed them then with a pink scratchy tongue and I picked them up again, one after the other, under wary green eyes, holding them gently lest I break them. They seemed the softest things I had ever touched, their eyes chalky and blue, their voices squeaky and small. I carefully returned them to their mother, her eyes soft, her fur glossy, her whiskers spiky white, and all the time she was purring so hard that her whole body shook. I lay beside them all on the mat, watching the tiny bodies squirm, then, one by one they fell asleep, wrapped around their mother, her purring soothing me until I, too, felt my eyelids droop. And that was where Father found me some hours later.

· · ·

I GAVE no thought to my mother as he took my hand and led me outside, my mind was full of kittens.

'Father, could I have one of the kittens – when they are grown enough to leave their mother? Could I, please?'

He didn't even look at me, but he dropped my hand.

'No Maria, you cannot. There will be enough to do, without a cat under our feet. Think of your mother.' I stopped, tears pricking my eyes, disappointment bitter in my throat. I was going to plead with him but the turn of his shoulders made me think the better of it. He said nothing further, just strode on ahead of me down the lane as I ran after him, trying to keep up, questions flooding my mind.

When we reached home, Father took off my apron, tidied my unruly curls then ushered me upstairs. Mother lay in the bed, pale and drawn, blue shadows under her eyes. She beckoned me to her, smiling wanly.

'Maria, you have a new sister. Say hello to her. We are calling her Ann.' I looked around. The room had changed in my short absence. The family cradle had appeared, scuffed and worn with use, positioned next to the bed. I walked over to it and gazed inside. A poor red wrinkled thing lay there, mewling like the kittens, tiny hands clasping at the air. I touched my fingertip against one palm and the fingers curled over mine, stronger than I expected. 'Is she not beautiful?' My mother's voice, questioning.

'She is not as pretty as the kittens.' I glanced at Mother's face, knots of jealousy tightening in my insides, then my heart sank as I realised I had said the wrong thing. I saw Father glowering from the back of the room.

'Maria, apologise to your mother!' His voice rose in anger and I knew I should not bait him further. I looked down and kicked the toes of my boots hard against the leg of the bed. My mother flinched at the sound.

'Is she your best girl now?'

Mother's face creased in sorrow.

'Come here, Maria, sit by me.' She patted the coverlet beside her and took my hand. 'You will always be my daughter. But you are six years old, the eldest, since God saw fit to take my babes away from me, so you must look out for your little sister as she grows.' I kept my head lowered, not wishing my mother to see my tears. 'Will you be a good girl and help me with her? Now I have two best girls?' Mother's voice was cracked, pleading, so I nodded my agreement but inside I felt sick. All that I thought familiar had shifted, ousted by this tiny shrivel of a being. I would have to share my mother's love and I wondered if there would be enough to go round, for this babe would demand so much. I always thought that, after the deaths of my brother and sisters, Mother would care only for me. But now there was a replacement. My mother's betrayal bit at me, sharp as the teeth of kittens.

CHAPTER

TWO

L ife went on, as it must, but all was changed. Mother did not recover quickly from the birth. It seemed to take all her strength to dress herself and stumble down the stairs each morning, and, when she did so, she seemed constantly sad and distracted. She did her best to look after the babe but more and more she relied on me. I know now what it was, for I have felt the same. But then I did not know what was wrong with her, where my mother had gone, for it seemed as if she had left me. I blamed myself. I tried to help her as best I could, but she was often tearful or impatient with me, and there were days when I could do nothing right. Little Ann flourished though, growing rapidly, and she slowly wormed her way into my affections, loosening my resentment, soothing me with her gummy smiles and gurgling laugh. She charmed everyone, even my father who had always seemed aloof and frightening to me. He called her his little Annie and I often caught him watching her, his eyes soft. He tried to teach her to say her name but her little mouth could not form the word, instead saying Nan-ee. And it seemed to suit her so Nancy she was from then on. It was hard to be sad when she was around and even Mother seemed to brighten slowly.

One day, when my sister was nearly two years old, I was shelling peas with my mother, sitting close to her on the back step in companionable silence. We were both watching Nancy toddling on unsteady feet as she explored the garden, her eyes wide in astonishment, talking her nonsense words to each flower and bee. I was happy at my mother's side, leaning into her, feeling her thin frame pressed against me, taking in her smell and warmth, breathing with her. Then Father's voice broke through my contentment, breaking the spell and anxiety burst, fluttering, into my chest.

'Maria, come in here.'

His voice was sombre and sharp and my heart beat faster. I struggled to my feet, carrying my bowl – Mother reached out to me, but then withdrew her hand, pushing it to her mouth with a sob, and I gripped tight to the cool hardness of the bowl to steady myself, the peas dancing and swirling green and shining round the curl of the rim. Mother tried to smile.

'Go to your father, Maria, there's a good girl. He wishes to speak to you.' She watched me with shimmering eyes and, as I turned to enter the dark parlour, I glanced back at her and the thought came to me that she knew what he wanted and she was frightened.

Father was sitting straight in his high-backed chair, hands braced on his knees, looking stern, and my heart began to thud so loud that I thought he must hear it.

'Yes, Father?' I tried to stand straight but wobbled a little, hindered by the bowl. Trying to be the good girl I knew he expected.

'Maria, you are to leave us. You are to go to the Rectory at Layham. I have arranged work there, you are to help the Rector's wife in the nursery.'

This was the last thing I had expected. Fear made my words stutter.

'To leave here? But what have I done . . . ?'

He held up his hand for silence.

'Your mother is no longer able to earn the money she once could, her time is now taken up with Nancy. Your little sister needs her more than you do. You can be a wilful child, you need discipline and something to keep you busy, your mother has cosseted you for too long.' He raised his chin in my mother's direction and I knew she was unmoving, listening on the step. 'You are eight years old now, and the Rector and I believe you to be suitable for the tasks he has in mind. He has agreed to teach you your letters too, which he need not do. And he is paying me. So you are to go into service, and I pray that this will help you to become a good and useful girl.'

I turned to the door as tears filled my eyes and poured down my cheeks.

'Mother?' I could not imagine a life without her.

She came to me then, rising stiffly from the step, bending to take my hands.

'Your Father has arranged this for the best, Maria, and I am sure you will be happy at the rectory. The Pritchetts are good Christian people.' I reached out, wanting her to hold me close and not let me go, but she pulled back, clasping her hands in front of her, her fingers working. Father nodded his approval. Then the enormity of what he had said struck me like a fist.

'Do you not want me anymore?' Sobs were wracking me now, my shoulders shaking, and she could stand it no longer, and stepped towards me, putting a hand on my head. I nuzzled against it, seeking security, affection, but she stood stiffly and did not answer. 'You promised . . .'

Father stepped forward, pulling me away from my mother.

'That is enough now. Maria. I will take you to the Rectory

tomorrow. You are expected. That is all.' He stood and walked away.

Sheer terror overcame me.

'Mother?' My mother stepped back, shaking her head. She could not look at me. 'Ma?'

'Your father has decided. It is for the best.' She shimmered through the wall of tears then a loud wail came from outside. 'I must go to Nancy, she must have fallen.' She did not look at me. She turned her back and walked away, out into the sunshine as, inside the dark parlour, the bowl fell from my shaking hands and shattered on the flagged floor. The peas, rolled towards her, bright and green and sweet, mingling with the dust.

The following day Father and I travelled to Layham, me sat high on a borrowed horse in front of him, grasping at its coarse mane for all I was worth. Father held a small pack under his arm which contained my clean dress and apron, and I wore my best boots. My mother had tried to kiss me farewell but I was so angry with her, so numbed with betrayal, that I pulled away from her and would not even say goodbye.

I wish I had. I wish I had run to her, held her, breathed her in, and never let her go. For my lasting memory was her standing in the doorway of our cottage, her arms wrapped around my sister.

CHAPTER THREE

The weeks and months that followed are a blur. I no longer remember what I did, or what I said. The first tasks given to me at the Rectory were to wash the clothes and napkins and tidy up after the children. Small things, but I was keen to learn and I tried to help Mrs Pritchett with whatever she asked. She and the Reverend were kind people but distracted by their many children and their parish duties, and the house seemed to be always in a state of upheaval. But the children and my work served to stop me from thinking of the home I had left behind and I was glad of it, for the missing of my mother was a shard of flint in my heart, sharp and cutting. Once a month I was given an afternoon off and Father would come and collect me on the horse and take me home, but those visits were strained and unnatural. There was so little time with Mother and she was always distracted. Nancy was growing into a bubbly child and I couldn't help laughing at her antics, but each time my mother bent to her with the smile on her face that once was just for me, the flint dug deeper.

· · ·

I HAD BEEN at the Rectory nigh on a year when Reverend Pritchett called me to his study. I knocked and pushed open the door hesitantly. I had never been allowed in that room until now and my heart was thumping, for I remembered the time my father had called me to him, of the change that came after. Reverend Pritchett sat behind a large dusty desk, covered with papers and books. A fire crackled in the hearth and all around were more and more volumes, shelves of them, from floor to ceiling. Hundreds of books. I looked around me wide-eyed, finally remembering to close my mouth which had dropped open. The room smelled of burning applewood and the air was full of the dry scent of paper. The shelves gleamed with leather and gold, the spines raised and powdery, and I wondered how a person could understand so many words. The Reverend leaned forward, resting his arms on his desk and looked at me. His eyeglasses twinkled on the bridge of his nose and his smile was warm.

'Mrs Pritchett and I think it is time you learned to read, Maria. I promised your father I would give you some teaching.' My heart steadied. 'You are a quick learner and we believe that all girls should have some reading and writing to stand you in good stead for your future. Our own little ones are young as yet, I will hone my teaching skills with you, so I will be ready for when they are grown enough.' I nodded, my eyes still sweeping the room in wonder. He laughed at my expression and then reached across the crowded desk for a slim volume. 'We will begin with this, Maria – '*Moral Tales for Young People*' – I believe it to be most suitable. Would you like that?' I took the proffered book and opened it carefully. Words danced before my eyes, alive with possibility. I looked back at Reverend Pritchett and beamed at him.

'Yes, please, Sir.'

And so it began. The memory of that room, the smell of leather and woodsmoke and age; the crackle of pages as I turned them, one by one, under the guidance of the Reverend, my finger pointing to each word as I sounded out the letters, his own taking its place when I stumbled. I treasured those times above all, and the stories I read set up a longing for more. There was a whole new world in those books, like a distant dream, glimmering, just out of reach, the promise of something more, and I craved it.

BUT LIFE and God have a way of dashing such dreams. Two years after I was sent to the Rectory, Mrs Pritchett came to find me one day. There were tears in her eyes as she ushered me into the drawing-room where I found the Reverend sitting before the fire, solemn-faced, his fingers steepled before his mouth. Mrs Pritchett stood beside me, her hand on my shoulder, dabbing at her eyes with a lace-edged handkerchief. My panic rose at their solemn faces.

The Reverend cleared his throat.

'Maria, I have some grave news for you. You must be brave. Sit down, child.' He patted the chair beside him but I was frozen to the spot. He looked up at his wife, then at me, and sighed deeply. 'Maria, your father has sent word that your mother passed away three days since. I'm afraid this means you must leave us, for you are needed at home to care for him and your little sister.'

Mrs Pritchett rubbed at my shoulder and turned me towards her. I gazed at her mutely. A single tear was running down her cheek and she swept at it with the back of her hand as she bent to face me.

'Maria?' She gazed at me, concern writ large on her face. 'Maria, do you understand what my husband is telling you?'

'I must go to her. I must see her.'

'Child, it is not possible, She was buried yesterday. Your father thought it best – she is no more.' Mrs Pritchett looked at her husband beseechingly. He bent toward me and his voice, when he spoke, was soft, seeking to offer comfort to my already hardening heart.

'Your loss is great, my child, but your mother is in a better place now. She has been called to God and He will tend to her now.'

I did not even nod. I found myself unable to move, fixed to the spot, too stunned even to respond, as my dreams of something better cracked and shattered around me.

CHAPTER
FOUR

The Reverend gave me two of the reading books as a gift and a small box for my belongings. I waited on the doorstep, my world crumbling around me. I had been happy at the Pritchetts, it had become my home which, once again, I was being forced to leave.

'Go with God, Maria, and may his blessings be upon you.' He and Mrs Pritchett stood with their children, waving sadly as Father lifted me onto the horse and we trotted away, my box under his arm, the books clasped tightly in my hands. I could not look back for fear I would break.

AT HOME, the silence embraced me like a shroud. Mother was everywhere and nowhere. Her presence still filled the cottage but it was empty, full of shadows. Nancy ran to me as soon as she saw me and clung on as if she feared that I too would leave her. I kissed her and petted her, hastening to reassure her, keeping her close, a part of Mother that I could still touch. Father said little. He never spoke to me of her although he gave me her earrings, to wear when

I was older. The box given to me by the Reverend, along with its books, was put under the bed I now shared with Nancy without a word, and I resumed my old place at the meal table. It was as if those past two years had never been.

The months that followed hung bitter with resentment. Father became distant and cold, never offering a word of solace. He never touched us, never spoke to us unless it was to question or demand. Even Nancy, always so full of mischief, learned to keep her silence. She was four now and always inquisitive and questioning. She often cried out for our mother in the night and I did my best to console her but my heart also wept. I tried to do my best but I was sometimes overly harsh, so much so that her lips would quiver and her eyes fill with tears at my clipped words. It was as if I could not help myself. At those times guilt clutched at my heart, but the truth was that a part of me resented her. Nancy was the reason I had been sent away, the reason I was not at the bedside when my mother died.

But it was not just that – I missed my lessons and the warm family atmosphere of the Layham Rectory. The Pritchetts had always been kind to me and the contrast between their warm, chaotic house and this one was stark. There was no warmth at home any more; that had died with my mother, and our house had become a place of silent, unspoken grief. Death embraced it. I rose at daybreak to prepare Father's breakfast, which he ate, unspeaking, the only sound that of his chewing and the slurping of his tea. Rarely, he would thank me with a nod, but most of the time he did not even acknowledge me. I carried out my duties as best I could, for I was only ten years old, but it was as if I was invisible, of no importance. My hours were filled with washing, preparing meals and tending to Nancy. My only solace was snatched moments in the garden, listening to the song of the birds and the soft soughing of the trees as I tended to Mother's plot, trying to keep it as she would have done, running my finger over the soft blooms of the roses and trying to conjure her face. We went to Polstead church on Sundays, dressed in our best, Nancy and I standing silently while Father shook hands with the Reverend Whitmore, nodding to our neighbours, always sombre and aloof, saying little, before striding down the hill towards home, with us trailing behind him. This was my life now, and, as it went on, my memories of Layham faded and my hopes for the future were extinguished, blotted out by drudgery and grief.

CHANGE CAME ONCE AGAIN. Some eighteen months after Mother had passed, Father called Nancy and me to him. He sat in the same chair in the parlour as before, hands again on his knees, and I shook as I remembered the last time this had happened. I clasped Nancy's hand tightly and it was as if she sensed my fear for she stood, feet together, silent and wide-eyed.

'Maria, Nancy.' Father looked at us in turn. Nancy's hand gripped mine even tighter. 'You are to have a new mother. I am to marry again.'

Nancy looked up at me, her face all confusion, and I blinked in astonishment.

'Married? But surely . . . ?' I took a deep breath. 'Mother has not long been gone. How can you you think of it?' The furrowing of his brow was enough to warn me, it should have silenced me, but I could not stop. 'Do you think nothing of Mother? Who is the person you are to marry?'

He glowered at me and I felt my hand shake as Nancy started to tremble. I reached for her thin shoulder and squeezed it, seeking to reassure her, but she moved behind me, still shaking, clutching at my skirts.

'I will ignore your rudeness on this occasion for I realise this must have come as a shock to you. This house has been too long without a womanly touch.' I stiffened, affronted. I had thought I was enough. I had done my very best. 'The lady's name is Ann Holder and she has consented to be my wife. The banns have been read and it is planned that we will marry shortly, on the sixth of October. She is to be your new mother and you will obey her in all things, as you do me.' He paused and fixed me with a hard stare. 'You will treat her with the respect due to her as my wife, Maria, d'you hear me?' I stared back at him, unflinching, then felt a movement behind me as Nancy peered up at him from around my skirts.

'I should like a new mother.' she said.

Father gazed at her, then up at me.

'That is good, Nancy, for you need a mother's guidance. Maria, do you have anything to say? To offer your good wishes perhaps?' My face was rigid and no words came. 'Very well then, but you will welcome her into this house, that is an order. I will not have any of your sullenness and moods. Do you understand me?' I nodded, but inside, as my resentment grew, so did a question. Why had I not been enough?

CHAPTER
FIVE

N ancy and I did not attend the wedding. It was a small affair, being Father's second time married, so the first we saw of his new wife was when he showed her into our cottage. She was dressed in a velvet cloak, the like of which I had never seen and which I immediately coveted. As she pulled back her hood I could not help but exclaim. She was so young. I had thought she would be of my mother's age, but Ann Holder was many years younger. She was round-faced and comely and her hair, pale and straw-coloured, fell in curls about her face as she removed her bonnet. She was pretty in a country sort of way, curved and womanly. She was clearly nervous and plucked at Father's sleeve with long fingers.

'Will you not introduce us, Thomas?' My eyes widened. I had never heard Mother use my father's name, she always called him Father, as we all did. I looked at him, expecting him to remonstrate with her but he did not, just looked down at her and smiled.

'Of course. This is my younger daughter, Nancy – Ann – your namesake.' She smiled and twittered at this. 'And this is my eldest, Maria. Children, this is your new mother.'

Nancy bobbed a curtsey, looking shyly at the newcomer.

'Am I to call you Mother?'

'Would you like to do that, Nancy?' The stranger bent down and gave my little sister her hand.

'Yes, please.' I gasped at her treachery.

'You are a pretty little thing, I'm sure we will get on famously.' Nancy skipped on the spot, beaming. I forgot that she was only six and motherless, all I could think of was how our mother was already dismissed in her mind, replaced by this cuckoo in our nest. Ann smiled at her again and stroked her hair and then turned to me.

'And you, Maria? Will you call me Mother also?' Behind her, Father's eyes caught mine and narrowed in warning.

'My mother is dead.'

She paused for a moment.

'Then perhaps you will call me Ann?'

Father stepped forward.

'She will not. She will call you Mother, for that is what you are to be. You must not put up with her nonsense, Ann, I have warned you of her wilfulness. She has her mother's looks but not her gentle manner, I'm sorry to say.' He turned to me. 'Do you understand, Maria?' I nodded, sullen. I would do as he ordered but she would never be a replacement. I thought of my mother, lying in her shroud deep beneath the earth, usurped by this stranger, and the very next day I went to kneel at her graveside to offer up a prayer that she would understand that, although I may have to call this woman Mother, she would never be so.

Ann Holder. She was but nineteen years old, only eight years older than me and twenty years younger than my father. She took over the cleaning of the house and asked me to help her with the washing, which I did, unwillingly, making my feelings clear by my constant frown and the violence of my scrubbing. She took over the baking from me and turned out to be a good cook, something I acknowledged with reluctance. My father now tucked into his evening meals with relish, smacking his lips in a most unsavoury manner whilst Ann stood beside him, simpering. It did not take her long to put her mark on our cottage either. She brought in knick-knacks and ornaments, removing those things that my mother had treasured, with not a thought for their significance. I found them later stuffed into a cupboard and took one, a small dish patterned in blue and white that I knew Mother had treasured, secreting it in the box under my bed alongside the reading books. My sister Nancy followed her around like a puppy, always eager to please, and the two of them grew close, but I could not accept Ann's presence in our house. She tried, I will give her that, asking my opinion, making me little gifts of handkerchiefs and ribbons, but I did not relent.

A change had come over Father too, a change I put down to the noises that came from their bedroom most nights, and it was no surprise when he announced that Ann was to have a child.

MY STEPMOTHER BECAME SLOWER as her pregnancy began to show. I watched her when she was not looking, saw her blossom and begin to glow, and my resentment grew. I thought of my mother, her last pregnancy, how she looked so thin and poorly. I remembered that I was sent away afterwards and I began to fear for Nancy and me, but I dared not ask what was to happen to us. As the weeks went on I watched Ann Holder as she let her stays out and saw that she began to rest her hand on the growing bump, as if protecting it from the world. Father seemed pleased at this further proof of his virility and his pleasure lifted the mood of the household a little. He was no longer so morose and angry and I found that, little by little, my resentment of her was lessening into tolerance.

We were sitting with our sewing one day. I was taking in

mending as my mother had done to bring in some money for our growing household and was trying to concentrate on keeping my stitches neat and swift, whilst continually stopping and helping little Nancy with her needle, which was always coming unthreaded. My sister's stitches were large and uneven, like teeth, and I kept having to lean towards her to show her how she should do it.

I could sense that my stepmother had something to say and knew that she was hesitant, but I kept my gaze lowered, resisting. Finally, she paused, pushed her needle into her work, then set it down on her lap and cleared her throat.

'Maria, I have something to ask of you.' I passed Nancy's sewing back to her and straightened in my chair, looking at my own work, at the line of hemming, the stitches even and small. 'I would be so glad of your help when the babe comes if you would give it? I know you are only young still, twelve isn't it? But your father tells me that you helped care for the children at Layham Rectory, so you have some experience.' I swallowed and raised my head. This was the first time she had asked me for help and as I looked at her I saw her vulnerability.

I hesitated.

'I will help where I can. I have little experience, the Rector's children were not new-born babes.'

She looked grateful.

'You still have more experience than I.' She gave a wry grin. 'And it will stand you in good stead when you have babes of your own.'

I shook my head.

'I will never have a babe. Where would I find a husband in this place?' I bit my lip – I had said too much, given something of myself. She leaned forward and took my hand.

'Time moves fast, Maria, these years will be gone in an instant, and you are such a beautiful girl, you will break hearts, I am sure of it. You will not be short of suitors.' She paused, thoughtful. 'It is a woman's lot to marry and bear children, it is their role in this life and is where security and happiness lie. I married your father, not for love, but for children, a family of my own. And love will grow, it always does.' I looked down at her hand on mine and, for the first time, I did not move it or pull away but looked up at her as if with new eyes. She had called me beautiful.

CHAPTER
SIX

The birth of Ann's child was not an easy one but the midwife was matter-of-fact as I ran to boil water and find clean cloths. The bedroom smelt metallic and sharp. The bloodied rags, as I bundled them up to burn them, were red and sodden, and I wondered why women went through such horrors. I was told to leave the room then, but her cries and screams echoed downstairs and Nancy and I clung to each other. Then, a small, shrill wail and the tension in the house evaporated. The midwife came to the top of the stairs and called us up.

Ann had been washed and dressed in a clean shift and she looked happy, though tired.

'Maria, Nancy, you have a brother.' I gazed for the first time at the babe, watched as his tiny fists clenched and waved, saw his fat little legs and my heart melted. The strength of feeling was overwhelming, unexpected, I could not draw my eyes away from him. He was perfect. My stepmother held him out to me as Nancy beamed at my side.

'Here, Maria. Hold him carefully, thus –' She was smiling as she moved my hand to support his head. 'The midwife has told me that a newborn babe's neck is weak, his head must always be supported. Yes, that's the way, you have it now.' I looked up and smiled back at her then stopped myself. But she saw it. 'We are to name him Thomas, after your father.' I nodded and looked into the little face, marbled eyelids now closing, pale lashes brushing his cheek as he gave a small sigh. His pink mouth pouted into a rosebud and his eyes quivered as he fell asleep in my arms. I held him to me and breathed in the smell of him, gently cradling the soft downy head in my palm.

It was then that it came. A rush of longing so sharp that my breath caught.

MORE BABIES FOLLOWED, each more adorable than the last, for my stepmother was fertile. Two years after little Thomas she gave birth to another son, Ambrose and then, three years after that, to another, George. Our cottage was full of small children, noisy, untidy and demanding, but I loved my half-brothers dearly. I was seventeen, and the longing to be a mother myself had grown. My days were spent in caring for the house, as my stepmother's time was taken up with her boys. She was always rushing to and fro, dealing with all that a growing family brings, but still finding time to chat with everybody, installing herself firmly in our village. Despite all, I could never bring myself to call her Mother. She was kind enough to me, although there was always a distance between us – I knew I had grown into the image of my mother and Ann saw me as a rival. She treated her boys differently than Nancy and me. They were clearly her favourites and she always, after Father, gave them the choicest meat at the table, made sure they were washed and cared for, always smart. Nancy and I were left to make our own way, Father saying little, expecting us to fend for ourselves. My mother was never mentioned and, after a time, it was as if she had never been. It was left to me to hold a place in my heart for her, as

Nancy happily accepted her replacement and grew closer to Ann as she got older. They said later that Ann was company for me but that is not the truth, for she was always occupied elsewhere. I had no friends but I never thought of myself as lonely. It was as if my mother's death had made me live inside myself – I felt the danger of opening up to someone, only to have them whisked away from me, so I kept my thoughts and dreams to myself. There were a few girls in the village with whom I passed the time of day but I had no special friend. Plenty came forward later though, claiming that they knew me well. But that was later.

MY STEPMOTHER continually nagged my father to better himself, for she had heard tell that there was a shortage of men to catch moles throughout the county and she saw an opportunity. She was not satisfied for my father to remain in the parish and eventually persuaded him, by constant complaining, to offer his services to local farmers and landowners outside our village, clearing their fields and gardens of vermin in addition to his parish duties. Father was always reluctant to change, preferring to carry on as he always had, but my stepmother had ambitions and besides, with seven of us in the cottage now, it was true that we needed more money. She knew lots of people hereabouts, did Ann, so she put the word about and soon Father was inundated with requests. He began to travel further and further away, sometimes not returning home for days, lodgings being provided while he carried out his work. He had the country habit of hanging the moles by their tails from the fence where he was working that day, to show how successful he had been and he hung them on our fence too. I still remember those tiny velvet bodies swinging in the breeze, the stench of them in the summer, remember how I averted my gaze when I walked past. But it worked and his fame soon spread. And, as Ann had predicted, his new role proved lucrative, for he now earned more than the local schoolmaster – as the money rolled in, our living improved. There was better food and more of it, toys for the children, new gloves and ribbons for Nancy and me. My stepmother began to dress better too, taking even more care over her appearance, making sure her boys were clean and well-dressed, acting every part the prosperous wife in new bonnets and ribbons, strutting around the village as if she owned it. For a while, things were good. Ann was content, everyone happy and even Father seemed to revel in his new-found notoriety. But it was not only our fortunes which changed in that summer of 1818. For that year the Corder family came into our lives.

I KNEW of the Corders of course. Everybody did. John and Mary Corder and their brood. They lived in the large, half-timbered house partway up the hill, overlooking Polstead Pond, and managed the farmland hereabouts, renting it from the Cookes of Polstead Hall. Although only tenant farmers, they all acted like lords of the manor. Theirs was a large family; Mary Corder had birthed ten children, but only four sons and two daughters had lived past infancy. They were well-to-do too, and looked down on the rest of us, making the most of their status and wealth. They all appeared in church every Sunday, Mr and Mrs Corder modest in black, but with their children in the finest cloth and newest fashions. There were those, spiked green with envy, who put it about that Mrs Corder was not as saintly as she appeared to be, for it seemed that she had given birth to their first child only five months after her marriage. But it was not uncommon in those days for couples to lie together before they solemnised their union by marriage, and this tittle-tattle was soon forgotten. No, their marriage was strong, despite the loss of so many children, and I was never one to gossip about others.

After all, who am I to judge, after what I did?

SEVEN

Of all the Corder family, it was the brothers who were renowned in the village. They were all handsome, not especially tall, but they carried themselves like lords. Always finely dressed, they rode good horses, and their mother, it was said, doted on them. They were known to be fun-loving and charming but, as they grew into manhood, it seemed that there was not enough entertainment for them in a place as sleepy as Polstead, so they began to pay frequent visits to Bury St Edmunds and London in search of good drink and better company. Oh, yes, the Corder boys were the talk of the area, and the local girls flushed and simpered, twirling their hair around their fingers at the very mention of them. I once would have done the same but I was grown now, a woman of twenty, too old for such nonsense and too busy to think about it. I knew the Corder boys were beyond the reach of us village girls and fully expected them all to make good matches with the women of quality they met on their travels, so I paid them no heed.

. . .

THE ANNUAL CHERRY fair was the event of the year. For two days each July, the whole of the village seemed to congregate on the village green amongst stall upon stall of glistening black cherries. That summer I was sitting on the grass with some other girls from the village, watching the comings and goings, listening to their chatter; who wore what, who was with child, who was pursuing whom. The sun was warm on my face and I had removed my bonnet and smoothed out my hair, pushing the dark curls from my face. I closed my eyes, letting the talk fade as I enjoyed the moment until a shadow fell across me. I opened my eyes. Thomas Corder, the second son, and many say the most handsome, was standing before me. A group of his friends stood a little way off, pretending not to watch, but I saw their eyes flashing between us, their knowing smiles.

He bowed gallantly and, as I struggled to stand up, he held out his hand to assist me.

'Maria Martin, is it not? I have not seen you for some time.' He smiled slowly, that wry grin that I came to find so irresistible. 'You have become a beauty, Maria.' He held a long piece of grass between his fingers and was twirling it against his cheek. His eyes were the clearest, deepest blue and I looked into them, unsure what to do.

'Thank you, Sir.' I remembered my manners and bobbed a curtsey and his smile widened. 'Are you enjoying the fair?'

He looked long at me.

'I am, but I lack pretty company. Would you walk with me a little?' He offered his arm. My heart was thumping hard against my chest, I did not know how to respond. The village girls had stopped their gossiping and were staring blatantly at us; his friends were in a cluster, watching. I felt myself blush as I realised that all eyes were on me and I brushed my skirts down, dropping my gaze from his face, wishing the earth would swallow me up.

'I do not think that would be appropriate, Sir, but I thank you for asking.'

His smile faded a little, replaced by an expression I could not read.

'Very well, another time, perhaps? He lifted my hand and brought it to his lips. I felt their smooth coolness send a flush of excitement through me, then he let go. 'I hope we will meet again soon, Maria.' I stood, fixed to the spot as he nodded and strode back to his friends and I watched as they smiled and patted him on the back, moving away to mingle with the crowds, then they were lost from sight. The girls next to me began talking all at once and I could see their sidelong glances at me. I did not move, just feeling the print of his lips burning my hand as I brought it to my mouth but, inside me, small flames of pride and excitement flickered into life. Thomas Corder had spoken to me, and I knew that I would never be the same again.

CHAPTER
EIGHT

They said afterwards that it was I who pursued him, who led him into sin, but that is not what happened. After that meeting at the fair, it was Thomas Corder who sought me out. I saw him more frequently in the village, watching me, and he often walked past our cottage on his way to the fields, lingering by the gate to see if I was there. I knew then that he was dangerous, that his interest in one such as me could never be heart-felt, but I was flattered and excited by his attention. It made me feel different; important and desired. I knew it could never come to anything, but a little part of me hoped that, maybe, it would.

It was a hot August day and I was tending the roses in Mother's garden. I liked the quiet contemplation, the rhythm of the scratch of the hoe, the heavy smell of the pink and red petals as they opened in the summer sun. Each time my skirt brushed against the bushes the bees rose in a cloud and I apologised to them for disturbing their work. Superstitious I know, but the old ways have much to teach us. A single rose had broken from its parent, lolling from the stem, so I picked it up, thinking to place it in some water so that it would not die so swiftly. I was smoothing its velvet petals with a fingertip when I heard a cough in the lane. I turned. He was leaning on the hedge watching me. I curtseyed, my eyes lowered as I knew my stepmother would expect of me.

'That is a beautiful rose.' I looked up at him. 'Almost as beautiful as you.' I saw the expression on his face, how he was looking at me and it was as if the sun had come out.

'It is, Sir. My mother grew them until she . . . now I look after them. It is a remembrance.'

'And it does you credit. Your father is the mole-catcher, is he not? I have seen you in the village on occasion.' He had a way of looking at you, deep and mesmerising, his eyes crinkled, his mouth smiling, pale hair falling over one eye. I shook myself.

'Was it my father you came to see, Sir? He is away working at present but I could give him a message. Are there moles you want dealing with?'

His smile widened.

'Why, yes, that would be ideal. There are certainly plenty of moles hereabouts.'

'I will leave him a note, Sir, asking him to call on you, if that would be convenient? Should he come up to the house?'

His eyes widened in surprise.

'You will leave him a note?'

I bristled at the implication.

'Of course. I can write and I can read too. I was a servant at Layham Rectory when I was younger, the Reverend Pritchett taught me my letters.' I drew myself up to my full height. 'I am not some illiterate country girl, Sir.' He laughed then and I felt my stomach lurch.

I held his gaze as his eyes roamed over me.

'No, I can see that. You are a lady of quality, that's for sure, it is in your bearing – if not your manners.' I stepped back. I knew I should not have spoken so boldly but he seemed to draw it out of me somehow. He saw my discomfort. 'Do not worry – I admire a girl with spirit.' He stood up and doffed his cap to me. 'I will see you again soon, Maria Martin.' He turned and walked away towards the Corder fields and left me, my mind all a-tumble, gazing at his retreating back.

HE PLAYED WITH ME THOUGH. Teased me like a cat with a fledgling. Four days came and went, leaving me in a fever of expectation. Ann sensed my distraction.

'Maria, what is the matter with you? Pull yourself together, girl, there is much for us to do. This floor needs scrubbing for a start. And you have mending to do, it won't wait.' She cocked her head and looked at me keenly. 'Are you coming down with something?' I shook my head. 'Well, perhaps it is your courses then, that can turn a maid's head curdled.' I did not speak, for to tell her what I truly thought of would have broken the spell. I just took the bucket and brush from her and lowered myself to my knees.

It was the fifth day when he came by again, this time riding on a fair grey horse. I heard the clop of hooves on the road and glanced up at the window from the wash tub, drying my hands on a cloth, and straightening my apron.

'I will go and turn the sheets on the hedge, they must be part dry by now.' My stepmother looked at me enquiringly but said nothing.

Thomas Corder was waiting by the gate.

'Maria Martin, good day! What a pleasant morning, do you not think?' I thought he was mocking me, but he stopped and dismounted, leading the grey over to where I stood. I was struck dumb. He seemed even more handsome that day, his fair hair blowing in the warm breeze, his eyes crinkling as he smiled at me. 'You are looking truly beautiful, Maria. That green neckerchief brings out the colour of your eyes.' The compliment was so unexpected that I flushed – I could feel it heat my face, spreading to my chest and I put my hands to my throat to mask it. But he saw; he saw me, and he knew. 'Will you not speak to me?' He stood closer now and his grey began to nuzzle my hand so I stroked its head, thinking what to say.

'Do you ride to London, Sir?'

He laughed then and shook his head.

'No, not for a while. My father is concerned about the amount of money my brothers and I have been spending and so we are confined to Polstead for the time being.'

My curiosity got the better of me.

'Is London expensive then?'

'It is, and gaming can run through your gold like water through silk. So I am here. Looking at you.'

His look emboldened me.

'So you are.'

He grinned.

'I would like to walk out with you if you would permit me?' I was so astounded that my mouth opened and he leant forward and, with the tip of his finger, stroked under my chin, pushing upwards to close it. His breath smelt of honey.

'I must ask my father's permission . . .' My voice tailed off when I saw the look on his face and inside me, deep down, something awoke and stretched. He moved his finger up from my chin to my lips.

'Let it be our secret, Maria. Let us keep it to ourselves.' He reached for my hand and lifted it to his lips. I expected him to brush his lips against it as he had at the fair, but he did not. Instead, he turned it palm up and ran the tip of his tongue over each fingertip in turn, all the time watching my face. I closed my eyes against the sensation, feeling it heat and then melt me. I stepped towards him, liquid, my eyes still closed, moving to him by instinct, but at that moment, from inside the cottage, my stepmother called to me. Thomas stood up and dropped my hand. His voice was low, his eyes searching behind me.

'So will you meet with me? Tonight? I will be by the field gate at dusk. I will wait for you. I know a place up by the Red Barn, d'you know it?' I nodded. 'It is owned by the Corders – we will not be seen there.'

I hesitated, looking up at him through my lashes as I had seen the other girls do.

'I am not sure. I am needed here to help put the boys to bed.'

He smiled knowingly.

'You will be there.' He put his foot in the stirrup and mounted in one smooth motion, then picked up the reins, clicking the horse into movement, and rode away without looking back.

I stood for a moment then looked at my hand where he had kissed it; the fingers were still tingling. I felt changed in that moment, hopeful, opened. As I turned back, I thought I caught a swish of movement behind the window of the cottage, but I gave it no further regard, for my mind was elsewhere, filled with thoughts of Thomas Corder.

And that is how it began.

CHAPTER
NINE

I was never one of those fast women, those tuppenny whores. I did not give myself to just anyone as the papers later suggested. I had always vowed I would wait for marriage, to stay pure until then. But I was twenty years old, aching to be loved, and the power of Thomas Corder's desire overwhelmed me.

I did meet with him that night, and for many nights following, but I did not give in to his entreaties and persuasion. Not then, not immediately. But when he saw I resisted he began to say how he was falling in love with me, how he wished us to lie together, to show our love for each other. He would hold me close and caress me, kissing me softly, running his hands over me. I allowed him liberties, yes, and his hands were knowing and sure and so often I thought 'Why not?' But, in the end, it was not his touch which undid me, stirring though it was. It was his words. It was the tone of his voice when he loosened my hair and buried his face in it and told me how much he desired me and loved me. How he wanted to take me away from this place.

'You do not know what you do to me, Maria.' We were lying in the long grass by the Red Barn and I had pushed him away once more. We were both hot and panting with desire. 'I cannot imagine life without you now.' He reached for me again and I clung to him, melding my body to his. He nuzzled my ear with his tongue, biting gently, so gently. 'I want you, Maria, I want you so much. Please let me love you. I know you want me as well.' I was so afraid, but weak with lust, so close to the brink. 'Oh, Maria, you don't know how you make me feel. Do you not understand how much I want you?' He ran his hands over my breasts, my hips. 'I must have you, we must be together somehow.' He took a strand of my hair in his palm and pulled his fingers down the length of it. 'Perhaps it would be possible to be together. Maybe I could find a way?' My hair shone dark against his white hand, the curls springing back as he dropped it and moved his hand to my breast, kneading it gently over my bodice. I felt my desire rising again, but then a thought stopped me, fast as a pail of cold water.

'Are you toying with me, Thomas?' I felt him pause then. 'Do you mean what you say?'

He pulled away and looked at me, his eyes veiled.

'I would never toy with you. Do you not know that by now? I love you, Maria, I want to be with you, but you are not yet old enough to marry without your father's permission, are you? And I am not sure if he would approve of me.'

I clasped his hand in mine.

'I will speak to him, Thomas, I will make him see how suited we are.'

He looked at me with such an expression that I felt all my resolve slipping. I pressed my lips to his and felt his mouth open, his tongue pushing at mine. Then his mouth moved to my ear and he blew, softly, gently, as I melted into his embrace.

'Let me, Maria. I will take care, you need not worry. I will look after you – I want so much to make you mine.'

'Thomas, I am afraid. What if . . . ?'

'I will be careful, Maria, I promise. Nothing bad will happen to you.' His eyes crinkled as he smiled in the way I loved, then closed as he moved his mouth over mine again. I shut my eyes against the sensations. 'Let me, please. Let me.' His lips brushed my ear, his voice was soft and full of desire, his body strong as it moved over mine and in that moment I was lost.

I believed him, you see. All the lies. He said he would speak to my father, but he did not. He said he would be careful, but he was not. I was too free with him that summer, I know, but I had trusted all he said, everything he promised. I had ignored the voice in my head that was warning me of the danger, the risk. Night after night we lay in the long grass by the edge of the field and watched the sun go down. Insects buzzed, birds sang sweetly, and the warmth of the days stayed long into the evenings. It seemed perfect. Until it wasn't.

The autumn had nearly gone and winter was drawing in when I knew. My breasts hurt and I often felt dizzy and sick. When I looked in the drawer where my monthly rags were kept I realised that I had not needed them for some time. I went cold with horror. Thomas had promised me he would be careful but often we had been carried away in our lust, we had become lax. And now I was to bear the consequence. I did not know who to speak to – Nancy was still only fourteen and not to be burdened with this. I had no option.

My stepmother was downstairs, the children playing noisily by the hearth as she washed the dishes. She looked up as I stood before her.

'Maria?' My eyes stung with tears and she moved towards me, drying her hands on her apron. 'Maria, what is wrong?' Her voice was concerned but I did not speak, then I saw realisation dawn in her face. 'Do not tell me – surely you cannot have been so witless as to . . . ? You foolish, foolish girl. What will your father say?' Her face was like thunder, her voice rising. 'So, who is it? Some farm hand who has been and gone, some gypsy from the fair I have no doubt. Throwing yourself away on anyone who gave you a second glance. What will people say?' She was white with anger as she glanced at the boys then took my arm and drew me into a corner, her voice dropping. 'Well, who was it? Or are you going to tell me you didn't know his name – is that it?

My face reddened and I bit my lip to stop myself crying. That she thought so little of me stung almost more than my predicament. I swallowed hard but even then my voice trembled as I spoke.

'He will marry me, that I am sure of. He promised he would take care of me. He loves me, he truly does.'

'So, tell me his name, this worthy man who will make an honest woman of you. Is he from round here?' I took a deep breath. 'Well, who is he?'

'It is not some farmhand. It is Thomas Corder.'

She froze and then put her hands to her hips and bent forward. The noise coming from her made me think she was crying and I moved towards her but, as she straightened I realised she was laughing.

'Thomas Corder? And you think he will marry you? Well, you are more moon-struck than you look. Of course he will not marry you. He has had his fun and he will drop you now like a hot coal, you mark my words. Did you imagine yourself mistress of the Corder farm one day, is that it? Thomas Corder indeed.' She stopped laughing and wiped her face with her hand. 'He will not marry one such as you, Maria, for all his talk. You have given your virtue up for nothing, and now you must face the consequences. Has he told his father?' I looked down at my boots. 'No, he hasn't, nor his mother either. You have been a roll in the hay while he is stuck here in Polstead, that is all. I've heard how the Corder boys are confined to home this summer. I know of their spending and loose ways, the whole village does. All but you, it seems.' She sighed and rubbed her face, then gazed at my stomach, assessing. 'I never thought to warn you, maybe I should have, but I thought you too sensible and now, by the looks of you, it is too late to do anything about it.'

I looked at her in horror.

'I could never do that. It is wrong.'

'You are twenty years old, how could you not know better?' She cocked her head to one side. 'You haven't told him, have you?' She rocked back on her heels and sighed dramatically. 'What will people say?' I moved to speak but she held her hand up. 'No, I will not hear one word from you. You have done enough damage to this family's reputation. Just when your father is making a name for himself around here. You will go to Thomas Corder and tell him he is to be a father. He must provide for you and the child – if it is his bastard?' She saw my expression and lifted her hand to silence me. 'You mind you ask for enough, Maria, for he has had his pleasure, now he must pay for it. Thomas Corder indeed.' She turned back to the sink, muttering to herself, as I moved, steadying myself on the door jamb, and slowly, shakily, made my way up the stairs to the room I shared with Nancy, stunned by her harshness. I would tell Thomas that night. He would know what to do. I trusted him.

But he had lied to me. He lied.

CHAPTER

TEN

To this day I can still see Thomas's expression when I told him; the shock and horror, the way he swept his hair from his face with the back of his hand as he shook his head, trying to gather his thoughts. We had met again in the Red Barn. It was bitter cold that evening and I wrapped my shawl tight around me. I could not stop shivering, whether through the chill or fear, I did not know. I had practiced the words I would use but in the end, it came out in a jumbled rush.

When I saw his look I stopped speaking and my heart sank, for I realised my stepmother was right.

'Is it mine, Maria?'

'Of course it is.'

'How do I know that?'

I clutched at his arm, shaking, but he pulled away, and I could see calculation in his eyes.

'I have been with no other man, Thomas, you know that. You were my first, I had never . . .'

'So you say, but how can I believe you? I know how you village girls are, leading a man on with never a hint of shame.'

Anger seared through me.

'You know that I have never lain with another. You know I was untouched when you first loved me. You saw the blood.' He hesitated then. 'You know this to be the truth, Thomas.' I could not believe that he could accuse me of such a thing, after all we had been to each other.

He had the grace to look shamefaced.

'I am sorry. I know I was your first, Maria, it is the shock that made me accuse you. You must forgive me. I was not expecting this, it has taken me by surprise.' He rubbed his hands over his face, shaking his head as if to clear it. I wanted so much for him to take me into his arms, tell me he would look after me, that all would be well, but I already knew that it was hopeless. 'I must think what can be done. And you are certain you are with child?' I nodded, dumbly. 'Very well. But no one must know of this, word must not reach my parents.' His eyes widened in fear. 'You have not told anyone?' He moved towards me, gripping my shoulders and I cried out as his fingers tightened. 'You must not speak of this, especially in Polstead, for you know how people like to gossip.' I did not say I had told my stepmother for fear of angering him further. He let go of me and began to pace up and down as I sank to my knees, the roof of the Red Barn looming high above me. 'My father's heart is weak as it is, and as for my mother, if she hears of this . . .' He looked down at me, his face set. 'I will do what I can.'

I reached up to him.

'Oh, thank you, Thomas, I knew you would help me.'

His brow creased and he rubbed at his face. He could not meet my gaze.

'We cannot see each other again.'

A sob ripped my throat.

'But I love you. You told me you loved me. You said it over and over. All that we are to each other, the promises we made.' I could not stop the tears then. 'You said you loved me, Thomas.'

He gazed at me as if for the first time. 'I did, in my way, I suppose. You are a beautiful girl, but surely you never thought – ? It was just fun, something to pass the hours until my father feels he has punished me enough.' I felt my face fall, saw his bemusement as my heart cracked open. 'You believed it all, didn't you.' He took my hand then, his expression softening. 'Oh, Maria, surely you did not think I would marry you? I never meant that.' I looked at him. 'They were words, that was all. I wanted you so much, I would have said anything to have you.' I pulled away, for at that moment I couldn't bear him to touch me. He reached out and ran a long finger down my cheek, wiping the tears which still streamed. 'I will find some money for you and the child. I am sorry it has come to this but I thought you realised.' He stepped away from me and his voice tightened. 'It is best this way, Maria, and remember, please, for my father's sake and for all I mean to you, not a word. You will know what to do, where to go, I am sure, and I will give you money when I can.' He drew his coat closer, pulled up the collar and pulled his hat low over his face. He slunk to the door of the barn and looked from left to right to make sure he was not seen, then hurried off into the dusk. I sank to the ground, all my strength and courage used up. I felt hollowed out, full of terror for the future, humiliated and above all, witless. My stepmother had called me that. She was right.

CHAPTER
ELEVEN

And then the scandal broke. But it was not mine; I was spared for now. It was Ann who told me. I had kept close to the house as my condition began to show, not wishing to see Thomas for fear I would beg him again not to leave me. It was a cold night and we were sitting sewing by candlelight while Nancy saw the children to bed.

'It seems you are not the only one caught out in the village.' I stiffened at her tone and she looked down her nose at me with a smirk. 'Hannah Snell, lives up the hill. In the family way by John Corder. Those boys – no morals any of them.'

Hannah Snell, the prettiest of the village girls, who had looked down her nose at everyone, particularly me. Hannah, also fallen.

'What will happen to her now?'

Ann sighed deeply.

'Her parents are so angry and ashamed that they have thrown her out.' She looked at me meaningfully. 'Old Mr Corder has said that he will not have his eldest son throwing himself away on some village harlot and has banned John from associating with her.' I wondered if, like me, Hannah may have held hopes for a union, and, too late, found out that she had been misled. Ann cleared her throat and looked hard at me. 'The girl had no alternative, being homeless, and in winter too. She presented herself to Cosford Workhouse. She had no option and they have now applied to the magistrate for support for the child. John Corder has been named as the father and a bastardy order has been issued. His father is said to have taken it hard, for he is not in the best of health himself.' She looked down her nose at me. 'Although I suppose you know that, being associated with the Corders as you are.' I could hear the spite in her voice and I stopped my stitching and looked up.

'All know Mr Corder is unwell, it is no secret. But the Workhouse? How will Hannah fare there?'

'She will be given board, food and occupation to keep her busy – they spin yarn for the Norwich markets I believe. But it is a brutal life and not a fit one for a babe.' I looked down at the sewing in my lap and thought of Hannah and her beauty, her head held high, dark eyes flashing, her nose in the air as she passed me. She was so full of life and passion. How desperate she must have been to take that journey to the workhouse, her last resort. I shuddered and Ann saw. 'Be thankful that the same will not happen to you, Maria, for we are Christian folk. I would not wish to see you in such a place. But you will need to be obedient, to do as you are told, else it would be the work of a moment to put you out onto the street. We will see what Thomas Corder comes up with.' I saw she was thinking ahead, always the businesswoman. She spied an advantage to letting me remain here and heard the rattle of silver. She had me now. Hannah's disgrace would be held over me, a stick to beat me. I was lost.

. . .

It was Hannah's fall from grace that convinced my stepmother that we should tell my father. I had been hoping in vain that the problem might go away, but each day my stomach swelled and now there was no avoiding it. Although my stays still covered my sin, my stepmother insisted it was time to tell Father that he also had disgrace brought upon his house. She waited until Nancy was out and then took my arm and pulled me to where he sat at his place by the fire.

'Maria has something to confess.' She looked at me. 'Go on, tell him.' I wrung my hands, unable to form the words; my mouth was dry, my throat constricted.

'Out with it, girl.' Her voice was sharp but I could not speak. I felt sick, my hands were shaking. My stepmother saw and seized her moment.

'Your daughter has brought shame to our household, Husband. She is in the family way.' My father stiffened. 'But it's not some farm hand. No, Thomas Corder nonetheless, if you can believe that? No common worker for our Maria.'

Father looked up at me, his face blank.

'Is this true, girl?'

I held his eye – I would not show fear in front of them.

'He promised we would be together.'

'And has he kept to his promise? He will marry you?'

My face fell.

'No Father. He has said we must not see each other again, that his father must not find out.' I could not bear to look at him, my shame was so great. He stared at me and cleared his throat as my stepmother broke the silence.

'He has told her that he will pay for his carelessness. I have thought about this and I think there is a way.' My father looked at her and nodded for her to go on. "We could bring it up as our own. Her condition could remain hidden, we could adjust her dress, keep her close confined.' It was as if I was not in the room, that I was of no importance, but I listened to her plan. 'It's that or the workhouse.' A cold dread threaded through me at the thought of that place. 'Consider it, Husband. It is not unheard of. I could name a family or two hereabouts who have done the same. Who would think twice about it? And if there were money coming in too, from the Corder boy, well, it may suit us all.'

I was reluctant to admit it but I wanted my child to have a good start in life and this was an answer. Country people are more tolerant, families blend and meld to fit their circumstances and very soon one person's scandal becomes old news, as another drama takes over. It has always been this way and now I was thankful for it for, if Father agreed, I would have a roof over my head and my child would be cared for. For all my dislike of Ann, she had turned out to be a good mother to her boys, and she had taken Nancy under her wing, so I knew my child would be safe and happy with her. My father looked resigned.

'It is the answer, I can see that. If you are happy to take this on?'

My stepmother nodded.

'I am. And Maria will help, I have no doubt.' Neither of them even looked at me, did not see the tears streaming down my face. They both looked away as my fate was decided.

FATHER LEFT ALL the arrangements to my stepmother, and she was more than willing to take over. I wondered if he felt as strongly as she did the disgrace I had brought to our house, for he cared little what people thought of him, it was my stepmother who was worried about the opinions of others. And the Corders employed him, we were reliant on them, and I knew he would not challenge them. But that event changed him, for, from that day forward, he barely spoke to me and his silence caused me much pain. No, it was she who kept me indoors as my condition began to show, who helped me let out my stays, who made the arrangements for the birth and, when my time came, it was she who helped Phoebe Stow deliver the child. The birth was a blur. The travail was long and hard and I cannot remember much of it now save that the pain was more than I ever thought it could be. After a day and a half, I thrust a squalling scrap of humanity into my stepmother's waiting hands – a girl, perfect in every way, and I named her Matilda. I was still weak, still lying in, when Nancy told me that news of my condition had come out.

'They are all talking about you in the village, Maria. That Phoebe Stow never could keep a secret, despite being sworn to secrecy.'

'What are they saying?' I had to ask.

'Just that you've had a child, that the father is unknown. That is all.' I breathed a sigh of relief. 'And Thomas? Does he ask about me, about his child?'

Nancy sighed.

'He is going about as normal, flirting with the village girls as always. It is as if nothing had happened. Well, it hasn't to him, has it?' Her face grew angry. 'It is us that have to put up with the gossip and shame.' She turned and gazed out of the bedroom window. 'It seems to me that it is always the women who suffer, who take the blame. Why is that?' She turned back to me, her eyes flashing. 'I will never allow this to happen to me, never. The disgrace.' She saw my face then and softened. 'Oh, Maria, why did you do it? Did he force himself on you? I have heard of such things.'

'No, he did not. I wanted him, Nancy, it was me as much as him. But he promised me he would be careful, that nothing would happen to me. He talked of being with me, of speaking to Father. I believed all he said. I trusted him.' I could not go on, I was crying so hard. Nancy sat on the bed beside me and smoothed my hair from my face.

'Do not take on so, it is done now. And you are to stay here. Mother will bring up Matilda and the shame will go and the village will find something else to talk about.' Her words were soft and sympathetic and I clasped her hand.

'Thank you, Nancy.'

'What for, I have done nothing?'

'For being kind when no one else has. For caring about me.'

'Of course I care for you, Maria, you are my sister. But you should be kinder to Mother than you are, for she has resolved your situation.' I nodded – she was right. If it had not been for my stepmother I could have been facing the workhouse now and I decided to try and treat her better in future.

BUT AS ANN took over the care of Matilda, my pain and resentment grew. My babe was brought to me when she needed feeding but that was all I was allowed to do for her.

'You agreed to this, Maria, you agreed to me bringing her up as my own.' She had taken the babe from my arms and was looking down at her, her face soft. 'Poor little mite. Well, I will make sure you are well cared for, brought up right.' She bent and kissed the tiny, smooth forehead then looked at me sharply. 'Better than your mother, that's for sure.' I watched as she left the room, Matilda in her arms, and my spirits sank.

She visited Reverend Whitmore and persuaded him to baptise my babe. She came back from the vicarage, flustered but pleased.

'Well, he agreed, despite his reluctance to embrace a bastard child into the church. I asked if he would put my name down as the mother but he refused, said it was against the law. So your name went down, but the father's name was left out. At least we keep our respectability, no thanks to you. But it's cost us. "*A contribution to the church*" he called it. Thirty pieces of silver I say. But it is settled and that poor child will not risk going to limbo for your sins.' The thought of my child unbaptised had tormented me so I was grateful to her, but I realise now that it was all done for her own benefit. Father went along with her wishes as always and so did Nancy, who was besotted by the new babe and was forever stroking and cosseting her. It was as if I did not exist.

CHAPTER

TWELVE

Three weeks after Matilda was baptised I was still lying in, still weak from the labour, when I heard a loud knock on the door. There were voices in the hallway, my stepmother's and a man's, deep and sure, then a bang as the front door was closed. My stepmother came up the stairs and held out her hand. In it was a leather purse.

'Well, at least he is paying for his pleasure – see, two pounds, from Thomas Corder.'

'Was that Thomas? Did he come?' I pulled myself upwards onto one elbow, lifting my hand to my hair, half hoping to see his slender frame in the doorway behind her.

'Lord no, he wouldn't come, would he? He wants nothing to do with you now he has had his way. No, it was a friend of his, Peter Mathews, who said he'd come on Corder's behalf.' She pocketed the coins in a swift movement. 'Well, this will help to start with.' From the crib, little Matilda began to cry and I slowly started to swing my legs out of bed to go to her, but Ann moved swiftly past me and picked her up. 'You'd best feed this little one.' She thrust Matilda into my arms and I wrapped them around her tiny soft body, her arms pushing at me, so strong now that she was hungry and searching for food. I lowered the neck of my nightgown and her rosebud mouth fumbled for a moment then latched itself to my breast. I watched her suckle as if from a vast distance. Three weeks and she still did not feel as if she belonged there; she never seemed to fit me. And already she was being taken away from me, for Ann watched me steadily, waiting for me to make a wrong move and I knew that once Matilda was weaned she would no longer be mine at all. Ann had taken my mother's place and now she was taking mine.

THOSE FIRST WEEKS were not as I expected. I had helped Ann after the birth of my half-brothers, watched her tenderness with them, her brisk efficiency with their napkins, with washing and feeding them, it all came so naturally to her. For me, it was as if a black cloud had descended. My body was recovering but my mind was not so fast to follow. Everything seemed unreal, as if shrouded in fog. I seemed to constantly hear my babe crying, as if from under-water, and I felt as if I was wading against the flow, grasping for the bank with numb fingers, to reach for her as she was pulled from my grasp. Ann allowed me to do nothing for Matilda apart from feed her, the one thing my stepmother could not take from me. But in everything else, it was as if she were not mine. I was not allowed to change her napkin or bathe her, I could not dandle her in my arms or sing softly to help her to sleep. It was all done for me. I was up and moving around the house now, slow and cumbersome, helping out with basic tasks, but when they were finished I returned to my bed whenever I could, and let the sorrow overwhelm me.

It was two months later that there was a knock on the front door which woke the babe. For once I was dressed and alone with her in the house. I picked her up, trying to calm her and carried her in my arms as I opened the door. An older man stood there, tall and dark and immaculately dressed. His smile was kind and my anger at the disruption melted away.

'You must be Maria.'

'I am, Sir, how may I help you?'

He reached into his embroidered waistcoat and brought out a small leather purse.

'From Thomas Corder.' He saw my hesitation. 'I am a friend of his, I came before and saw your mother.'

'Step-mother.'

The man nodded.

'I am Peter Mathews, Thomas asked me to give you this.' He held out the purse and I took it, tucking it into Matilda's blanket. He gazed at the babe, now sleeping in my arms. 'A beautiful child. Like his mother.' He glanced back up at me and I felt myself blush.

'How is Thomas? When will he come to see his daughter?' I tried to keep the pleading from my voice but he heard.

His face softened. 'He will not come, Maria. Thomas is in London now and I do not know when he will return. He thinks it best if he does not come, as gossip has been avoided thus far. His servants have been sworn to silence so as not to upset his parents, and they rarely venture into the village. No one but us knows who the father is. You understand, I'm sure.' But I did not. I did not know how a grown man could ignore his own child or the woman who bore her. I did not understand how a child, conceived in such love, could now be called a bastard. There was much of the world I did not understand then.

I looked down at my sleeping babe. How could he not love her – love me? Tears filled my eyes and Peter Mathews saw.

'Are you unwell, Maria?' I lifted my eyes to his and saw sympathy in them – and something else.

'It is the birth, Sir, it has taken more than I expected from me. I am just saddened that Thomas chooses to ignore our child.' Peter looked down at Matilda, waking now, her mouth pursed in hunger, as she raised a tiny fist towards him. I saw him stretch his finger out to touch her, then withdraw it as if she might burn him. 'She needs feeding. Thank you for bringing the money. Please tell Thomas . . .' My words failed. Tell him what? That we were well, that his child was beautiful – that I still loved him?

Peter Mathews bowed.

'I will tell him you and the babe do well. I will come again, Maria, in a few weeks. Thomas has said he will do his duty by you and I will make sure he does.' He turned on his elegantly booted heel and walked back towards the village as Matilda lost patience, wriggled in my arms and began to cry loudly. I watched as he walked away then shut the door and sat down heavily on the chair, opening the front of my dress to feed her. I looked at her downy head, her face smooth with contentment as she suckled, and a sadness seemed to well up from deep within me. How could I care for something as small and fragile as she? I did not know how to do it and I was alone. Tears fell then and I brushed them away as I moved her to the other breast. As I did so she opened her eyes and looked at me, all the time her mouth working, as if to give me hope. Her hair was dark like mine, her eyes blue and knowing. One little hand pushed at me as she suckled and I held out my finger and stroked it, feeling the tiny fingers close around and clasp it tightly. She was perfect. She was my daughter and I swore to do the very best for her that I could. I closed my eyes and held her, letting myself be absorbed by the sharp pulling at my breast, the peace and quiet, the stillness of the house, and for the first time since she had been born, a small contentment came over me.

The very next morning I found her in her crib, stone-dead.

CHAPTER

THIRTEEN

W hen I think of the time that followed it seems unreal to me now. My stepmother organised everything for I could barely get out of bed. Little Matilda was laid to rest in the churchyard, next to my mother, just eleven weeks from the day she was born. Reverend Whitmore hurriedly said the prayers for the dead over her tiny shrouded body, then they put her in the cold earth and everyone behaved as if she had never been. That very day the crib was put away, the small clothes shut into lavender-lined drawers and I was expected to return to my role as housekeeper. But I was not the same. In the days that followed I kept thinking of her deep in the ground, alone and in the dark, with no one to comfort her. I wanted her back so much, my arms ached for the feel of her small body. My stepmother was losing patience.

'Maria, you need to get out of bed and keep yourself occupied.' She was packing cabbage leaves against my breasts, binding them tight to ease the pain. 'God has chosen her, she will be with Him now. A little angel in Heaven. It does no good to lie here fretting.'

Her eyes filled with tears and I caught a glimpse of the pain of loss behind her brisk manner.

I tried, I really did, but I wept all the time and the black cloud that had descended on me after the birth grew bigger, heavier, weighing down my every footstep. Each movement was an effort, each word a struggle. I woke every morning with a surge of dread which flooded through me and did not leave until I fell into my bed at the end of each long day, clasping at sleep like a drowning man. I went to church and tried to pray, but my thoughts constantly drifted to my babe, outside in the churchyard. Everyone said it was a beautiful autumn, that the leaves had never shown so much colour, how the days were remarkably warm. But I saw nothing, felt nothing. I carried out my tasks as if I were a ghost.

IT WAS when I dropped and broke the second plate in as many days that my stepmother snapped.

'For goodness sake, girl, pull yourself together. You are not the first to lose a child and you won't be the last. It's time you stopped moping around the place looking like death warmed up. Tidy yourself up, go outside, I'm tired of you bringing misery to this house all day. Think of the boys, of Nancy – you are bringing us all down with your moods.' I said nothing, just lowered my head and picked at the stuff of my skirt. She moved closer, her stale breath warming my face. 'You brought this upon yourself, Maria, you made your bed and now you must lie in it, for better or worse. That poor babe, to be saddled with a mother like you, no wonder she decided to leave this world.' She did not see the slap coming. My hand flew through the air without thought, landing on her smug face with a loud smack. She cried out and put her palm to her reddening cheek, as I dropped my hand to my side, shaking. 'How dare you! How dare you hit me. Your father will know of this, my girl.' For once words seemed to fail her as I stood there, unmoving, then she rallied. 'Get out of my sight.'

She was panting, near to tears, and I remembered Nancy's plea and held out my hand.

'I did not mean – it was when you spoke of Matilda so. It was not my fault she died, I could not help it. I would not have wanted it for the world but it happened and I do not know how to live now, how to go on.' I could no longer speak for the sobs which shuddered through me and I wanted her to come to me, to hold me and comfort me, but she did not. She stared hard at me then just left me there and walked away. She walked away.

WE SPENT the next days moving around each other cautiously, like cats, unsure when the other would bare her claws. Nancy curled up against me in bed a few nights later and put her arm around me.

'Mother is still very upset, Maria. You should apologise to her.'

I stiffened.

'I will not. She told me that I had been a bad mother, that I hadn't deserved to have Matilda.' My voice caught at the speaking of her name. 'She thinks it was my fault she died.'

'It was not your fault, Maria, and she was wrong to say that, but she has been good to us and you should not have put your hand on her. She has not told Father what you did. But you should make things right with her, for else how are we all to live?'

And I was going to speak to her, to try and put things right between us, for the sake of the family. I was trying to find the right words to say, but then George, her youngest, fell ill with an inflammation of the lungs. He was only five years old and it was heartbreaking to see him lying so still, his chest moving erratically, the sound of wheezing filling the house. For a while, I feared that he too would be taken, and the memories of Matilda came back to haunt me, filling my waking hours, darkening my dreams. Ann, for all her faults, loved her children dearly and she spent hours by George's bedside, nursing him back to health. She feared for little Thomas and Ambrose and kept them away from their brother to avoid them being afflicted. When she was too tired or needed her rest, Nancy or I took over. As he slowly got better, so did matters between us, and by the time he was up and about things had returned almost to normal.

One morning when Ann was in bed, sleeping after her broken nights with George, Peter Mathews called again. I answered his knock and he bowed to me.

'Maria, news has reached me of your sad loss. Please accept my condolences.' I stared at him, the words stinging, as he cleared his throat, suddenly looking awkward. 'Thomas has asked me to inform you that, as there is no longer a child, he considers your financial arrangement at an end.' He reached into his coat and brought out a small purse. 'He sends this to cover the burial but says that there will be no more.' He glanced behind me as my step-mother came down the stairs and shouldered me out of the way, shoving me back into the hallway. She took the purse from him and tipped the few coins into her palm, then put her hands on her hips and stared at him.

'What do you mean, there will be no more? He has barely paid enough to cover the costs we have had, which, I must say, have been substantial. Is this how a gentleman behaves? No, Sir, it is not! Remember, Maria has kept any mention of his name away from connection with this unfortunate episode.'

Mr Mathews looked from her to me then back again, all sympathy gone, his face blank.

'How much?'

I stepped forward, biting back my tears.

'Sir, we have been paid sufficient. As you say, there is no child now.'

'Five pounds.' Ann's voice rang sharp, and her eyes narrowed.

'That is a lot of money, Mrs Martin.

'Five pounds buys Maria's continued silence. Mr Corder will not be troubled by us again.'

He looked her up and down, judging the situation, then glanced at me.

'I have four pounds with me, Mrs Martin. It would take your husband all summer to earn that. Will it suffice?'

She looked him up and down then held out her hand. He reached into his coat, unfolding four notes which he pressed into her outstretched hand. She looked down, nodding in satisfaction.

'We understand each other, Mr Mathews. You need not call on us again, the arrangement is at an end. I trust this is satisfactory to you – and Mr Corder?' She spat his name out and Peter Mathews stepped back.

'It is, Madam. I will relay your message to Thomas.'

'You do that, Sir.' She stepped away from the door and disappeared into the dark of the cottage, counting the notes in her hand as she went. I stood there, hot with embarrassment, not knowing what to say to him. He looked down at me then and his smile warmed my heart.

'I am truly sorry for your loss, Maria. It has been a pleasure to meet you but now I must leave. I am back to London tomorrow.'

'Will you call again?' I found I didn't want to lose this last contact with Thomas.

'Your stepmother has told me not to and I suppose I must abide by her wishes.' He looked down at me and his eyes softened. 'I should not come again.'

But he did.

CHAPTER
FOURTEEN

There were few whispers about Peter Mathews later. No one said that Peter Mathews was a seducer, as they had with Thomas, that he had taken advantage of me. It was claimed that it was I who lured him. For Peter was a gentleman, you see, and gentlemen are always protected by their like. But it was he who pursued me. At first, he called every few weeks to ask after my welfare. Gradually my stepmother mellowed in her attitude towards him, for he flattered and flirted with her until her objections were silenced – she was ever one to defer to her betters.

As I slowly began to recover from the loss of Matilda, Peter surprised me with gifts, small at first – ribbons, a little brooch, a handkerchief embroidered with flowers – and it was these kindnesses that kept me from brooding on my loss, from sinking back under the dark cloud that possessed me after her birth. He brought light into my life again and I was grateful for it and began to look forward to his visits. He was older than me by some fifteen years and lived in London, but he was a frequent visitor to these parts and had known the Corder family for most of his life. And he told me of London. He brought it to life for me with his stories, that far-off city that I had often dreamed about visiting when I was a child. He had kin hereabouts, so he visited them and would use this as an excuse to call on me. I never knew what his occupation was, just that he was a gentleman, the youngest of nine and was supported by his father, as gentlemen so often seem to be.

My stepmother still frowned on our arrangement.

'He is only after one thing, Maria, mark my words. You threw yourself away on Thomas Corder and you are set to do the same thing again.'

'It is a friendship, that is all.'

'Stupid girl to believe that. You will not bring scandal to this door a second time, d'you hear me? Your father would see you in the workhouse if it happened again. And I hope you don't think Peter Mathews will make an honest woman of you? Soiled goods, that's what you are, and no gentleman would consider for a moment lowering themselves to marry you. No, he's after for free what he has to pay for in London.'

She was right, I knew it deep down. But slowly it dawned on me what it was that angered her, why she was so cruel towards me. For whenever Peter came to the door she flew to remove her apron and put a hand to her curls, pinching her cheeks to brighten them, and she fairly simpered when he spoke to her. It was jealousy – she was only eight years older than me and was tied to my father, a man twenty-one years her senior. She had borne three children to an old man and her world had narrowed, tied as it was to the cottage and her boys. Peter Mathews represented freedom and choice to her, all the dreams that had been taken from her when she married my father. She looked at me and saw what the future could have been like for her. Her earlier prettiness had gone, taken from her by life and time, and she looked older now, a pale shadow of the bright young girl who came into our house. No, she was jealous of me and the attention I received. But I did not heed her warnings, for my mind was full of Peter.

. . .

I DID NOT RUSH into anything, I had learned my lesson. He visited me on every occasion he was in Suffolk and we would walk and talk – he made no demands of me. We seemed charmed, Peter and me, and I did not give any thought to the future, just lived for the times I was with him, for he took me away from myself to another world. When he was away from me I spent my time dreaming of him and gradually he became all I thought of as I went about my daily tasks, my stepmother tutting and sighing. I so wanted to go to all the places he talked about and I pestered and pestered him. And eventually, he gave in.

I told my stepmother that I would be away for a few nights. She knew I was going with Peter but she kept her lips tight-buttoned, although disapproval was writ large on her face. Father was away working and it was only Nancy who voiced any concerns, only Nancy who cared.

'Are you sure this is wise, Maria?' I was packing my bag, clothes strewn over the bed. 'He is taking advantage of your good nature, you know.' I stopped what I was doing and looked hard at her.

'I love him. And I so want to go to London, to see all those places we have long dreamed of. I may never get another chance and I cannot live out my life here in Polstead knowing that there was something better and that I had not known it.' I took her hands. 'Be happy for me, Nancy, I beg you. You are the only one who cares for me here. I must take this chance, and who knows what will come of it?'

She took my hands in hers.

'I wish you would not go. I fear for you.' She paused, solemn. 'Be careful, sister, that is all. And be happy.'

'I will, and I will bring you a gift. What would you like?'

Nancy beamed at me.

'I will be happy with whatever you choose for me.' We clung to each other for a long time, then I continued my packing.

PETER TOOK ME TO LONDON, and it was everything I had imagined it would be. We ate in oyster houses, drank champagne from tall shining glasses served by obsequious waiters. We saw shows and visited pleasure gardens and tea houses. Peter treated me like a Queen, taught me to be a lady. He showed me how to speak with care, how to eat at table, how to dress and undress. Yes, he had his price and it was in London, in his rooms, that I finally surrendered to him. The small gifts changed to more generous ones. He bought me clothes finer than I had ever seen; a silk shawl, fashionable shoes, white kid gloves and silk stockings.

'This is the greatest city in the world, Maria, and you must dress accordingly. Someone as beautiful as you should be appreciated. You should be shown off as the stunner you are.' His rooms had a long mirror and for the first time, I could see the whole of me. My body was not willowy as it once was, for time and childbirth had made it womanly, soft and curvy. But he did not mind. He made me proud to be the way I was, made me feel cherished – he made me feel loved. In those days my eyes sparkled and my dark curls shone and when he peeled off the silk stockings, slowly, one by one, he made my body sing too. I am shamed now to confess it but I loved the feel of his weight on me, the absolute delight of being naked in his arms, moving together, the darts of pleasure it gave me, the satisfaction it gave him. Yes, Peter Mathews taught me many things. He bought me a black silk gown and a green umbrella and, on our last evening, I wore it to a restaurant where all was fine white linen and the glitter of glass and cutlery. It was a charmed world, far away from where I grew up, a fantasy land. Peter let me be the person I had always dreamed of being.

I remember the feel of that dress now. The silk whispered as I moved, warm and smooth against my skin, the bodice tight, embroidered with tiny flowers. It showed off my figure, my clear complexion and rosy cheeks and it made my eyes glitter; I had caught sight of myself in the seamstress' mirror and knew how well it suited me, how well he had chosen for me.

I liked myself then, for the first time. I felt happy, attractive and was proud of what I had become. Peter did love me, I knew it. I did not hold out any hopes for our union, I had learned my lesson there, but I wanted to enjoy myself, and feel appreciated and desired, and he never lied to me. For a time, I was allowed to feel special, beautiful and loved. Was that so little to ask? Doesn't every girl want that? Would anyone have behaved very differently if they had been me? By the way they spoke of me afterwards, it was as if I was the one to blame for the ill that befell me and, yes, I was partly responsible. But for that short time, Peter allowed me to be who I had always wanted to be and I make no apology for that. I paid no heed to the day of reckoning I knew would come. I lived a life I had always dreamt of.

But I paid the price eventually.

CHAPTER

FIFTEEN

When I returned home after that visit in my new dress and cloak, carrying a hatbox and the green umbrella, my family quickly brought me down to earth. Ann must have heard the carriage, for she was waiting in the parlour as I walked through the door, Father beside her, his face taut and pale. My stepmother put her hand proprietorially on his shoulder as he spoke first.

'What do you you look like? I'll tell you, girl. Some London whore, that's what.' His voice was harsh and bitter and I felt all my new-found assurance shatter before him like glass.

'Peter bought me these clothes. He likes to see me look beautiful.'

'Get your head down out of the clouds, girl. He likes to have a pretty wench on his arm, 'tis all. You could be anyone, but for some reason, he's chosen you. It won't last and then where will you be?'

I felt myself begin to tremble as my stepmother leaned forward, her eyes glittering.

'So how have you paid him for all this finery, eh? Well, we all know the answer to that.' She puffed herself up like a robin in the snow. 'You can't hide it from me. You've become his mistress, haven't you, bedding him into buying you beautiful things. You are no better than you should be. Your father would have done well to have taken a switch to you when you were young, for look at you now.' Father dropped his head at this as Nancy came into the parlour and my stepmother pointed to her. 'What sort of example are you to your sister?' I looked at Nancy but she would not meet my gaze and I knew in that moment I was losing her. She was becoming my stepmother's creature and I was on my own. I drew myself up and bit my lip to stop myself from crying.

'Peter and I . . .'

The ferocity of my stepmother's voice startled me.

'There is no '*Peter and I*', can you not see that, you stupid girl?' Her face was vicious. 'He is using you, just as Thomas Corder did, and he will throw you off just as quick when he tires of you.'

'He enjoys my company, we are happy together. He says I make him laugh.'

'I am sure he does, for you are giving yourself to him for a few silks and petticoats. He is laughing because he realises just how cheaply he's had you.' I clenched my hands into fists but kept them by my side. I would not lash out at her again, not in front of my father and sister. I was better than that now, better than her and her spite and malice. 'You will bring shame on this family once again, Maria.'

'He is careful and so am I.'

She hissed at me like a snake.

'Careful? Pfft. It is us who have to endure the gossip and whispers in the village and just look what it did to us last time. No, I will not tolerate that again.'

I gathered my things and moved to the door, then went slowly up the stairs to the room I shared with Nancy. I put the hat box down, took off my new dress and folded it carefully over the chair, then fell onto the hard bed and wept.

. . .

THE ROOM DARKENED into night as I lay there until I had cried myself out. Then, the creak of the door, and Nancy came in.

'Oh, Maria, why do you do these things?' Her voice, gentle, undid me and I started to cry again.

'Oh Nan, do you hate me as well?'

'No, not hate you. I just – I just wish you would be the sister you used to be. I miss you, Maria. This house was not the same while you were away.' She turned and gazed longingly at the hat box. 'May I look?' I sat up, wiping my eyes, and nodded. She stooped over the hatbox, untying the ribbon slowly, savouring the moment, then lifted out the Leghorn bonnet that Peter had bought me only three days before. The straw rustled seductively under her touch. 'Oh, Maria, look at this. May I try it on?' It was a little too big for her but she tied the ribbons under her chin. I found the silk shawl Peter had given me and handed it to her.

'Here, this is for you. I promised you a gift.'

She took it in her hands and stroked the shining softness of it then opened it out and pulled it around her shoulders. She turned to me and I saw the old Nancy, my Nancy, in her dancing eyes. 'It is beautiful, thank you. Now I am as lovely as you.' She smiled then and I smiled back, but my father's words rattled in my head and the shine went off the day.

PETER and I had two more visits to London. It was as if money did not matter to him, for he spent often and well. He began to play the card tables and I was horrified to see the amount of money that he lost, but the more he lost the more he kept gambling. I could not bear to see it and my speaking up about it was the cause of our first falling-out.

'You forget yourself, Maria. I am not to be told by you what I may or may not do. I have raised you up and I may as easily bring you down. Have I not treated you well?' His face was blank and I saw a hardness in him that I had not noticed before. It made me step back and I bowed my head.

'You are right, Peter, and I am sorry. It's just that it seems wrong to me, all those coins, all that waste, when I think what they could do for others who have so little.'

'It brings me pleasure.' He tilted his head in the way I found so endearing, and looked at me under his lashes. 'As do you.' He kissed the tip of my nose, then slid his face against mine to nuzzle at my ear and my body melted. For Peter knew how to arouse me and I matched his passion with my own. 'We shall not argue. Come here, let me look at you.' He reached towards me, releasing my hair from its pins and shaking it loose to hang over my shoulders. He looped a finger into the neckline of my gown and drew me close towards him, undoing the fastenings with a practised movement, and buried his face in my neck, winding my hair through his hands as he pulled me to the bed. I do not know if that was the time. I like to think it was, for that night we were loving and laughing and full of life. But this time or another that followed we were not careful, Peter did not release me in time, but, in our pleasure, we did not heed it. For we were happy and that was all that mattered.

BUT HAPPINESS often goes unrewarded and it was that summer that I began to feel the tenderness of my breasts, sickness that I could not shake and I knew my stepmother had been proved right once again. I had not seen Peter for some weeks as he was away on business, but my stepmother's eyes were sharp, her judgement shrewd and, in the end, it was she who challenged me about my condition.

'So it's happened again, has it?' She nodded towards my stomach and I lifted a hand to the small curve protectively. She sighed. 'I'm not surprised, with the way you have been going about. So what is he going to do about it, your Peter Mathews? I suppose it is his?'

'Of course it is!' My anger dropped away as soon as it came. 'I have yet to tell him. I am waiting for the right moment. He has written to me saying he will be here in the next two days so I will speak to him then.'

She drew closer then, her voice dropping to a whisper.

'There is a woman over Sudbury way – she can make such problems go away. And he will pay, I am sure of it.'

I look at her in horror.

'No! I could not do that, not after Matilda.' My voice broke as the memories flooded back. 'I will not do that, it is wrong in the eyes of God. I will speak to Peter, he will know what to do.'

She stepped away from me and nodded.

'Do not leave it too long to speak to him, I dare not think how he will take the news. It's a shame you did not think of God before you went out enjoying yourself.' She paused. 'I suppose you want me to tell your father?' I nodded miserably. 'Very well, but I do not know what he will say. He has given up on you, Maria, and so have I. You are a disgrace to this family, no example to your sister and brothers. You should be ashamed.'

I was, and never more so than when I told Peter about the coming child. I saw the love leach from his eyes, his face tightening as he stepped back from me as if I had the pox.

'This is a shock, Maria. I wish you had been more careful. You know how much I desired you, you should have taken better precautions.' He rubbed his face with his palm. 'But it is done now. I will take care of matters for you. You will not have to go through this alone.' For a moment I thought he meant that he would marry me and I gasped in surprise, but my smile was soon lost. 'I can't wed you, Maria. Surely you did not imagine I would? I am a gentleman, it would not be fitting for me to marry one such as you, so far below my station. I'm sure you understand why that cannot be.'

'But what am I to do?'

He looked down at me and wiped the tears from my eyes.

'Do you not know of a woman who could . . . ?'

I looked at him angrily.

'I will not take the life of my child. I have lost one already, I cannot lose another.'

Peter sighed heavily.

'Oh, Maria, I wish that this had not happened but it has and I will help you as best I can. I will make sure you and the child are properly cared for. I can do that for you at least.'

I could not help myself.

'Like Thomas Corder did?'

He placed a finger under my chin and lifted it so that I looked him in the eye.

'I am not Thomas Corder. He was a careless young man who used you and then shirked his responsibilities by deserting you. I am not he. I am fond of you, very fond; I suppose I loved you in my way and we had fun, did we not, we were happy?' I nodded, mutely. I had no words. 'I will send you money each month and give you expenses for the lying-in. You will not go without, Maria, I will ensure that. But things will not be able to go along as they have, you do see that, don't you? A child changes everything. No, you will be safer staying here in Polstead with your family.' He paused. 'And I think it may be best we do not see each other for a while.' He let go of my chin and walked away as my tears fell, darkening the black silk dress he had bought me.

CHAPTER
SIXTEEN

Peter was generous, I will say that for him. All through that autumn, he sent money each month and with it, I was able to buy the necessary things for the coming child. I could not bear to use the clothes I had so lovingly sewn for Matilda, I thought it to be a bad omen, so I began again, my needle always in my hand, stitching my life away. As the days grew shorter and darker and my body grew larger, I became listless and tired. My legs and ankles swelled to bursting and at times I could barely walk, so I stayed indoors as much as I could, not wanting people to see my shame.

The child, a boy, was born just before Christmas. The birth was quicker than it had been with Matilda but it exhausted me more and I could do little for myself for the first two weeks. My son. His baptism had been arranged for a few days after Christmas, my stepmother again managing to persuade the Reverend Whitmore, even though this babe too was a bastard.

'He wanted even more this time. Peter Mathews will have to cover that cost as well. Do you have a name for the child?'

'I had thought to name him for his father.'

She hesitated.

'That will not be appropriate. Peter's name must not be mentioned in connection with this, you know that, especially not on the baptism records.'

'But . . .'

She looked at me intently.

'It cannot be. That is the price for his continued generosity. No, there must be no suggestion of the father's name. You must think of another. Perhaps Thomas, after your father? It may serve to placate him little.' So my boy was baptised Thomas Henry and Peter's money continued. But I was past caring then, for the blackness had descended on me far worse than before. I relied on my stepmother and Nancy to do everything for the babe except feed him, but even the effort of that left me listless and numb. Once again I could not believe this scrap of a being was mine, he felt as if he belonged to a stranger, and this time, I did not feel that rush of love, that sense of belonging that I had finally felt with Matilda. I felt nothing.

BUT DESPITE MY INDIFFERENCE, Thomas Henry thrived. He was active and lusty and his cries echoed around the cottage incessantly, so that I often had to cover my ears to get some peace. I tried to comfort him, to play with him and comfort him, but it was my stepmother he cried for. I began to long for quiet but there was none to be had indoors so, once I had fully recovered from the birth, I took to walking across the fields, going further and further as my strength returned. It helped, you see, the rhythm of the walking, the chime of birdsong, the flutter of new leaves in the trees, the crunch of my boots on the track through the woods. Spring came in all its glory that year, shoots peeking through the soil, the lowing of cattle and the bleating of newborn lambs. Everywhere was fresh and green. It was all there for me to see, in all its abundance, but I was blind to it. Mostly, I felt alone and unloved, thinking that all that was ahead of me were weeks of drudgery and greyness, for the colour had bleached from my life when Peter went. As spring moved into summer, then autumn, I walked and walked, enjoying the peace, dreading the time when I would have to retrace my steps and return home. But the blackness did not lift. I was perpetually sad, tearful, and uncaring. I felt empty and alone. There was nothing here for me any more.

WE HEARD about the death just before Christmas. We were about to sit down for our meal when a knock came on the door. My step-mother was busy in the kitchen so my father went to answer it. I heard a man's voice, mumbled words, my father's gruff reply, then he came back in and sat down heavily, his face grave. We knew better than to hurry him so we waited in silence.

'Old man Corder has died.' Always a man of few words, Father was blunt and unemotional. My stepmother dropped the forks she was carrying and put her hand to her chest dramatically.

'Oh, how terrible! Poor Mrs Corder. But he is your main employer. We cannot afford to lose those wages. What will this mean for us, Thomas?' She turned to my father, who was already loading his plate with food. He forked a mound of potato into his mouth, then looked up at her.

'Nothing, I expect, One of the sons will take over. Thomas probably, as James already has his own farm. The unmarried daughter will no doubt take care of her mother, as the other is wed.' He took another forkful. 'Moles still need catching, I will not be short of employment.' His jaws worked as he looked around at our surprised faces and pointed to the food with his fork. 'Eat up, before it goes cold. Your mother hasn't made all this for you to ignore it.' We helped ourselves and each other to the food and began to eat in silence. But my stepmother never could remain quiet for long.

'The word in the village was that Mr Corder was careful with his money, miserly some say. He gave those boys too much freedom until he had to settle their debts. Then he pulled them in on a tight leash.'

'Nothing wrong with being careful with money.' My father's head was bowed to his meal, his mouth full. 'Boys will be boys, best for them to sow their wild oats young so that they can settle down and marry.'

'Certainly, a few wild oats have been sown around here.' She glared at me and then looked thoughtful. 'So the father is dead – that will make Thomas Corder a rich man, no doubt.' I caught my breath at the mention of his name but my stepmother carried on regardless. 'Shame the babe died, we could have asked for more money.'

I threw down my fork and stood up from the table, my chair screeching on the flagged floor.

'Will you never stop reminding me of him?'

'Sit down, Maria.' My father's voice was stern and I obeyed. 'Your mother only wants what's best for you, for this household.' I looked at him through narrowed eyes.

She wants only to make trouble. The words were on the tip of my tongue but I swallowed them and addressed myself to my dinner as we settled again. I had almost forgotten Thomas, for I had not seen him in the village much since it had happened. I had tried hard to forget Matilda, too, but she was always in my thoughts; I often crept away to visit her and my mother, sitting by the grave-side deep in thought. I looked across to Thomas Henry, sat up at the table next to my stepmother. He had a bowl of pap in front of him which she was spooning into his mouth whilst trying to eat her own meal. He was a beautiful child, there was no doubt of it, but he was not mine now. I watched his face as he waited for each spoonful, mouth opening like a baby bird, his eyes fixed on her, doting and unwavering. She had taken him from me too. I glanced over at Nancy, but her eyes were on her plate and she did not speak. I had no one.

THE BAD WEATHER that winter kept me indoors and I became increasingly frustrated and irritable, snapping at the children, ignoring their cries for attention, and their tears when I did not respond. I tried to keep myself distracted – we had begun to take in mending again and my stepmother had put word about. People knew I was skilled with a needle, and so I was kept busy. The rhythm of the stitches soothed me, kept my mind from the blackness that always filled me. But the day came when I opened my bedroom casement and leaned out and smelt the warm sharpness of another spring on the breeze. The air felt cleaner, fresher, and I carried out my duties quickly that morning, then, throwing my warmest shawl around me, I stepped outside. Mother's rose garden was bedraggled and brown but there were the beginnings of green shoots bursting from the branches and I vowed to tidy it as soon as the ground had dried out a little more. But now I needed to walk. I moved to the gate and swung it closed behind me, then strode along the lane, past the pond and up the hill, to the footpath that ran beside the Corder house. Freedom flooded through me as I lengthened my stride, enjoying the warmth of the weak spring sun on my face, the feeling of the movement of limbs too long confined. Soft air filled my lungs and I coughed a little as I became out of breath, but I carried on, along the edge of the field then into the woods. It was a quiet place, calming and few ventured there. There were puddles and ponds, fed by a small stream, which had swollen with the rain. I had walked here with Thomas often enough to know every inch of it but I had avoided it these past years.

Now I saw that the trees were taller, the undergrowth more tangled and I realised that it was not only I that was changed. I had been an innocent. Such a lot had happened in those years; the loss of Matilda, the time with Peter, the birth of Thomas Henry, but it struck me then that my life had not moved on. I was still the same as I had been, but now I felt soiled. Two children born out of wedlock, the space for a father's name blank on each of the baptismal records. I was not the only one, many other girls had been caught like I had, and the blame was always laid at our door. But how were we to know, when no one spoke of such things? Men were a part of this too, they should share the blame, but it was always the women who had to bear the shame and the scorn. It was us that were outcasts. My rage flared within me as my spirits fell. The blackness that still dogged me began to descend, so I shook my head to clear it and increased my pace. I walked on, rounding a corner to the tree-fringed pond and then I saw him. A figure, leaning against the trunk of a tree that leaned out over the water, a book in his hand. I gasped and looked around me, thinking to escape, but there was no point. It had to happen some-time. For there stood Thomas Corder.

CHAPTER
SEVENTEEN

'Thomas?'

It was only as he turned that I realised my mistake.

'No, not Thomas. Were you to meet him here?' His voice was lighter and, when he straightened, I saw that he was not as tall. But the likeness was great, the fair hair falling over his eyes, the same snub nose, although this face was melancholy and drawn. And he wore eyeglasses, which glinted in the sunlight as he took them off.

'No, I thought –'

'That I was he. I'm afraid not.' He closed the book he had been reading and moved towards me and held out his hand. I was so taken aback that moved closer and shook it. 'I am his younger brother. William Corder, at your service.' He bowed and then straightened, his shy smile disarming me.

'I am Maria Martin.' His expression did not change but he shuffled his feet a little, then looked down. 'You have heard of me I see.'

He lifted his head and gazed at me.

'Yours is not a name that is mentioned in our household, I'm afraid to say, but Thomas has spoken to me of you, though not for some time now. I am glad to see you well after your . . . unfortunate experience.'

Although he had chosen his words to take the sting from them, still my anger surfaced.

'You mean the child I bore your brother, the one that he ignored. The one that died?'

'I am sorry, I did not mean to upset you, Maria. If it is of any comfort, I believe my brother did not treat you well in that matter and I am sorry for it.

'It is not for you to apologise for your brother, but I thank you all the same. It is good to hear his failure acknowledged rather than the wrong all being mine.' My anger bled away as I remembered. 'I am sorry for the loss of your father. His death must have come as a terrible shock to the family.'

His face fell and he looked down at his boots, scuffing one over the other.

'It did, though my father did not hold me in much esteem. I had caused him a few problems – money, you know – and he'd hoped I would join the Navy but even in that, I failed him. My eyesight is not good.' He held out the spectacles, then tucked them away into his pocket. 'No, it would be fair to say that I am the black sheep of the family, although my mother was pleased when I told her I was considering taking holy orders but – I don't know – nothing seems to fit me somehow.'

I smiled at him.

'I understand how you feel. I am also a black sheep. I do not fit either.' As I spoke the words aloud I wondered that I could confess such a thing to an acquaintance of a few short moments. He looked at me and then smiled back. He was handsome.

'Then we are twin souls, Maria Martin. Are you returning home now? May I walk with you? Only to the end of the track, you understand? It would not be done for us to be seen.'

'I understand.' He proffered his arm and I took it.

And in that moment our fate was sealed.

WILLIAM CORDER. So much has been said about him, thousands of words written about him. The papers have prised out every aspect of his character and blackened it, so his very name has become a byword for evil. Everyone in Polstead had something to say about him later, very little of it good, but I knew him better than anyone, for it was I that fell in love with him, and he with me. From that first meeting we did not stop talking to each other, sharing every thought and hope, and getting to know each other inside out. William told me how he had been sent away to school, and then returned, when he was sixteen, to help his father run the farm. He had been wild at this stage, visiting low establishments with his older brothers John and Thomas, gambling, lying to get money, even stealing once. He told me how his father, despairing of him, had said that any money owed would be taken out of his inheritance.

'So I do not expect to receive much as a result.' We were walking across the fields one day, enjoying the companionship.

'Were you so very bad?'

I was smiling at him, trying to lighten the moment.

'Bad enough. But at least I do not frequent taverns as my brother Thomas does, my father cannot hold that against me. I do not like the taste of strong drink, never have.' He paused and looked at me. I nodded for him to go on, wanting to know all I could about him. 'Things improved when I was nineteen. There was a service at Boxford Meeting House, Non-Conformists, you know. I knew my parents would be angry at my attending but when I heard the preacher speak it changed me, Maria. It made me realise that what I had been doing, the way I'd been behaving, was wrong, and I finally felt that God had a purpose for me. I revisited my bible after that and I found truths in there that I had not noticed before. But even this did not please my parents – they are strict Church of England and despised the Dissenters I began to mix with. My mother did think it had cured me of my wickedness, but I am not sure I believe much of it now.' His voice trailed off, then he looked at me and smiled ruefully. 'As to my father, I shall have to wait until his Will is proved to see what he finally thought of me. He was not a man you could love, although I tried, and I know I was a poor son to him. I stole from him and lied to him and now he is gone I cannot ask his forgiveness. No, I was never a son he could be proud of.'

I took William's hand and gripped it hard. He had such a poor opinion of himself and such people often seem to attract trouble into their lives without realising it. I wondered if he was one of them.

'But you can be that good son to your mother now, she will need you, all of you, to help and support her in her widowhood. You can make amends in that way.'

He smiled at me then.

'Yes, that is true. Thank you for listening. I have never had someone who understands before. I find it easy to speak of these things with you.'

'I do not judge you, William, only the Lord will do that, and I am not without sin myself. I do understand.'

He took my hand and raised it to his lips.

'We are matched then.'

'It seems so.' Laughter bubbled out of me then for the first time in many weeks and the sensation seemed strange. But the world lightened a little and I began to hope.

EIGHTEEN

Ours was a fire slow burning. We were hesitant, cautious, just lonely people in need of company at first. I liked him, he attracted me and slowly, gradually, what we had blossomed into something deeper. He was not as haughty-looking as Thomas, nor as confident as Peter, but he was kind and fair. He was little taller than me and walked with a stoop, often with his left arm holding the lapel of his coat, which I found endearing. And he listened to me, truly listened. As spring turned to summer and our walks grew longer, I told him of my time at the rectory, of the kindness of the Pritchetts, and after a while, when I knew him better, about the death of my mother.

'That must have affected you greatly, Maria. And to have another take her place so soon –'

'I did not have time to grieve, it was all so sudden. I was summoned home to care for Nancy. And then he brought Ann into our household. I can never think of that woman as my mother, despite Father's insistence. She took my sister's love from me, and Nancy was my only link to the past – my sister is her creature now, has been from the beginning really.'

'Perhaps, being younger than you, she needed a mother more? She was only four years old after all, and would sorely miss a mother's touch, her care.'

I had not thought of it in that way before.

'Maybe you are right, and maybe I should be more charitable, but it hurt me so much and still does, truth be known. And then when your – when Thomas rejected me –'

William took my hand.

'Do not speak of him, I can't bear to think of you with him.' A hardness had crept into his voice and, with a jolt of pleasure, I realised he was jealous.

'I rarely speak of him, it was long in the past. I do not even think of him now.'

'You thought I was him the first time we met. You called out his name.'

'It was the shock, that was all. I had not seen him for such a long time and you look so alike. I was surprised to see him – you – there.' I can feel the tension in his hand. 'Thomas had nothing to do with me after I told him I was with child, you know that, and that is how it will remain. Our babe . . .' My voice catches. 'My Matilda, she was not meant for this world. She was taken from me so quickly. I had no one left.'

His grip tightened and I thought to pull away but did not. His voice was harder now.

'What of Peter Mathews? Do you still think of him, wish you were with him?'

'No, I do not. Yes, he is the father of my child and visits occasionally to see him. He sends my father money each quarter year for the upkeep of our boy and is generous, but it is long over between us, whatever it was we had.'

'You loved him?'

I paused then.

'I believed myself in love with him, yes, he was good to me and showed me a life I could only have dreamt of. But it ended, and that was his doing and I am not sure now if it was love. But he provides for Thomas Henry.'

'I do not want you to see him again, Maria. You are my friend now, not his.' I was surprised by his ferocity and depth of feeling, and I did not want to anger him further.

'If that is what you wish. I can ask my stepmother to deal with him as she already does. I am grateful for his generosity, that is all. There is no feeling there, I promise. But if you wish I will not speak to him again.'

'And you will tell him?'

'I will if it gives you peace of mind.'

'Do you swear it?'

'I swear it.' I did not hesitate. Peter was lost to me anyway, and I was reassured as the tension loosened in William's shoulders and he clasped my hand gently once more and gazed into my eyes.

'And what of us, of me – do you have feelings for me, Maria?' He bowed his head, awaiting my reply, and I looked at the fair lashes shading his pale blue eyes, the freckles on his upturned nose and I moved into him and kissed him softly. His hand slid around my waist and he pulled me to him as his lips sought mine. He was nervous, inexperienced, pursing his lips, so I pushed my tongue against them until he opened his mouth a little and softened into the sensation. Our first kiss. It was sweet and gentle, like him. He was kind, he never forced me. He courted me with soft words and, as the heat of that summer grew, we sought the shade and privacy of the Red Barn. And then came the Cherry Fair.

THAT JULY WAS hot and dry. Polstead simmered with excitement in the heat, for the annual fair was upon us. Our cherries were known far and wide to be the best-tasting and this had been a good year. Polstead Blacks they were called and all the fields around here grew them. The blossom in the spring was sweet and delicate, scenting the air, and the cherries when they ripened were small and black-skinned. People came from all around to buy them and the fair was the one excitement we had all year. Everyone dressed in their finest clothes and paraded between the stalls, which were heaped high with cherries and other produce. There was a puppet show and a fiddler played as girls danced. Children dodged noisily in and out, drawing curses from the stall holders, but it was all good-natured. I had been one of those children once. Nancy and I had chased each other around the stalls, through the legs of the crowds, picking up fallen cherries and stuffing them in our mouths, laughing at the staining as our lips and tongues grew dark. I had not done that for many a year, preferring to keep to myself. But this year was different. For this year I had William.

'I shall meet you by our pond in the woods, Maria, in the afternoon. Everyone will be at the fair. I am only sorry that we cannot meet there, but our liaison must remain hidden for now.'

I had wished to hear different from him, wanted with all my heart for him to say he would meet me there. I had imagined walking proudly through the crowd, head held high, on the arm of William Corder, and seen in my mind the jealous faces of the other girls, the surprise and pride when my father and stepmother saw us together. I had dreamt of it every waking moment but it was not to be. William was right, I knew that, it was too soon for our relationship to be known, but I was deeply disappointed. Just for once, I had hoped that one of my dreams might come true.

MY STEPMOTHER WAS PUTTING on her best hat and straightening my father's neckerchief when I came down the stairs. The boys ran through the house, shouting and laughing, full of excitement, and she called to them to be quiet then turned and looked at me.

'You are not ready? Are you not coming to the fair with us?

Everyone will be there. You did not come last year, nor the year before that.'

'Not this year.' I looked at my father. 'I am sorry Father, I just do not wish to be with so many people.'

'Very well. Your stepmother will be disappointed.' Her head bobbed in agreement, the ridiculous bonnet perched on her curls, but I had little concern for her feelings. She gathered her boys around her sighing heavily, but I knew that she did not want me there really. Nancy had already gone to meet her friends, a group of giggling, shallow girls, heads full of the latest fashions and handsome boys. I stood in the doorway and watched them leave, waving as they wandered down the lane, then ran to my room and put on my best dress. I smoothed it down and looked at myself in the speckled mirror. I looked well enough so, snatching my bonnet, I strode out along the track to meet William.

THE SUN BEAT down as I crossed the field but the wood was cool and welcoming, shadowed, the trees barely moving. I wiped my brow with my handkerchief, not wanting to arrive flushed and damp. He was waiting in the place where I had first seen him and he took my arm, drawing me down on the soft grass under a tall willow which bent over the water. Sunlight glimmered on the surface as I removed my bonnet and loosened my hair.

'I am glad you are here. I have a gift for you.' His eyes were sparking with pleasure. 'I know you must have wished we could go to the fair together but I hope this will make up for that. Now, close your eyes.' I did as I was told and heard a rustle, then felt his breath, soft on my cheek, as he moved closer. I could feel his body, the heat of him. Something brushed my lips and I started back in surprise and heard him laugh. 'Trust me, I will not harm you.' I opened my eyes to see him holding a basket of cherries. 'I bought these especially for you. We will have our own Cherry Fair here.' He

a

held one out to me. It was black, gleaming in the afternoon sun like a dark gem, suspended on a narrow green stem the colour of new shoots. I opened my mouth and felt the weight of it as he placed it on my tongue, closed my eyes and bit. A slight pressure, the skin broke, sweet salt, a tingling burst of sharpness, then the hard surface of the stone. Juice ran down my chin and, laughing, he brought up his neckerchief to wipe me clean. He offered me another, then another; I could not have enough.

'Oh, Maria.' The way he said my name, soft and low, made long-forgotten sensations rise in me. I opened my eyes and looked at him. His face was close now, the corners of his blue eyes creased in a smile and his look was kind, loving, and full of desire. 'Maria, my love.' He bent forward, brought his lips to mine and I was lost.

CHAPTER
NINETEEN

We were so happy that summer. The weather continued hot until the farmers were complaining loudly of the lack of rain. The crops shrivelled and the ground turned to dust but it seemed that nothing could touch William and me.

On the last day of August Peter called. He had ridden to our gate and asked to see his son. My stepmother took Thomas Henry out to him and Peter dismounted and bent down to him, reaching into the pocket of his coat and holding out a carved wooden soldier. Thomas Henry clasped it in his chubby hand and laughed at it while my stepmother thanked him effusively. I watched them from the doorway, keeping my distance, as Peter glanced up.

'Maria.' he said. 'The child is a bonny boy.'

My stepmother looked hard at me, waiting for me to reply.

'You have my stepmother to thank for that, it is she that cares for him in most things.'

'Then I thank you most sincerely, Mrs Martin, you are turning him into a good and obedient boy. He is a credit to you both.' He smiled at her and she brought her hand to her cheek and blushed. He turned back to me.

'And you, Maria? You are looking well – glowing some might say.' His gaze was searching and I knew in that moment that he had heard about William and me. 'I have just come from the Corder house.' I was praying that he would not say anything in front of my stepmother, who sensed something flash between us and was looking enquiringly from one to the other.

'I am in good health, thank you.' I bent to pick up my son as Ann went past me into the darkness of the hallway. Thomas Henry grabbed at my hair and wriggled hard, wanting to be released, so I set him down and he toddled after my stepmother, waving his toy soldier delightedly. When she was out of earshot I turned back to Peter. His expression was shrewd, an eyebrow raised.

'I have something to say to you.' I cleared my throat, suddenly nervous. 'I am not able to see you again. It would not be right. I have met someone else. You are welcome to visit your son but I must no longer speak with you.'

Peter's face did not change. He was gentleman enough not to betray his feelings.

'I understand. I wish you well. I will, of course, continue to send money for the boy each quarter.' He moved towards his horse, placed a leather-shod foot in the stirrup, launching himself into the saddle.

'I am grateful. He will be well cared for. My stepmother –'

'I understand the situation, better than you think.' He bent down from his horse towards me, his voice low. 'But be careful, Maria. I would not like to see you badly used.' He straightened and clicked his tongue and his mount moved off. I stood in the doorway watching his retreating back and considered what he had said. Badly used? As if he had not used me, like Thomas before him. I sighed deeply at the way men smooth and bend the truth to suit themselves. And then I dismissed all thought of him.

. . .

As that winter tightened its grip William and I began to meet in the Red Barn. I had not been there since the night I told Thomas I was with child. Now I looked at it with new eyes. It was tall and imposing and stood alone in the middle of a field; painted a deep blood red, it caught the rays of the setting sun, which added to its mystery. Now it was full of the summer's harvest and William had begun to keep the key in his pocket for safety. Afterwards, the engravings in the newspapers and broadsheets made it look small and insignificant, but it was not. It soared like a church. When you opened the outer door and stepped inside it felt almost holy; tall and imposing, with a feel of great age. There were two bays, one a wagon shed, and one a chaff house. But that winter the whole barn was full of wheat, dry and sweet-smelling. And it was quiet, so quiet, sweet-scented, but with a faint musty smell from the packed earth floor that reminded me of cold pews and hymnals. No one came there so we often stayed, wrapped in coats and shawls. It became our private place, lying on a bed of straw in each other's arms, sated and warm, before creeping back to our homes, hand in hand. He was my comfort and I his. We would talk about every-thing and he would sometimes read to me, looking distinguished in his eyeglasses. I took them from him once and put them on. My world instantly distorted and I felt as if I would fall. It was like looking through water, everything rippled and shimmered.

'I can see nothing!'

He laughed and took them from me.

'I don't need them all the time, fortunately, but they do help when I need to read.'

We were happy that winter, speaking of our dreams, of London and fashions and how slow life was here in Polstead and how we both longed for something more. William was a thinker, slow to react, against my sharpness and speed of thought, and his plans were often fantastical, such as could never become real. He seemed to think that if he believed in something truly enough then he could make it so. It was his one weakness.

This time of contentment could not last. I had grown lax, just wanting the comfort of William's arms, the weight of his body on mine, and had given no heed to the consequences. You would have thought I would take great trouble not to find myself in the same position as I had twice before, but I did not, for I was past caring what others thought of me. I only lived for the present. William had lifted the black fog that had long surrounded me and had shown me the affection that I had always yearned for. Our love grew slowly and was all the stronger for that. I realised that my previous feelings for Thomas and then Peter had been infatuation. No, what William and I had was true. He was the youngest son, of no significance to the family, no father now to object, and I dared to hope that we might have a future together. He made my spirits soar and I wanted that feeling to last forever.

BY NOVEMBER I knew I was with child again and my heart sank. I did not know how my father would react and the spectre of the workhouse loomed. I worried how I would give William the news, or how it would be received. I hoped against hope that he would be pleased but I was terrified that he would not be, that he too would leave me and I knew I could not bear it again. I was beginning to show and I could not hold it off for much longer. My stepmother suspected, I was certain, for I had seen the looks she had been giving me, but we had not spoken of it and I am sure my father would not have noticed as he barely gave me the time of day. But I had to tell William.

I waited until one evening when we were in the Red Barn, close in each other's arms.

'William, I have to tell you something but I am afraid to speak it.' He looked at me and gently smoothed a curl back from my cheek.

'You can tell me anything, Maria, do you not know that?'

I took a deep breath and closed my eyes.

'I am to have a child – our child.' He did not move. 'It will be in the spring, I think.' I dared not look at him, I did not want to see his expression. Then he did a small thing. He took my chin in his hand and kissed my lips slowly and sweetly.

'I am to be a father? I can scarce believe it. Oh, Maria, you have made me a very happy man.'

I looked at him then and saw he spoke the truth and all my fears dropped away.

'You are truly pleased? You will not leave me?'

He smiled broadly.

'Of course not. We have made a child together and we shall care for it together.' He rested his hand over my stomach. 'My child, growing here. It is like a miracle.' We did not speak then of what would happen when the babe was born, William just held me and told me over and over how much he loved and cared for me, how proud he was, until I knew he would not let me down. I was calm then, confident that all would be well. But God seeks to punish the wicked and bring down those who rise above themselves.

CHAPTER
TWENTY

I could not have foretold what happened next. Of all the disasters that could have rained down on our heads, none could have thought of a tragedy such as this. William's younger brother, James, took ill.

'Oh, Maria, you should see him. He has had a cough for a time. We Corders all have a weakness in our chests but Mother said it was merely a summer cold. But now, to see him brought so low. He is not yet twenty years old and looks like an old man.' William's voice was sad and defeated. 'A few days ago he collapsed in the fields and they brought him back on a trestle, for he could not even walk the distance home.'

I took his hand.

'William, I am so sorry. How is he now?'

'His breathing is laboured, as if he has to pull for every lungful, and his skin is grey. He is wasting away before our eyes. The doctor has confirmed it, but we had so hoped that we were wrong. Mother had assured us it was nought but a cold, but now – ' He brought his hand to his face and rubbed at it as if to take the vision away. 'James has consumption and is not expected to live. The doctor cannot say how long he has, but it is not long.' I held William's hand as his eyes welled with tears, then he took a deep breath, composing himself. 'John has his own farm to manage, so Thomas and I will need to take over the running of the farm and lands here, even though I know little about it. I must help shoulder my share of responsibility. It will mean that our meetings cannot be so frequent. I am sorry, Maria.' He bowed his head as the tears flowed and I held him tightly. 'Oh my love, if only it could be different. I do not wish to do this. I do not want to be a farmer.' I had no words with which to comfort him, so I just held him until his body stopped shuddering and his tears ceased. He looked at me and my heart broke to see him so distressed, so I took his hand and placed it on my stomach.

'Your child is here, William, I am here.' I stroked his hair back from his forehead as you would a small boy. 'You have us to console you. I will be your comfort, though we cannot be together.'

'I have thought about it all night. There is my inheritance from my father – we could leave here.'

I turned to him, surprised by his words.

'Leave? Both of us? But what of the farm, your mother?'

He looked me in the eye and smiled in that shy way he had, and my heart surged.

'We could marry.'

IT WAS SAID. All I had dreamed of, William was now offering me. 'We could go to London as man and wife, or maybe live in Ipswich. I could find work as a clerk and you could set up a dame school. You can read and write well, and I could help you. Or you could take in mending as you do now. We could do anything we wanted. We would be free.' I could not speak, my mind was whirring with thoughts and dreams jostling for a place in my head. Then he paused and his voice softened. 'But we cannot do it yet. I would need to tell my mother of you and the child, and set things right with her. And with James so ill – they will need my help.' He took my hand and brought it to his lips. 'We could be married, Maria, if you would like that?' His voice sounded surprised, as if someone else had said the words, as if the idea was new-born in his mind. Then he dropped my fingers and placed both his hands on my stomach. The babe kicked at his touch and he smiled shyly in amazement. 'You, me and our child – we would be a family.' And the world seemed better then as if things would come right for us. I dared to hope that the life I had long dreamed of was finally to be mine, and with a man I truly loved.

But death came swooping and stole away my dreams.

It was the day of Thomas Corder's twenty-sixth birthday. I had glimpsed him just before Christmas at a distance but had not spoken to him since I told him about Matilda and now had no wish to. He was in my past and I was better for it. I had heard rumours about him and the local girls, but they did not trouble me, for I had the promise of a better life. No, Thomas was nothing to me any more. William had told me that his mother was preparing a luncheon for him in celebration, and all the Corder family were to be in attendance, even James, still so ill. The weather that January had been sharp and bitter, but on the day of his birthday the sun was out. It was the sort of day that cleanses the senses and raises the spirits. Polstead was clothed white with frost, silent and waiting, like a bride-cake and I imagined the family, tight with anticipation, assembling in the beamed house on the hill and wondered if I would ever be a part of that.

I did not see it happen. They said afterwards that Thomas had spied a friend from the frozen side of Polstead Pond and went to greet him. I did not see him place his feet, one after the other, testing his weight on the ice as he began to walk across it, laughing as he went. They said that he was calling and waving to his friend as his strides became longer, more confident and that he forgot to take care. I did not hear the crack as the ice broke under him and he slid beneath the frigid water, making no sound, until only his hand showed above the surface, his fist clenched white. They got there as quickly as they could, the men from the village. The smallest of them slid on his stomach with rope in hand, edging his way carefully to where Thomas was as the others held him tight. The man tied the rope firmly around the exposed wrist and they all hauled Thomas out, pulling him as quickly as they could to the safety of the frozen grass. They turned him and pumped his arms to try and get the water from his lungs but it was all too late. Thomas was dead. I did not see them lay him on a trestle brought from the Cock Inn, or watch as six of them carried him solemnly to his mother's house, one going ahead, cap in hand, to tell her the terrible news, the rest of the village following.

I did not hear his mother's screams, nor see her fall to the floor, stricken with grief. It was only later that I heard that Mrs Corder had been watching her favourite son from her bedroom window and had seen him die.

CHAPTER
TWENTY-ONE

T hen I made it all worse. As if William did not have enough to face with the sudden death of his brother, I brought shame upon him. I did not think. It began when the first quarter's letter came from Peter with a banknote for five pounds for his child's welfare. The payments were always addressed to my father, that was the arrangement, and Father would cash them and give my stepmother the money for Thomas Henry. But I so badly wanted new muslin gowns for the coming child, new, clean clouts and a new lace cover and soft blanket for the crib. I had seen such things in the shops in London and craved them for myself. I could not ask William for money, mired in grief for his brother as he was, and I had none of my own; my earnings from what mending I did were given straight to Father, my step-mother saw to that. Thomas Henry had everything he needed and more, thanks to Peter's generosity, and I thought it would not matter, just this once. It was all my doing – I saw the letter and I kept it and the five-pound note, and when my stepmother asked where that quarter's payment was, I told her that it had never come.

'Then you must write to Mr Mathews and ask for it.' I should have confessed then. I should have retrieved the letter and banknote and given it to her, borne her anger. But I did not. Instead, I promised to write to Peter, but I didn't. No, when William said he had business in Colchester, I asked him to cash the note and bring me the coins.

But my stepmother did not leave the matter alone. When at last I confessed I had not written to Peter she produced pen and paper and stood over me until I had, then sealed the letter herself and took it to the post office. I was not thinking clearly. I was expecting William's child and my mind was in a flurry of fear, so when William called to the door one morning I was not expecting the news he brought.

'Maria, I must speak with you.' His face was flushed, his voice urgent and he kept running his fingers through his hair distractedly. 'We are found out.' Father was at work, my stepmother was shopping in the village and Nancy had taken the boys out to feed the ducks. The cottage was empty so I drew him into the parlour.

He sat, coughing hard, and clutched at his chest so I ran to fetch him a cup of water.

'Here, drink this and tell me what has happened.'

He gulped it gratefully and composed himself.

'The postmistress from Colchester has called on my mother. A solicitor was with her. They were asking after the five-pound note I cashed for you.' I went cold. 'It seems that Mathews instigated an investigation into the whereabouts of the letter he sent to your father in January with the banknote, after you said it had gone missing. He went first to the post office, then called at the bank and they told him that it was I who had cashed the banknote. They had recognised me. The postmistress asked if my mother had any knowledge of a missing letter. Mother summoned me and, in front of her, the solicitor suggested that I had stolen the letter, opened it and cashed the banknote in the Hadleigh bank.'

'Oh, William. What did you say?'

'I denied all knowledge of the matter first, I could not think what else to do. Since Thomas died my mind has been in turmoil and I could not let Mother find out that we had been keeping company together.'

I was unable to speak. I never thought that he would be accused of stealing. My words came out in a whisper.

'What then?'

He bowed his head and his voice, when he spoke, was full of fear.

'Oh, Maria, I agreed to go to the post office in Colchester and put the situation right. But I do not know how. What should we do?'

He reached for my hand. His was cold and trembling and I rubbed it between mine, thinking hard, then it came to me.

'I will write a letter to the postmistress. I will tell them that I received the banknote and gave it to you. This will absolve them and stop the investigation. I will write to Peter and say that I asked you to cash it for me. He will believe that. And that will absolve you too. The fault will be entirely mine.'

William looked at me, tears filling his eyes.

'I could not bear for my mother to think me a thief, not on top of all she is going through. First Father, then Thomas. She believes me reformed. She trusts me. Thank you, Maria. I will think of a way of explaining to her how I came to be cashing it for you.'

'Does she not know we have been walking out together? She must have heard rumours.'

He looked at me and cleared his throat.

'I have not yet told her, but she may do. Servants talk. But that is the answer – I will tell her we are acquainted. And you will write those letters? You promise?'

'I will do it today. This will all be forgotten in no time. Do not worry, William, it will be as if it never happened, you'll see.'

I wrote the letters as I had promised. Peter's reply was curt but he agreed to let the matter lie in the interests of all, given Mrs Corder's recent bereavements. So I thought that it was over, that things would carry on between William and me as they had done before. But it was not to be.

CHAPTER
TWENTY-TWO

T homas's death changed everything. He had been running the family farm, with the help of William and James, since the death of his father and since John had returned to his own acres. But now William was left to manage it alone. And his brother's death, coming only thirteen months after that of his father, and the illness of James, seemed to break something in William. He became closer to his mother, who doted on him in a way that seemed almost unnatural. He was required to inform her whenever he went out and she fretted until he had returned. He still had not spoken to her about us, or of my condition, although I had calculated that our child was due in two months' time. He promised me he would tell her all when the time was ripe. I could not put my finger on what had changed in him, but it was clear that something had. He became bolder, more reckless, as if he no longer cared for his reputation and standing. His mother had become frightened of thieves and he wanted to make her feel safe so he took to carrying a pair of pistols that had been a gift from his late father. But he was no longer afraid to be seen with me and we often walked out together so our relationship was no longer a secret in the village. Careful alterations to my gowns, the tying of my stays and wearing my winter cape kept the secret of my condition.

WILLIAM CALLED whenever he could and this familiarity, and his wooing of me, meant that my father and stepmother now welcomed him as one of their own, the coming child grudgingly acknowledged. He was full of ideas of how he would re-shape the farm, and bring in more machinery, although this would mean letting some of the men go. He had great plans to buy the farm from the landowner, not caring that he did not have the money to do so. When he talked of such things his eyes became wild, his manner excitable, his plans more extraordinary, and I did my best to calm him, for such ferocity of feeling did not seem good for him. He seemed full of an uncontrolled energy which sometimes frightened me, although he was always kind and gentle – I put it down to his concern about the farm and worry about my condition. I was heavy with child by now, my feet swollen, my back aching and I was often sharp with him; and all those little things that I once found endearing about him became an irritation and we began to argue, but we always made up in the end. Our excursions to the Red Barn had stopped by necessity, as I was unable to walk any distance and our intimacies became limited to a hand held, a stolen kiss, as my stepmother always seemed to be present and we were rarely left alone. I was not good company in those last weeks and poor William had enough with his own troubles. But he tolerated my moodiness and did not respond when I was unkind to him. He always spoke to me with kindness and good humour and he made sure I wanted for nothing. I knew I was being unbearable, but I could not seem to stop myself, sharp words pouring from my lips without restraint. He promised me that he would arrange for my confinement away from Polstead to avoid any attention from the parish constables and this was a big relief to me. Although Thomas Henry was recorded by the church as being a bastard, the parish constables had turned a blind eye, as he was supported by his father and was part of our family, but to have another illegitimate child would raise eyebrows and could bring the attention of the law to bear on me. And so we went on together, trying our best, but all the time the dread grew in me that I would drive him away and that he, too, would leave me.

WILLIAM WAS true to his word and when the time for my confinement came he rented rooms in Plough Lane in Sudbury, taking me there in his gig, showing me every attention. The weather was mild for the time of year and William often suggested that we walk out a little as he thought it would be good for me. He was a man who needed things to occupy himself, he never could sit still for long. He still carried the pistols but one had become blocked, so, as the gunsmith in Sudbury was well-respected, William took them for repair, asking me to go with him to collect them when they were ready. I was glad of the excuse, for the landlady, Mrs Goodwin, although most kind, and lavishing every care on me, did not believe in a woman in my condition being seen outside. Of Mr Goodwin, I saw little, save to hear his voice conversing with William when they sat in the parlour.

My pains started one evening in late March. Mrs Goodwin took one look at me and helped me to bed, then sent for the midwife.

'Please, will you send for William? I am afraid.'

She smiled down at me.

'It has already been done, my dear. Now don't you worry, I am sure he will be here soon, but you will not be alone, I will be here and you will have the midwife. Your man would only get under our feet now, wouldn't he?' She laughed and busied herself preparing the room. There was a soft knock on the door and I sat up, hoping it might be William, but it was Mr Goodwin, carrying a crib which his wife set down beside the bed. Then the midwife arrived and examined me. As my labour began in earnest, Mrs Goodwin stayed with me as she had promised, frequently mopping my brow with a cool cloth and speaking softly to encourage me until, after a long and painful night, the child was born. It was she who handed the tiny bundle to me, cleaned and wrapped tight.

'You have a son, Maria, and bonny he is too.' I looked down at my babe, mewing in my arms. He was tiny, smaller than ever Matilda or Thomas Henry had been, and I felt a jolt of fear.

'He is so small. His cry – it sounds weak. Is he completely well?'

The midwife bustled over then, wiping large hands on a cloth.

'He is healthy enough, tho' small, as you say. Maybe he has arrived a little early?'

I looked at her doubtfully.

'I do not think so.'

She smoothed his downy head gently and he snuffled and pouted.

'He will improve, I am sure of it, he will grow hearty and strong and be a joy to you.' I looked at him again, watching as his blue-veined eyelids closed in sleep, then she took him gently from my arms and laid him in the cradle. I closed my eyes in relief as exhaustion overwhelmed me, and I lay back on the pillows and slept.

CHAPTER
TWENTY-THREE

When I woke some time later William was sitting on the edge of the bed, holding my hand.

'A son, Maria, to follow on from me and bear my name. I am so proud, so very proud.' He bent and kissed the top of my head. 'I hope the travail was not too troublesome?'

'It was bearable.' I did not tell him more, about the pain and the blood, for men do not wish to know such things. 'But I am concerned about the babe. He looks so fragile.'

William put his finger to my lips.

'There is no need for concern. Mrs Goodwin has told me of your fears but assured me that the midwife is pleased with him and that you worry for no reason. Be happy, as I am.' He kissed me again and stood up. 'I am sorry to leave you but have to get back to the farm. They are sowing this week and I need to supervise. I will tell your family that you have a son. I have left money with Mr Goodwin for your continued care and will come whenever I can to see how you both are until you are well enough to return home.'

'And when I do – will you speak to your mother then?' I may

have imagined his face blanching but in my weakened state I was not certain. 'If you do not approach her yourself, she is bound to hear from someone that there is a new babe in our cottage.'

I did not imagine his hesitation then.

'I must bide my time, pick the right moment. She is still so distressed about losing Thomas, and James's illness has worsened. It is not a good time.'

I raised myself on one elbow.

'But when will be a good time, William? I thought that, after the babe was born you said . . .'

He looked down into the crib.

'We must think of a name for him. One that he will grow into.' He rubbed his hands together. 'I must leave now, Mother is expecting me, and I've told you how she can be.' He smiled and bent to kiss my cheek. I could not see him through the tears blurring my vision. 'I will tell her soon, my love, I promise, but not yet. We must keep this a secret for now. I love you, Maria, remember that. Look after our little one and I will come and see you again in a few days. If there is anything you need, just send word by letter and I will provide it.' I smiled at him wanly and wiped my eyes. He kissed me again and smoothed my face with his hand, then turned to leave.

As he closed the dark oak door behind him I let the tears fall.

THE FOLLOWING day the blackness descended on me again. Mrs Goodwin's best efforts to console me could not stem my tears. I wept for myself, for my broken dreams, for my tiny son who lay, too quiet, in his crib. For I knew deep down that he was not right. He was weak and placid and I knew I was going to lose him, just as I had my poor Matilda. My heart broke over and over again at the thought. Even a letter from Nancy could not console me. She said how pleased everyone was that the birth had gone well and asked after my health. She had taken over my mending and was busy with that, and she hoped I would be recovered enough to come home soon. Lastly, she sent me her best love. I crumpled the letter in my palm and closed my eyes.

William visited me frequently. I do not know where he told his mother he was on these occasions but he came and that was enough. He, too, tried to offer me words of consolation but I could not heed them for a deep sadness overwhelmed me and some days I could barely speak. I was anxious and restless, constantly looking into the crib to make sure my babe was still living. Mrs Goodwin brought me broths and soft-cooked eggs, fresh bread shining with butter, but I could eat nothing. It was she who had to raise me to wash and dress myself, for I had no interest, no strength – I felt hopeless.

'You must look nice for Mr Corder, he has been so kind to you.' I looked at her blankly. 'He is due to call today. Here, try your good dress on.' She held it up and gazed at it. 'It is so pretty.' I took the silk from her and ran it through my fingers. It was soft, smooth as my babe's cheek, but, as I took it from her, I felt its icy coldness. It was an omen.

It was the middle of April before I was well enough to travel. William arrived in fine style in his gig and I sat up high next to him, my cloak tight around me and our little one wrapped up warm against the spring chill, held close to my heart. He was still not feeding as he should, often pulling away from me and screaming, and I blamed myself, for he did not seem to be growing. I was doing my best but it was not good enough – I felt inadequate and unsure. I looked down at the tiny child in my arms as the country-side flew past, William whistling softly at my side. Birds were singing and all was green, the sun was shining and a soft mist rose from the damp fields, but I could not see its beauty. Out of the blue,

I felt a desperate need for my mother. I tried to remember her smile, the touch of her hand, the smell of her, but those images were gone from me, leaving me all the more bereft. Tears started in my eyes and I brushed them away with my sleeve lest William saw, for I did not want him to know how very low I was. That I did not know what to do.

It was my stepmother who took charge. She was waiting at the gate with Nancy as we pulled up, the horse snorting and prancing at the pull of the reins. I looked around to see if anyone was about as William pulled at the harness, then jumped down and helped me from the bench. My stepmother rushed to me but gave me no greeting, just took the babe from my arms.

'Look now, Nancy, isn't he beautiful? But so tiny.' She looked at me sharp. 'Are you caring for him properly? Is he feeding well and often?' She did not give me time to reply before whisking him indoors. Nancy smiled at me uncertainly then followed her. I stood, looking at my shoes, my face burning, wondering how I could stay here, then William patted my arm.

'She will help you, Maria, she is a good woman, though hard on you.' He placed a cold finger under my chin and lifted it so that I looked him in the eyes. It was as if he read my thoughts. 'I will tell Mother very soon, I promise. I will not desert you, not like the others. I am the better man.' He looked confident and I tried to smile at him, knowing he was seeking reassurance.

'You *are* the better man and I am lucky to have you.' I paused as anxiety bubbled and broke loose in me. 'But what will happen to me and our child until then? News will get out, there is no keeping of secrets in a village like this. And what if the constable hears? We have not even named him yet.' Thoughts of Hannah Snell and the workhouse fitted through my mind like bats as William took my hand and kissed it.

'I am a man of my word. We will marry, I promise. Let all this settle, and I am sure that my mother will accept us as husband and wife. She adores me and will want only to see me happy. And I will be, with you and our son.'

I so wanted to believe him. But I know how a woman's mind works and the Corders were higher than us. Her son and a mole-catcher's daughter, and a soiled one at that? I was not so sure.

CHAPTER
TWENTY-FOUR

We had not even had time to decide on a name before my babe grew weak and then stopped feeding altogether. His cries were pitiful to hear and even my stepmother did not know how to help him. One night, I thrust him into her arms, for I could bear his crying no longer. I had tried everything I knew to comfort him and all my attempts to feed him were in vain, for he just pulled his mouth away.

'Please, take him. I cannot bear it.'

'I will try him with some pap.' She went to the table where a pan stood. The bread and water mixture was thin and pale and she tested the heat of it by spilling a little onto the inside of her wrist, then poured some into a small shaped silver bowl. 'I was given this by my mother when my first was born, in case he did not feed properly. I have never had a use for it until now.' She took my babe from my arms and held him close, then pushed the small spout to his lips. He pulled away instantly, screwing up his face and screaming. She tried again with the same result, and he kicked out in distress, the liquid soaking the front of his smock, so she put the pap bowl down and stroked his small frame, crooning to try and settle him. Finally, his crying subsided and he lay quiet, looking at her with glassy eyes. I pulled my shawl around my shoulders and slumped by the fire, watching, hoping, not knowing what more I could have done, as she sat down next to me, holding him tenderly.

HIS EYES WERE OPEN. That's why I did not see the moment he died. I had always imagined that people's eyes closed at the moment of death, but his did not. His face just whitened and his body stilled.

'He is gone, Maria.' My stepmother's voice was small and shaking – it did not sound like her at all. My heart was beating fit to burst, my head reeling.

'No, see, he still looks at us – ' I looked at her in anguish.

'He has gone to the Lord, child. He is free from pain and sorrow now.' She passed her hand gently over his face and closed his eyes. 'Will you hold him, say farewell?' Her voice was the softest she had ever used to me and that was when I knew she was telling the truth. She proffered the tiny bundle to me and I took him from her with shaking hands. He looked so small and perfect, it was hard to believe he was no longer of this world. The pain I felt when Matilda died was nothing compared to this, the loss of a second child.

'What must I do? I don't know what to do.'

My stepmother rubbed her face with her hand and, at once, became her brisk self again.

'You must send word to William. He must decide' I looked at her blankly. 'This babe has not been baptised, Maria.' She spoke the words slowly, carefully, as if I were a child. 'He cannot be buried in the churchyard.'

'He cannot rest with Matilda and Mother?'

'The Reverend will not allow it. Because he was not born in this parish he must be buried in the place where he came into this world. You must take him back to Sudbury.'

I looked at her aghast.

'I cannot. What would happen to him there? He must stay near me. I want him near me . . .' My voice tailed off in a wail. 'I can't take him away.'

She leaned forward and her tone sharpened.

'Listen to me, girl. He is a bastard. You are not yet wed to William. It was all I could do to persuade Reverend Whitmore to baptise your two other children and, God knows, it cost a pretty penny, but he can do nothing for this one. An illegitimate child must be buried at the expense of the parish he was born in. That is the law. Polstead will not pay for his grave for he is not their responsibility.'

It was she that sent for William, and told him what had happened. He sat down next to me in the parlour and took my hand, his face etched with grief. I told him how our child had died, and what my stepmother had said and he was silent for a long while. I was unable to stop sobbing and he made moves to comfort me but when that failed he turned away from me and put his head in his hands.

'Your stepmother is correct in all she told you.'

I looked at him, horrified.

'It cannot be true. I can't lose our boy, he must stay here, close by. I must be able to visit him.'

'The parish will not pay for a child who was not born there. I know her to be right in that. We must plan this carefully, Maria, there may be a way around it yet. Let me think.'

He came back a day later and told me what we must do.

CHAPTER
TWENTY-FIVE

His face was grim when I opened the door to his knock the next morning. The cottage was empty save for me so I ushered him into the parlour and sat down at his side as he reached for my hand. His own was cold and trembling.

'I have thought of a way that you can keep the child close.' He could not meet my eye.

'Anything, William. I can't let him be laid to rest so far from me.' It was all I could think about.

'We will pack our things and take a gig to Sudbury.' He held his hand up at my cry of dismay. 'We will tell your parents that is what we are doing. Your father must believe that we have abided by the law. He is a cautious man and it would not serve us for him to know what we will do. We shall go at night so as not to be seen.' He stared at me. 'Maria, you must not speak of this to anyone, especially not your stepmother, you must swear it.' I nodded, my hands clasped tight in my lap, twisting. 'But we will not go to Sudbury.'

I looked at him in horror.

'But where? Where is he to be buried?'

William closed his eyes and swallowed hard, then turned to look at me, holding my gaze.

'We will take him to the pool in the woods. Where we first met.' He dropped his gaze. 'We will weigh his body down with stones.' My eyes widened, a great sob escaping me, and I put my hand over my mouth to stifle it. 'We will lay him to rest there, Maria. He will be close to you and no one will know but us. The parish records at Sudbury will not be checked. He will be safe and no one will find him. It will be as good as if he was buried in the ground.'

'In the water? We are to put him in the water?' I could not stop myself shaking.

'A newly dug grave may easily be found. He cannot be buried in the churchyard in this parish. If we were to bury him in a field animals may disturb him and then people would ask questions. If the body of a newborn babe should be found like that . . .' His voice tailed off and he rubbed his forehead with his palm as if the horror of what he had just suggested had pained him. 'It is the only way, I can think of nothing better.' He bowed his head and I watched as drops of water fell onto his lap, then his shoulders began to heave with quiet sobs. My heart went out to him and I flung my arms around him, nuzzling my face against his neck, feeling him lean into me. 'If there was another way I would find it. I just want you to be near him, as you wish.'

I shushed him and stroked his hair until he calmed under my touch.

'If that is the only way then that is what we must do. But are you certain? What if they find him?' A shard of fear punctured my heart. 'William, I would be accused of murdering my child – they would hang me!' I put my hands to my throat as if the rope were already there.

He kissed my cheek softly, then turned my face to his.

'You will not hang, my love, I will make sure of it. I have

thought of nothing else all night, I have not slept. This was all I could think of. It will work, I promise you.'

'But what if we are found out?' My breath was coming short and I put my hand to my chest and clutched at my bodice, coughing and gasping for air.

He put his arms around me.

'Breathe now, breathe.' I did as he said and began to calm. 'I will keep you safe, Maria, I promise. If we are careful and quiet it will work. And we will be able to go together to where he is, to pray for him if you like? As often as you please.'

I was still trembling, still terrified.

'But if they catch us, William? They will hang us for sure and I could not bear . . . those convicted of murder are hung in chains. Some are dissected, put on public show.' I was shaking uncontrollably and I saw my terror mirrored in his eyes. He too was afraid.

'It will not happen. We will not be caught. We will plan this carefully, each step, then we will hold strong and we will do this.' His voice was full of certainty as he lifted my chin and placed a gentle kiss on my quivering lips. 'Do you love me?'

I kiss him back.

'You know I do, above all others. I cannot be without you.'

'And I love you too. So we will do this one terrible thing together and then be married and live our lives in quiet contentment.

'Do you swear?'

'I swear, Maria. You will be my wife. But we must do this first, and quickly before your father or stepmother believes something is not as it should be. Where is our child?' I pointed wordlessly towards the stairs.

'And his body – it is ready for burial?'

'Yes.' My throat burned and my head ached with the pain of it all. 'My stepmother – she knew what to do. He is laid out upstairs.'

'Then pack your bag as if we were going to Sudbury. I will say that a gig will be coming for us. We will go this evening, at dusk We will walk up the road as if to meet it then take the path to the woods. But you must bring the child. Are you strong enough to do that?' I nodded numbly. 'Then we will take him to the pond. We will unwrap his winding sheet and fill it with stones.' I could not stop the tears. 'I will wade out a little way. We can speak the prayers for the dead. We can say our goodbyes and I will lower him into the water. It will be like a baptism. And afterwards, we will go to my mother's house. It will be dark by then, we can use the back stairs, no one will know we are there, and we can sleep. And the next day I will bring you back here. They will think we have been away as we told them. No one will know.'

We looked at each other in horror. There was no choice.

CHAPTER

TWENTY-SIX

When William had gone I rallied myself to pack my bag and, when Father and his wife returned with the boys and Nancy, I told them we were to take the child to Sudbury for burial. My stepmother was heartily relieved.

'It is for the best, Maria. When does William collect you?'

'He is hiring a gig, it will be here at dusk. We travel by night so as not to be seen. We will stay overnight tomorrow and be back the day after.'

'And the burial has been arranged?'

'William has seen to that.' I bit my lip to stop my tears at the thought of what we were about to do.

My stepmother turned to Father.

'Should we not accompany them, Thomas? Must they do this alone?'

My heart pounded in my chest.

'The arrangements are made now. I do not know where you would stay or if –'

My father cleared his throat.

'Let them be, Ann, they have made their choice. They wish this to be a private affair and understandably so, given the circumstances.' He looked disdainfully at me and I sensed his disgust. 'Best they do it quietly. Few knew of Maria's pregnancy outside of this family. No, the less we have to do with this matter the better.' He turned away and my stepmother followed, ushering the boys in front of her. The room fell silent. Nancy came forward and held me tightly.

'I am so sorry for your loss, Sister, but you do the right thing in taking him back there.' I hugged her back, craving her affection. 'I will go and say my goodbyes to him. Will you come with me?' She held out her hand.

'Nancy, I cannot. You go, you should say goodbye.'

'If you are certain?' I looked down at my feet and heard the pat of her slippers as she mounted the stairs. At that moment guilt overwhelmed me and my legs failed. I slid to the floor and let the tears come. It was there that my stepmother found me.

'Why so distraught? Women lose children every day, it is the way of things.' She put her hands to her hips. 'Unless there is more to this. You and William have been whispering in corners for days and you swore you would not take the poor mite to Sudbury. And why would he waste money on a gig when he could take his own?' Her eyes narrowed. 'There is something amiss here.' She bent and took my arm to pull me up and her fingers tightened sharply. Her hand was broad and strong and I gasped at the sudden pain but it only served to make her grip harder. 'What are you plotting? And do not tell me Sudbury for I do not believe you.'

'Father does.'

'Your father is a simple man, he takes people at their word. But something smells bad in this. What is it? What do you plan?' I could feel my arm bruising under her grasp.

'Leave go of me.' But she did not and the pain grew too much to bear. 'We are to bury him in the field.'

She dropped my arm as if it were a hot iron. I stood up and rubbed the place where she had held me, then looked her full in the eye. I would no longer be cowed by this woman. 'We are to bury him tomorrow, where no one will ever find him. And if you dare repeat this to anyone, William and I will say that it was you who suggested it. If they take me up for it, be sure they will take you as well.' She said nothing but backed away and turned towards the kitchen. I leaned forward and put my hands on my knees, I felt faint. But I had stood up to her and there was some small satisfaction in that.

William came for me just as the sun was setting. He had his bag and carried his pistols in his belt. He looked sadly at the bundle I carried in my arms.

'I have wrapped him in an extra shawl – I did not want him to be cold.' I realised what I had said and put my hand to my mouth.

'All will be well.' he said, then turned as my father and stepmother came to the cottage doorway. 'I will take care of her, Mr Martin, and the child. All will be done properly. Come, Maria, the gig will be waiting in the lane.' He picked up my bag with his. 'We must not be late.'

There was silence as we turned and walked away. I glanced over my shoulder, catching my stepmother's gaze and she nodded once, then took my father's arm and shut the door. We moved slowly but steadily, the little bundle weighing me down, keeping our faces expressionless. But inside I was quaking, barely able to control my emotions, my movements mechanical. We walked as far as the turn in the road where we could no longer be seen, and then William looked around us in all directions. There was no one on the road, everyone was at home, safe in their cottages.

'Come.' He took my elbow and steered me towards the path to the woods that we had trodden so many times before, watching warily as the fields fell away and the trees enveloped us.

. . .

IT HAUNTS ME STILL. I cannot rid myself of the memories; I still smell the freshness of that spring – it was April and everything seemed washed clean. But my soul was not. What we did that night was wrong and we both knew it. But we had no alternative. And we have both suffered much for it.

William did not need his lantern, for the moon lit our path. When we reached the pond he put our bags down as I held my babe tightly to me, nuzzling him in case there was any trace left of his smell, any essence of him, but there was nothing. He had already left me.

At the edge of the pond, there was a pile of flat stones, and I realised that William must have been here before, must have prepared for this, and my heart went out to him. He looked at me once then took the child gently from my arms. I stifled a sob as he unwrapped the shawl, and then began to unwind the bindings. It was the sight of a tiny white hand that undid me. It shone waxy in the moonlight, stone-cold, like a marble effigy, and I fell to my knees in despair as he tucked stones around the body then wrapped it up and pulled some cord from his pocket. I stretched out my hand.

'No, please.'

'We have no alternative, Maria. The parish will not allow him to be buried here and you do not wish to take him back to Sudbury. There is more risk of him being found if we were to bury him in a field. We have to do this.'

'Do not bind him.'

William sighed.

'If I do not, and the stones fall out, his body will rise and he will be found. If the water in the pond drops low this coming summer and anything is left to be seen, people will think that it is just a roll of rags that someone has disposed of. I must do it, do you see?' I nodded, unable to speak, as he tied the bundle firmly and wrapped it back in the shawl, shaping it until it no longer looked like what it was. He placed it tenderly on the ground then stooped to remove his boots, rolled up his trousers and stepped into the mud, which oozed through his toes and squelched at the weight of him. He turned to me and held out his arms. I picked up the small body, heavy now, and held my son close for the last time, then, sobbing silently, I handed him to William. He took him from me and, holding the bundle out in front of him, he bent forward.

Small bubbles rose as the body of my babe sank into the brackish water. I still see bubbles in my mind, popping over the brown of the shawl, blending with the dank water. The darkness was silent save for the rustle of the trees. We had intended to pray, to give our son a Christian burial as best we could, but we were so overwhelmed that it was forgotten in the moment and my son went to his rest unblessed. Another sin to lay at our door.

AFTER IT WAS DONE, we walked back slowly to his mother's house. It was a beautiful building, half-timbered, moonlight making the pale walls glow. We silently crossed the back garden and entered by the kitchen door, tiptoeing up the back stairs. The curtains had not been drawn in his room.

'I have told the servants I am in Sudbury. They have not prepared my room because of that.' William moved to pull the curtains but I stayed his hand.

'No, leave them. The moonlight makes me feel closer to him somehow.' I was brought low with distress and terror of being found out – my head pounded and I could not stop shaking.

'You are hungry, you have not eaten all day.' He crept down to the kitchen and returned with a piece of pie and some bread to eat, a jug of water, but my throat was dry and I could swallow nothing. After we had eaten we lay side by side on the bed, fully dressed. It got colder as the dawn came, but the fire stayed unlit as we each kept to our own place, our own thoughts. We did not hold each other that night but lay, like marble statues, on the tombstone of our memories. We had not even given him a name.

CHAPTER
TWENTY-SEVEN

As dawn broke we heard the voices of the farm workers outside, passing the Corder farmhouse on their way to the fields. Inside the farmhouse, we could hear the clatter of servants, but no one came up to William's room. We were safe. We waited in his room until the next evening, not eating, barely speaking. Night came once more, another dawn, then William raised me, took me back down the staircase and escorted me home, our burden gone but a heaviness dragging at us.

'You must be brave now, my love. Your father may ask questions and your stepmother certainly will. You know what you must say.'

'She knows.' My voice was dull and flat.

'Who knows? Your stepmother? Oh, Maria, what have you done?' His voice was sharp with fear.

'She was hurting me and she knew already. So I told her that we were going to bury the babe in a field. I did not want her to know the truth. I wanted to keep that place special, hidden, only known by us. So I told her we would put him in a field.'

He looks aghast.

'But she could tell the constable.'

I shook my head.

'No, she will not. I have told her that I will say it was her idea all along if she does. She will not speak of it, I am certain. She just wanted to find out the truth of the matter and, now she knows, she will be satisfied.'

'Are you sure?'

'I am, I know her. I am sorry, William, I had no option. She could tell that I was hiding the truth from her.' I paused. 'And, if she ever did speak out and they were to dig, nothing would be found and she would be proved a liar. No, she will not speak of it to anyone. She has too much to lose, she just could not bear that I had a secret from her.'

He said nothing. As we drew closer to home I could feel the blackness closing in on me, weighing me down until I could scarce move one leg after the other. William took my arm when I stumbled but otherwise, we did not touch. It was as if we were strangers, taking the same path but with different destinations.

He left me at the gate with a squeeze of my hand and I walked down the path and opened the door. I could see Father's shape in the parlour, huddled in his chair and I thought to go to him, but just then my stepmother came from the kitchen, wiping her hands on a cloth. Outside I could hear the boys playing happily. It was as if nothing had changed and I was a spectre, watching it all from on high.

'Is it done?' she asked. 'He is buried?' I nodded and closed my eyes against her probing gaze. 'He was not meant for this world, Maria, he was poorly from the first. Well, it's done now and perhaps you have learned a lesson from it all.' She looked behind me. 'Is William not with you?

'He went straight home to see his mother – you know how she frets.'

'Is it not time he told her about you – if she has not already heard? You know how gossip rages in this place.'

I sparked at her remark.

'He has every intention of telling her, it is just that, with Thomas dying so unexpectedly and with James gravely ill –' She raised an eyebrow. 'He has asked me to marry him and I have said I will.' This, at least, took her by surprise.

'Has he indeed? And how do you think Mrs Corder will take that, her favourite son, joined to the likes of you?' She smiles bitterly and I see in her eyes the green flash of jealousy.

I draw myself up to my full height.

'He will marry me. We will be husband and wife. He has promised.'

I walked towards the stairs but she followed me, her eyes narrowed.

'Is that what he told you? That's what he said when he was foisting his by-blow on you? You must be more simple than I thought. I always had you pegged for a bright girl, but look at yourself, Maria Martin. Coming up to twenty-six years old with three bastard children born to you, and you not even capable of caring for the one who lived.' She pointed a finger at me, all her resentment and spite spilling out as if she had opened a bottle and let the contents splatter where they may. 'Thomas Corder did not want you, nor Peter Mathews either and I am sure William will drop you like a hot stone now. You are spoiled goods, girl, not marriage material for the likes of the Corders. The babe was born, he died in my arms, and now he is buried and that will be an end to it, mark my words.' Her face was too close to mine, spittle striking me as her words poured out. 'You have looked down your nose at me often enough. Don't look like that, I tell the truth and you know it. You thought I was selling myself short when I married your father. Well, I was the same age as you are now and look at me. Married to an honest man, with four boys.'

'Three! Thomas Henry is my child, not yours.'

'Then you would have done well to care for him yourself. Who has looked after him since he was born?' Her finger was stabbing into my chest. 'Me, that's who, while you go gallivanting off with all and sundry, bringing the good name of this house into disrepute. You have hardly lifted a finger to look after your boy.'

My anger rose then, to match hers and I felt my face reddening.

'I tried! I tried my very best to care for him but you would not allow it! You took him from me the moment he was born . . .'

'Because you lay abed like some swooning maiden, crying and moping. What else was I to do? The child needed a mother.' All of a sudden my anger washed away and I was left empty. I felt the sting of tears but I would not let her see me cry. But she knew. 'That's right, turn on the tears like you always have. Leave others to clear up your mess. Well, you've made your bed, my girl, and you must lie on it. I want no more to do with you. Thomas Henry is happy here with us, you must do as you will. No good will come to you, that's for sure. You are nothing but a common whore.'

I LOOKED AT HER, all the fight gone from me, and turned without a word, taking the stairs slowly up to the bedroom. My sister was sitting on our bed, white and shaking.

'Oh, Nancy, you were listening? I did not mean for you to hear that. Here, come to me.' I held out my arms to her, wanting to hold her so much, but she pulled away.

'Mother is right, Maria, you have brought disgrace on this house. How do you think I feel, having the whole village talk about you, listening to them say that you will lie with any man? Have you never thought of anyone else, you with your frills and finery? Yes, I remember how you got those dresses, that hat. By laying with

Peter Mathews. Mother is right, you are no better than one of the common girls who travel with the fair. Perhaps that is where you should go, for it is certain you are not wanted here.' She turned away from me. 'I must go to Mother, she will be upset.' She slammed the door behind her as I sank to the bed. Even my sister had turned against me. I could no longer stay upright so I lay down on my side, curled my legs up to my chest and felt the darkness come.

CHAPTER
TWENTY-EIGHT

William called on me that evening. We walked across the fields to the Red Barn and sat, watching the sun go down through the open door. He had brought his pistols with him and, as we sat, he oiled and primed them, working the catch until the clicking sound thudded in my ears.

'Will you stop that, please? I cannot bear it.'

He looked over at me, puzzled by my irritation.

'We are safe now Maria, it is over. Our child is buried.' He looked around to see if anyone heard, dropping his voice. 'Can we not go back to how we were? I do not understand your moods. You are dark when I thought you would be light again. I did what you asked, I found a way to keep our child nearby and no one will ever know. It is our secret. We are bonded by it, are we not?' He took my hand. 'What is the matter, Maria, what ails you?'

I thought I could not find the words to explain how I felt. The blackness that pounded in my head, the constant sorrow, the feeling of being drained of all life, a mere shell. But somehow they came.

'I feel like the wheat when it has been flailed. As if all the life has been threshed out of me and taken away, and now I am but a husk, dried up and useless. I feel as if I might blow away to nothingness at the slightest breeze.' He looked at me and I could see he did not understand. 'And I am sore afraid. I cannot breathe, my mind blurs and I am tired, so very tired. Terror wakes me at night, invades me by day.'

'Terror? Of what?'

I look him in the eye.

'Terror that we will be found out. That I will be accused of murdering my son.'

'But that was not your fault. Your stepmother – he died in her arms. She knows, as does your father and Nancy. They would never say that you killed him . . .' His voice tailed off. 'You have nothing to fear. It is done. You will not be accused, for your family believes that the child is buried in Sudbury. You were not responsible for his death, it was God's doing.'

'God's doing? Where was your God in that?' I spat the words out and felt him draw back. 'A tiny babe, to be taken so soon. Where was the justice? They say that God loves little children. But what of their mothers? How does He think they will feel when He takes their children away? A loving God? No, I think not. A hard and cruel God, yes, but loving? No.'

William looked as shocked at my outburst as I had ever seen him.

'Maria, what you say is blasphemy. You have been brought up in the Church, you know what God means, how he cares and tends us.'

I looked him full in the face.

'Maybe I once did. But not any more. God seems to me to be cruel beyond belief.'

He reached for my hand and I allowed him to take it.

'We shall be married and all will be well. You will recover your health, we will have more children and all this will be but a memory.'

'But when? When will we marry? And your mother, what of her?'

'I will speak to her, I promise. I will tell her that I intend to marry you and will have no other. But it cannot be yet, for James is nearing death.' His voice choked. 'I must be with him at the end. But I will speak to her after, ask for her blessing. You have my word.'

I believed him then. I know he believed it too. But things were unravelling.

I DO NOT KNOW when we started to quarrel so badly. In the past, our arguments had blown over and we had made up quickly but now I was short-tempered and cruel and William stood by and accepted it, which inflamed me even more. I became obsessed with being found out and he could do little to calm me. I could feel my moods spiralling away from me, turning me into a harridan. I was not taking care of myself, my hair going unwashed, my clothes unaired and stale smelling. We walked out as we had always done but a distance had grown between us and I knew it to be of my making. And there was another reason for my growing anger.

'Have you been able to talk to your mother yet? Tell her of us?' He shook his head. 'Does she not know? The whole village seems to gossip about us.' I knew that this was not true but could not help myself from goading him.

He turned and took my hand.

'My brother has not much longer to live. I cannot, not before –' He looked down at his boots. 'I do not wish to upset her further. She has been through so much and she remains strong so far. I am certain she has not heard tales of us, for she does not go into the village at all. She and my sisters just sit by James's bedside, for they cannot bear to lose even a minute of the time he has left.'

'So now you say you will not marry me? After everything you promised?' My voice was stony and even as I uttered the words, I knew I should not, that I was being unfair. He dropped my hand.

'I will marry you, I am a man of my word, do you not know that by now?' He took me by the shoulders and looked at me. 'I will do it. I will go to Ipswich for a licence and we will be married.' He straightened and I could see excitement glistening in his eyes. 'I will go tomorrow. I have tarried too long and it has not been fair on you, Maria, I see that now. We will marry and you will come to live at my mother's house. I will be needed to take charge of the farm and lands when James is gone, and we will live there together and be happy. You will care for my mother in her dotage and we will have more children and live to a contented old age.'

'You mean this?' I knew how his enthusiasm took him over.

'I do. I will go to fetch a licence tomorrow and will call for you once I have it, so be ready.' He spins on his heel, raking his hair with his fingers. 'We will leave for Ipswich to be married. And once it is done I shall tell my mother that it is you I love and that we are man and wife.'

But now the moment had come, I hesitated and he saw it.

'If you wish, we can sleep together in my room overnight. We were not discovered before. You can stay with me and then, the following morning, we will leave to get married.' He took my hands and kissed me, his face alight. 'I could leave today to arrange the licence.' I still was not sure what to think. After so many months of secrecy, his plan seems rushed and ill-thought-through. To be married to William Corder was all I wanted, to be with him as his wife, but still I paused. I looked at the man I was to spend the rest of my life with. He sparkled. His excitement made him flushed, his speech hurried and I realised that he lived in a world of his imaginings. His plan seemed fanciful and unreal. But I so wanted it to be true that I believed him.

I told my father that we were to be married. He was surprised, my stepmother more so, but they guardedly offered their congratulations.

It was she that echoed my thoughts.

'So he is to marry you, in truth? He has truly gone to buy a licence? I had hoped to see you wed in Polstead Church.'

'We wish to marry without ceremony, a small affair.'

'Well, I can't say I'm not disappointed.' She turned to my father. 'And it is a shame that you will not be able to walk her down the aisle, Thomas.' My father merely grunted and I knew she expected more from him. But she was secretly pleased, I could see that in her manner, for to be linked to the Corders by marriage was a step upwards that she could only have dreamed of. 'Well, I hope he is as good as his word. He should have married you before the child was born, but I suppose he is making an honest woman of you now.' She turned her mind to practicalities. 'Now, what will you wear?'

I had not thought of this, for to do so had seemed to tempt fate, but she required an answer.

'I have the black silk dress . . .'

'The one that Peter Mathews bought you? And you think that appropriate?'

'Peter and I have no connection any more, save that of Thomas Henry.'

My chest began to thud, as a realisation dawned. My stepmother read my mind and her voice rose.

'What of Thomas Henry? What will become of him when you are married? Surely you do not mean to take him with you?'

'He will come to live with William and me.' There, it was said, the decision made.

She began to cry, loud sobs that shook her frame and my father moved to her side, patting her shoulder helplessly. 'No, Maria, I could not bear to lose him, he is like one of my own. Surely you could not be so cruel. I have been a true mother to him these past three years. It is me he runs to, me that cares for him.'

My father spoke then.

'Your mother has done everything for that boy, Maria, it would be heartless to take him from her. She is as a mother to him.'

My temper rose and I clenched my hands into fists at my side.

'He is my son. And what choice did I have in the matter? From the moment he was born, she took him from me.'

Her eyes flashed and she stepped in front of my father, her face thunderous.

'Because you lay abed like a lady of leisure. You cared nothing for him.'

'I was unwell.'

'It was I that changed his clouts, washed and dressed him, held him when he cried. I even had to bring him to you to feed him, you could barely be bothered to do even that. You are unnatural, that's what you are. You care only for your own pleasure – and look where that has brought you.' Her face was flushed, her hair wild.

'Married to William Corder, that's where it has brought me. Thomas Henry will grow to love me, his true mother. He is young yet, he will forget all of this. I can take good care of him, I know it, and he will be well provided for.' My heart was beating fast but I would not back down.

Then my stepmother was in front of me, her finger stabbing the air between us, her eyes narrowed, tears dried.

'And what of William Corder? Has he agreed to bring up another man's by-blow?'

The very air froze around us. I had not considered that he

might refuse for I had been too wrapped up in my own thoughts. William had asked me to end all contact with Peter. Would it be right to ask him to bring up another man's child when our own son had died? I went cold at the thought that he might deny me, but I could not let my stepmother get away with all she had said about me. I knew I should wait to ask William on his return but I dreaded what his answer would be.

'He is my child, Ann.'

For the first time, I called her by her name and she looked up sharply. 'I know that you have carried out much of his upbringing until now, but he is not your son, he is mine, and I will have him with me.'

I felt certain, confident. But I had not asked William.

CHAPTER
TWENTY-NINE

William returned from Ipswich on Sunday. The atmosphere in the cottage since I had told them of our plans had been as tight-coiled as a rope. I had kept to my room, parried Nancy's questions as best I could and packed my bag, ready. I had my umbrella and my bonnet, my best dress and my clean shifts. I paced between the door and the window, watching for him, and all the time my mind was churning over how I should ask him about Thomas Henry. I knew I was being unfair in taking my boy away from my stepmother, for she had been good to him, but he was mine and I loved him and wanted to give him a better life. He was a sunny child, chubby and just beginning to walk. William had seen him on his visits to our cottage but I do not remember how he was with him. I knew William to be jealous of his late brother and of Peter, because of their association with me but surely, he could not deny me the presence of my own son?

My mind was churning with these thoughts when I heard the clop of hooves on the road outside, a harrumph of breath as the horse stopped and footsteps coming slowly to the door. I flew down the stairs to meet him.

'William, do you have it? The licence?'

He kissed my cheek but paused.

'I am sorry, Maria. There is a delay.' He saw my face fall and pulled me to him. 'It was more complicated than I imagined.' He buried his face in my hair and breathed me in. 'Oh, my love, I am sorry, but it will not change our plans. I did not have the right papers with me. Come with me to my mother's house tonight and we will travel to Ipswich tomorrow, early, so as not to be seen, and when you are settled there I can return to the notary and arrange the licence. Is your bag packed?'

I blinked back tears and nodded.

'I will fetch it.' I ran upstairs and brought it down, placing it by my feet as my stepmother, hearing voices, came in from the garden. 'Ah, William,' she said. 'May I call you that now, as you are to be my son-in-law? William blinked. 'You have the licence? You and Maria are to wed?'

He hesitated only a moment as the lie tripped from his tongue.

'Yes, I do, Mrs Martin. I am unable to show it to you as it is packed in my bag, but Maria and I will be staying the night at our farmhouse and leaving tomorrow at first light. We will be wed this week, for certain.'

My stepmother smiled and nodded.

'Then I trust you to take good care of her. She has been like one of my own.' I stiffened at the hypocrisy. 'I will miss her presence in this household.' She lowered her head and put a sorrowful look on her face. 'And what shall I tell Mr Mathews, for he is sure to ask where . . .'

I step forward and lift my bag, passing it to William.

'We must be leaving now; Mrs Corder expects us.' William looked startled, but he was not the only one who could ignore the truth. 'Say farewell to Nancy and the boys for me. I will see them when we return.' She proffered her cheek as if expecting a kiss, but I ignored it and pushed past her without a backward look. My future was forward now, a new life in front of me and I could not wait to seize it.

I RETURNED HOME in the early hours, too numb to speak. We had gone to his house as he promised, through the garden gate and down the path to the back door, then crept up the back staircase to his room without being seen. The thought had come to me that soon this house may be ours, and I had turned to William and taken his hand.

'It is a beautiful room, a beautiful house.'

He smiled.

'It is.' He placed his pistols in the drawer by his bedside.

'Why do you still keep those pistols close?'

'We have had a spate of thefts hereabouts. The constable came to see my mother a while back, to warn her to be careful. My mother and sister are still nervous, so I keep them for our protection, in case there is a need. There is a small sword, too, downstairs. I thought of having it cleaned and sharpened so that I could wear it at our wedding. What do you think?'

'That is a fine idea. Perhaps we could cut our bride-cake with it?' I touched the fabric of the thick curtains, running my fingers over the slubbed satin, and moved to the bed. The sheet was turned down, ready for sleep and I looked at William. 'I do not mind that we do not have a license yet. I know it was not to be helped. But we will have it soon and be married, and this room will be ours.' I looked around, drinking it all in, then turned back to him. 'Hold me, William.' The desire to be in his arms was so great at that moment that all modesty fled. I took his hand and pulled him to the bed, unbuttoning my jacket with the other. 'Come, lie with me –'

Something was wrong. He looked startled, sheepish, as he let go of me.

'Maria, I cannot. Not here, in my mother's house. What if she heard us? I plan to tell her about us once we are wed. I will write to her from Ipswich so that she is prepared for our return.' He rested his head against mine and pulled at my ear with his lips. He was warm and strong and I felt my desire rise again, but then he pulled back.

I smile at him, coquettishly.

'We can be silent. Come, we have never slept the night together in a real bed before.' An image of us, a few short weeks earlier, lying side by side on the coverlet, unspeaking, sprang into my mind and I pushed it down instantly. 'Love me, let me love you.' I pulled him down to sit on the side of the bed, then moved close to him and put my arms around him. I slid my hand down his shirt, feeling his beating heart under my fingers. I caressed the smooth skin of his chest, then moved my hand lower. I felt brazen and powerful as he rose under my touch and I leaned to kiss him but he pulled away.

He took my hand and removed it from his person.

'I cannot do it.' He saw my disappointment. 'Not in this house, not yet. It would not be right.'

I should have been charmed by his thoughtfulness and modesty but I was not. Instead, I felt cheapened by his rejection and my anger began to simmer.

'Why so modest now?' I was trying hard to retrieve the situation but it began to spiral.

He stood hurriedly, straightening his dress.

'Because this is my mother's house and I will not sully it. We are not yet wed. Mother's room is just down the landing and I cannot risk her discovering us like this.' He turned to me and put his arms around me. 'I love you and I do not know how I would be without you now, it's just that I am unable to do that, here, now.'

He looked at me piteously. 'Please say you understand. I would do anything for you, you know that.'

I took a deep breath. Now was the time.

'Will you allow my son to live with us when we are married? For me?'

He pulled away sharply.

'Our son is dead.'

I took a deep breath.

'I CANNOT BEAR the thought of leaving Thomas Henry behind and this would be such a fine house for him to grow up in.' I chanced a look at his face – it was dark with anger and I took a step back.

'You expect me to agree to raise another man's son? I will not. We will have children of our own I have no doubt, and your time will be filled with them. Our children, sired by me. No, I will not have that boy to live with us. Mathews pays enough, let your step-mother care for him. After all, she seems to have done that since he was born.' His eyes narrowed in suspicion. 'Are you still in touch with Mathews, is that it? Do you still meet with him?' We were hissing now, trying not to be heard.

'Of course not. I gave you my word that I would not see him again and I have not.'

'But do you speak the truth? Can I trust you?' I had not seen him angry like this before and I stepped back, not through fear but because my fury matched his.

'He is my son. How can you expect me to desert him?'

'Well, I do. He will not come to live with us. I cannot allow it. You may see the boy whenever you wish but I cannot bear the thought of another man's child under my roof. Another man that you may still be in contact with. It is not right and you are unfair to ask.'

I started to shake.

'I have not seen Peter since last August. I told you that and I have kept to it. I have done all you asked. But Thomas Henry is mine and it is you that is unfair, expecting me to leave him behind.' I was blazing with fury and fear and knew I must leave before we said any more words that could not be unsaid. It seemed that I had to choose between my son and William. All of a sudden my anger departed as quickly as it had come and I was left, weak and bereft. I did not know what to do. William stood, rubbing his head with his hands, as I put my jacket back on, gathered up my bag and moved towards the door. William held out his hand to me but I pushed past him, back down the stairs and out into the dark garden. When I got to the gate I turned, just once. He did not follow.

THIRTY

M y stepmother was unrelenting in her criticism when she saw me the next morning.

'You have made a grave error, girl. What if he abandons you now? You do not have a ring on your finger yet. You would be wise to bow down to him, accept his wishes, apologise and make matters well with him again.'

'And leave you caring for Thomas Henry?'

'It is not as if you have done much of the caring 'til now, is it?' Her words were spiteful and they stung. Then her voice softened. 'Maria, he is not unreasonable in not wanting to bring up another man's child. He has made few demands of you and this marriage, well, it will be good for all of us. Maybe you could let the matter lie for now, marry, see how he is in a few month's time. He may change his mind once you are wed and settled. He is too good a catch to lose now, especially as his brother is bad. Think of all he will inherit.' There was some sense in her words but still I was torn. 'Go to him – I will take a message for you if you wish – speak to him. Tell him you have reconsidered.' Her eyes narrowed then, all trace of softness gone. 'If he leaves you and they find out about the dead child, well, the parish may become involved . . .'

My heart jumped in my chest and I looked at her in shock. I knew full well what she meant.

'You wouldn't tell?'

She gazed at me like a snake poised to strike.

'Two bastard children, Maria, and another dead – so far no one knows about the last, but if anyone were to find out the constable could obtain a warrant, take you up, and punish you. And do not forget he is a distant relative of Mrs Corder. She would want it hushed up. She wouldn't want to see either of her precious sons shamed. No, the blame would be laid squarely on your shoulders if she were to find out.' She paused and the air hung heavy with threat. 'You saw what happened to Hannah Snell. Why, you could end up in the workhouse like she did, or prison – or worse.' It was as if she could read my mind, see my deepest fear. 'We have always let Polstead think that Thomas Henry is mine. We were discreet at the time, and any who knows the truth would never speak of it. You are not the only one to pass off their bastard as their sibling, it happens all the time to avoid problems with the law. No, your path is clear. Leave Thomas Henry with me, make up with William and go and live your life.'

'He believes I am still seeing Peter.'

'There is little that can be done about jealousy save reassurance. And if Thomas Henry is left with me, then you will have no cause to speak to Mathews ever again.'

I sank into the chair, my legs trembling. I did not know what to do for the best. If I persisted in my need for my son I could well lose William. If I let William go, and word got out, I could go to prison and I would lose my child anyway. The very thought of that took my breath away. Deep down I knew Ann was right. A word to Constable Baalham and all would go ill for me, and I did not trust her not to be the one who told him. I knew Mrs Corder would not hesitate to make a case, the way she doted on her son. I would be portrayed as a foul seductress, a fallen woman, and I would have to live out the rest of my life here in Polstead with my head bowed in shame. I got slowly to my feet and pulled myself up the stairs to the bedroom. I curled up on the bed as cold hands drew me under.

WILLIAM CAME THAT EVENING. My stepmother called me down, for I had not moved all day, and showed him into the parlour. She shut the door behind her as I stood before William, head lowered. I listened for the sound of her feet moving away from the closed door, but they did not.

'Maria, I am sorry for my harsh words yesterday. I never thought that you would want to bring his son with you.'

'I have changed my mind.'

'Pardon?'

'I no longer wish to bring Thomas Henry with me. I have thought, and he will stay here.' I felt like Judas, waited for the thirty pieces of silver to rain down on my head. 'I was wrong to ask it of you. And I promise you that I no longer have any connection with Peter Mathews, save payment for the upkeep of my child.'

William sighed with relief.

'That is good, for I could not raise another man's child, particularly after that same man accused me of stealing from you.' He moved towards me and took my hand. 'So all is well between us? And we will be married soon? We will go this week then, to Ipswich, as we planned.' I was unable to speak, my head felt as if it was made of lead as I nodded. 'I only hope it will be possible. James has taken a turn for the worse you see. The doctor thinks he may only have a matter of days to live.'

Tears filled his eyes and I reached out for him, feeling his pain.

'I am sorry to hear that, I know how much you love him.'

'I sometimes think my family is tainted, Maria. First my father, then Thomas. John is not well and James, well the consumption is taking him so fast. Sometimes I feel their weakness in my own lungs, for my cough often worsens and it can be hard to breathe. If both my brothers die I will be left in charge.' He paused, sadness making him small and vulnerable, like a child. 'My mother remains strong for now but I can see she is brittle. She has had too much sadness in her life already.'

I held him tightly in my arms, letting his sorrow blend with mine.

'We will be married, William, and all will be well. And perhaps, in time, we will have children of our own to cheer your mother?'

He smiled at me then and his mood brightened.

'I will come for you tomorrow, we will travel on Wednesday. But we will not tell my mother just yet.'

'As you wish, but we cannot go on Wednesday – it is the day of Stoke Fair, and there will be many people around, what if we are seen?'

He thought for a moment.

'Thursday then.' He clasped my hand. 'I will call for you on Thursday. I will be so proud to call you my wife. And my mother, seeing my love for you, is certain to accept you and welcome you into the family.' He brought my hand to his lips, turned it over and kissed my palm gently. 'Whatever happens, remember that I love you.' He smiled softly and was gone.

On Thursday he sent me a message to say that his brother had only hours to live.

CHAPTER

THIRTY-ONE

He finally came to the cottage at midday on Friday. My eyes were thick and puffy with the tears I had shed, for I had not believed he would come at all. James had rallied a little, but it seemed to me that William's ties to his mother and dying brother were far stronger than his ties to me. I had spent the two days and nights since his last visit lying in my bed, wracked by grief, for myself, for my lost children. No one could stir me, not even Nancy, who eventually lost patience with me and left me alone.

I had not eaten, nor washed, and my hair, of which I had once been so proud, hung lank and dirty around my shoulders. I was dressed only in my old shift, which smelt stale and acrid. I had packed my bag, then unpacked it again when William did not come, and my clothes were spread around the floor where I had flung them. My head thumped and I felt weak and empty but worse, the blackness that never left me had grown and now pushed thick and dark at my thoughts.

And I was terrified. Terrified that they would find the tiny body in the pond, terrified of being taken up by John Baalham and put on trial. Worse still was the fear of hanging.

The disgrace and humiliation.

The terror of the scaffold.

The drop.

The rope tightening enough to stop my breath, but not enough to kill me.

For all had heard of such executions, where the victim was left to suffocate in agony. I buried myself under the blankets, pushing my fists to my ears, trying to block out the sound of the bolt shooting, the floor falling away, the voiding of my body, the creak of the rope as I swung, half dead, the jeering and shouting of the crowd. I could not rid myself of those thoughts swirling through my mind and nothing could console me.

I BARELY HEARD the tap on the bedroom door before it swung open. William stood there, a bundle under his arm, my stepmother close behind him.

'Maria, I have come for you.' He crossed to the bed and sat on it, placing the bundle by his side, taking hold of my hand. 'Your stepmother tells me that you have not left this room since I last saw you. I am sorry, my love, that I could not come to you earlier. The doctor said that James was near death. The Reverend was summoned and he gave the last rites. I could not leave. You did get my message, did you not?'

'She did.'

He looked back at my stepmother.

'Mrs Martin, could you leave us, please? I wish to talk to Maria.'

She bristled at this.

'But it is not proper that a gentleman should be in a lady's bedchamber unchaperoned.' He gave her a hard stare and she backed away. 'I will wait outside the door in case of any impropriety.'

William turned back to me and lowered his voice.

'She will be listening.'

I nodded and tried to smile.

'She will. She does not wish to miss any gossip.'

He reached out and smoothed a lock of hair from my eyes.

'Oh, Maria, look at you. That I should have caused this unhappiness. I know that you have felt low since we lost our child.'

'Before that. These moods have brought me down since I lost Matilda, they worsened after Thomas Henry, and after our son . . . I was told that many women have such sadness after the birth of a child and that these feelings would go away, but they have not, they have worsened. And now I cannot seem to rouse myself.'

He stood and bent to gather my clothes.

'Then maybe I can cheer you. I have come to say that we are to leave for Ipswich today. I have hesitated long enough. Let us go, now.'

I looked at him, aghast.

'But I am not prepared. My bag – '

'It will take but a moment to pack it, see, your clothes are here already.' He began folding my dress and shifts into the bag and I put out a hand to stop him.

'It is the middle of the day, William. We cannot go together. I thought we agreed to go by night.' I pulled myself up from the bed and stepped towards the window. 'The men are in the fields, we will be seen. And my father is not here, he is away working, I would not be able to say farewell.' My voice rose to a wail and he moved to hold me.

'I have thought of all that. The men are working on the lower field today, they will not come as far as the Red Barn.' He pointed to the bundle on the bed. 'I have brought you clothes. A disguise.'

His eyes sparkled. 'You shall dress as a man. If we are seen, no one will suspect two men striding along the track.'

I opened the bundle and pulled out a pair of trousers, a waistcoat, an old blue jacket, and a man's cap.

'I am to put these on? But whose are they, they do not look like yours?'

He hesitated.

'They belong to James.'

'I cannot wear the clothes of a dying man!'

'It was all I could think of. Mine would be recognised.' His voice flickered with impatience. 'They will have to do. Come, put them on. Here, take one of my pistols as well, it will add to the concealment.' He pulled it from his belt and passed it to me. 'I have already hidden my bag in the barn, we will pack your things and I will take them for you. You can change into your own clothes there. But you must hurry.'

I DID AS HE SAID. I packed my black velvet reticule, for I thought it would look well carried at my wedding, and the straw Leghorn hat that Peter had bought me in London. My wedding. I could not believe the day had finally come and, now it had, I was filled with a frenzy. I filled the bag hurriedly and passed it to William. He took it and, kissing me farewell, went down the stairs and I heard his footsteps, the creak of the gate as he went through it. There was a bowl of cold water, a piece of lavender-scented soap and a washcloth on the nightstand and I splashed my face hurriedly, trying to bring some colour back to my cheeks, then washed myself thoroughly. I wetted the cloth again and ran it over my hair, trying to freshen it. My stepmother helped me into a clean shift and laced my stays, then left me without a word as she went downstairs. I slid on a pair of black silk stockings and tied the garters. I pulled on the clothes that William had brought me with a shudder, fumbling with the unfamiliar ties and buttons. The blue jacket slipped over the top, a little too large for me but it would do. I twisted my hair up, held it in place with my combs and tucked it into the cap. As I lifted my face I caught sight of myself in the mirror. I was as pale as a ghost. I found my green silk neckerchief and tied it around my throat, then took up the earrings that had once belonged to my mother. As I held them between my fingers the thought of her set up a sadness in me that I could not shrug off. I felt frantic and unsettled, tears stinging my eyes at the same time as laughter welled up in my throat.

There was a knock on the cottage door and I heard William's voice downstairs. I pushed the earrings into a pocket then took one look around the room and stepped outside. As I turned at the top of the stairs all eyes were on me.

'Will this suffice?'

William laughed.

'Your own mother would not have recognised you.' He stiffened, realising what he had said, as my face whitened further. I was shaking by then, whether with anticipation or fear I know not. Was I to marry this man, who could be so careless in his speech? I paused then, all instincts telling me to go back upstairs, to bury myself under the covers, to let William Corder go. But I wanted to be married and safe and happy, so I did not heed it. I had come this far and I resolved to see it through. And once we were married, I would be mended and everything would be better.

My stepmother moved forward.

'It will suffice. Now, go, before something else happens to stop you.' She called back into the parlour. Nancy came out, shepherding the boys in front of her. I hugged my sister hard and saw tears in her eyes.

'Be happy, Maria. That is all I wish for you.' She kissed me once, twice, and then I bent to kiss my stepbrothers. Last of all I turned to Thomas Henry and held out my arms. I do not know what caused it. Maybe he saw not his mother, but a stranger. Perhaps it was the clothes that frightened him or my strangeness, but he would not come to me. I knelt there, reaching out my arms, desperate to hold him, but he refused to even kiss me farewell. Instead, he backed away to stand behind my stepmother, clutching her skirts with a thumb in his mouth, his eyes huge as she looked down at him fondly, stroking his hair.

He would not come to me to me. And that was the last time I ever saw my little boy.

CHAPTER
THIRTY-TWO

I crept out of the cottage by the back door, as if ashamed, and made my way across the field. William left by the front, saying a loud goodbye to my family, and walked up the road towards the Red Barn. We met at the field path and walked along it as if we were strangers, side by side as the fields fell away and we entered the woods. It was the middle of May. It had rained a little and the birds were singing loudly in the glistening trees. We did not speak or touch until, finally, we came to the pond. Seeing it so still and peaceful broke me. It was as if I was struck down. The memory of that night, my poor dead child sinking beneath the dank water, bubbles rising from the tiny body that no longer looked human, hit me with a force. A slow feeling of endless falling brought me to my knees.

'Come, Maria, get up. We must get to the barn.' William's voice was sharp, urgent. He looked around. 'No one comes yet, but they may do. We must go.'

'I cannot.'

'Oh, Maria.' His voice rang cold with frustration and worry. 'I have moved heaven and earth to give you your wish. We will marry, but we must go now. Please.'

I looked up at him as my tears began to fall.

'Is it not your wish as well?' The words were sharp in my mouth.

'Of course it is.' His voice was snappish with frustration as he took my arm and pulled me to my feet. 'But we must hurry. This is not the time for your moods. We will be back in Polstead in a week or two, but now we must go, and quickly.'

My heart was thumping and I could feel anger rising in me.

'I wish only to say farewell to our dead child, William, is that too much to ask? I have given up one for you and this one was taken from us. I have not even had time to visit my mother's grave and that of Matilda to say goodbye to them.' A great sob spilt from me. 'You are careless of my feelings, you do not understand how it is for me. You refuse to tell your mother of us, you accuse me of keeping company with Peter Mathews despite my assurances.' I knew I was being unreasonable, and that he had done his best, but I could not stop my tears or my nagging. I did not know why, but I was filled with an overwhelming sense of dread.

He helped me up, then pulled me away from the pond and back on the path.

'If you think so little of me, Maria, then I wonder that you still wish to be married. I do not have to marry you – it would be the thing of a moment to turn back and go home alone.'

My anger was like a flame, fanned by his words into a blaze.

'Your mother will never accept me, your family will not receive me.' He stopped and looked at me but said nothing, just shook his head, and then took my arm and steered me out of the wood and across the last field.

. . .

THE EVENING WAS MILD, the Red Barn a dark shape against the dusk. He took the key from his pocket and unlocked the great wooden door, pulling it open. The smell of hay and earth filled my nostrils, familiar and comforting, but there was no consoling me. I forgot the many happy hours and nights we had spent here in each other's arms, but instead stumbled inside, barely able to see for misery.

'Look, there is your bag. Get changed into your dress and we will leave for Ipswich.' He ran his hand through his hair, his voice resigned. 'We will do this thing, I am determined. We have come so far.'

'So far, yes, but you have no respect for me, I can hear it in your tone.'

'And I suppose Mathews showed you more, did he?' The name dropped through the air like a stone into water, the ripples pushing the air away. William looked shocked at the words as if they had come out of his mouth unwillingly.

'At least he made no false promises. He treated me like a lady. He took me to London and bought me things. He showed me affection.'

'And I do not? Maria, we do not have time for this. You must hurry.'

I ripped the man's cap from my head and took the pistol from my belt, then turned to my bag, crouching over it, pulling out my black silk dress and flannel petticoat. I shouldered off the jacket, fumbled at the buttons of the britches, my head lowered. My mind was spinning, thoughts whirling in a thick cloud of misery which was bearing down on me. I stepped out of the britches, letting them fall to the hard-packed floor and bent to step into my petticoat. I tied it and reached for my dress. It was only then that I looked at him.

He was pacing the floor, his hands tearing through his hair as he turned to me.

'I do not understand your moods, I do not know what it is that you want. I thought you would be pleased that we are finally leaving. Maria, we do not have to marry if you do not wish it. We can go home and say no more of the matter.' His voice sharpened and he looked at me. 'If you think so little of my intentions, maybe that would be for the best.'

A FEAR TOOK ME THEN, so strong it swept all in its wake. My mouth could not form any words of reply for I did not know how to answer. William was right. I had waited for marriage so long that I could not say now if it was still what I truly wanted and I could no longer keep from wailing. My fingers tore at my hair, so carefully pinned up with my best combs, causing it to fall heavy about my shoulders and over my face. William looked at me as if I was a madwoman and the thought came to me that maybe I was – perhaps it was madness that made me fight and argue with the one person I truly loved. My children were gone, my mind too, and I had made William, who cared for me more than anyone else, doubt me. And now he was going to leave me as the others had, as my children had. Madness it must be. I slammed my fists into my forehead, trying to get rid of the thoughts pounding there and he came towards me, worry in his eyes, and reached out his hands.

'Maria, my love, calm yourself. You will make yourself ill.' Even then I did not relent but gave him a look so withering and harsh that he backed away, uncertain of what to do. 'I am going to leave you to compose yourself. You must decide what you want of me. I will wait outside.' His face was a picture of abject misery, his head tilted to one side. 'I do not know what you want any more. I do not know what to do.' His shoulders drooped and he put his hand to his face as he stepped away from me and opened the barn door. I heard the wind whistling as he moved heavily through it and closed it softly behind him.

'William! Don't leave me.'

I BELIEVED that he had ignored my cry, that he had finally given up on me and would not return. The thought of being alone once more was too much to bear. The pain in my head was increasing so fast that I could barely stand. I looked wildly around me, my hair flying about my face and then I looked down. The pistol lay next to the discarded cap. Slowly I picked it up, feeling its heft, and cradled it in my hand. I do not know what I intended to do with it. I turned it, remembering our time at Sudbury, when we were full of hope, our babe due, filled with such happiness. It all seemed so long ago although it was but a few short weeks.

I thought of my poor Matilda, stone dead in her crib, and Thomas Henry, his angelic face scrunched up in fear as he pulled back from my outstretched arms.

My mind clouded further as, hard on its heels, came the memory of our dead son, gone but four weeks since, so quickly he was unnamed; I could feel the weight of him in my arms as I handed his still body to William, watching again as he gently took him from me and stooped to release the bundle into the murky depths. I could see again the dank water closing over my babe, the bubbles . . .

So much heartache, so much loss.

And now, after all that, after all we had suffered, I had lost William too. The thoughts sliced through me like knives, each one carving deep into my heart and shredding it to pieces. The torment, the losses – my mind was racing faster than ever, the thoughts and memories tripping over each other in their haste. The throbbing in my head was so intense, and I could scarcely see for the flashing before my eyes and I could bear it all no longer.

Everything I had held dear was lost to me.

The metal felt cold and hard against my palm, weighty. I gazed around once more at the Red Barn then I put the pistol to my neck and pulled the trigger.

CHAPTER
THIRTY-THREE

The pistol jerked, there was a flash, a burning intense pain, a smell of gunpowder and hot metal, and all went red. I felt myself slipping, falling, as the walls of the tall barn streamed crimson and the floor came up to meet me. The blood in my mouth stifled my scream. Then, a brilliant white light, colours, a shattered rainbow sparkling and falling like fine mist around me.

I thought I heard someone calling my name, faint in the distance.

I cried out then, for my lost children, for my lost love, the terror and the not-knowing as I fell down, down.

Then there was nothing, a complete emptiness and I shuddered at its bleakness. The pain was lessening now, the colours fading as I floated, empty, in a place of freedom where nothing could touch me.

In the distance, a small shining light appeared. It came closer and closer and I saw a narrow figure emerging from its brightness. The figure was familiar and loved and it reached for me. It was my mother who had come for me. She said but one word, *'Maria'* and I wanted so much to fall into her arms and let her bear me away, but I could not.

For William pulled me back.

CHAPTER
THIRTY-FOUR

I felt a blissful, cleansing freedom as my spirit rose up to dart through the air, like a summer swallow, higher and higher, into the roof of the barn. I swooped through the rafters, brushed against the thatch. Then there was a slow movement beneath me, the cord that bound me to him tightened and I pulled in and dropped down closer to see, as the air continued to swirl through me and around me. I hovered for a moment, unsure, and the light that was my mother began to fade as William cried out my name.

My earthly body lay on the hard-packed earth below me, motionless, my face a pool of blood. I saw the door of the barn swing open and there he was, come back for me as he promised. I watched as he fell to his knees at my side, his voice a howl of pain and I stretched out my arms to him. I could not hold him but in my altered state I found I could see inside his mind, and it was fragmented with panic and loss and fear. He was touching my body now, feeling for signs of life, and all the time his tears flowed. He kept saying my name over and over and the word soared through the barn on motes of dust, swirling and spreading, winnowing through the slats and thatch, the spider's webs and bird's nests, the cosy homes made by mice and rats, until my name was absorbed into the very fabric of the Red Barn.

Time seemed to stand still. I watched William try to lift me into his arms, but when he realised that life had left me he placed me back on the ground, so tenderly and lovingly. It was then he saw the pistol. He picked it up, crying out as he recognised it and I could feel his terror in that moment. He slumped to the ground beside me, shaking, as he realised that no one had seen what happened.

That his pistol was here.

That everyone would think that it was he who had murdered me.

HE WAS NOT THINKING CLEARLY. His mind was distorted, confused, his emotions high, it was as if I could read him now, knew his every thought. He should have gone for help, he knew that, and I urged him to, but my words were too faint over the clamour in his head. He was numb with fear. I watched as he slowly came to his senses and placed my shawl over my face so that he did not have to look at the horror of it, then he crossed my hands over my chest in repose. He composed himself a little and ran back to the barn door and peered out of it to see if anyone came, if the shot had been heard. All was silent, so, with a backward glance he left me lying there. He left me. He walked out of the door and I heard the sound of the heavy key turning in the lock, then I was alone, floating; a spirit.

But he had not run away. I was hunched in a corner in the dark when I heard him returning. I watched him from on high as he unlocked the door, all the time warily looking around him. He was carrying a pickaxe and a spade and he came in, locked the door behind him and set the tools down. That year's harvest was still growing in the fields so the barn was empty save for some old husks and bedding.

It was in the alcove to the right of the barn that he started. He took off his coat and hat and picked up the pickaxe and brought it down hard on the earth, over and over, the muscles of his arms bulging, his shoulders stiffening with each blow. He thought the ground would be softer there, where the corn was usually stored, and so it seemed, for the earth crumbled beneath the blade. He threw down the pickaxe after a little while and exchanged it for the spade.

Carefully, slowly, he dug my grave.

WHEN HE WAS DONE he went over to the empty shell that had once been me. He bent down and pulled away the shawl and a sob burst from him as he saw again my ruined face. He tried to lift me by my shoulders but the weight was too much for him, so he found a discarded sack in the corner of the barn and rolled me onto it. Holding the edge of the sack and my neckerchief to ensure I did not come off, he dragged me the few yards to the hole he had prepared. He was as careful with me as he could be but my body was heavy and he could barely manage. He had no option but to roll me into the pit he had dug and I landed hard on my right side. I could hear his breath coming quick and uneven, see the sweat running down his face as he realised that the hole he had dug was not long enough; my feet lay over the side. He wiped his forehead with his sleeve, took a deep breath then stepped down beside me. He drew my legs up, then turned and took my head in his hands.

'Oh, Maria.' He put his lips to my bloodied face and kissed me gently. 'I am sorry that I brought you to this, my love.' His tears still fell as he turned my head. He rested it gently on my chest so that I fitted tightly into the space, then he climbed out, took up the spade, hesitated for a moment, and then began to pile the earth onto me. I watched my body slowly disappear as he shovelled, his movements getting faster and faster as his thoughts became more frantic. He stamped down on the piled earth to flatten it and then spread the remainder all around to disperse it. When he'd finished he stopped to draw breath then put his hat and coat back on and gazed at his handiwork. The soil was freshly turned, yes, but after a while, it would blend back into the floor and no one would know I was there. I swooped down to look at William's face. It was grey and tense, streaked with dirt, sweat and tears, and his hair was dull with dust. I so wanted to touch him, to smooth away the terror that was shaping him. I took his dear face between my palms but they passed over him, through him.

He shuddered at my touch.

THIRTY-FIVE

I followed after him as he returned to his mother's house, looking over his shoulder as he walked. The thread between us was still strong. He crept up the back stairs as we had done together and went into his room. He filled the basin with cool water, took up a sponge, and washed the evidence of what he had done away, then changed his clothes. I stayed near him as he sank down on his bed, waiting for the fear and shaking to subside.

That evening he sat down to eat with his mother and sister and they talked of everyday things; of James's health, of the farm, of how many men he would need for the coming harvest. And he kept up the pretence but I could feel his terror, it was a stone in his stomach that would never leave him.

TWO DAYS LATER, on Sunday, he screwed up his courage and went to see my family. I drifted in the air around him as he walked down the familiar road and round the corner to the cottage. I gazed at the garden where I had tended my mother's roses; I heard the chatter of the boys playing outside, and the creak of the gate as

William entered, but the image shimmered and shone as if veiled by tears. He knocked on the door.

'William? I did not expect to see you. Where is Maria?' My stepmother did not hold the door wide to let him in, just looked at him in astonishment.

'Mrs Martin.' I felt him hesitate a little, then he straightened his shoulders and looked at her. 'Our plans had to be changed at the last minute. Rest assured, Maria is settled in Ipswich, with the sister of a good school friend of mine, Miss Rowland. She will look after her, and provide company while I am here. It is but a small delay. It could not be helped.' The lies slid off his tongue like melted butter.

'But what will she wear? She took so little. And why are you not with her?' Her face had narrowed in suspicion.

'Miss Rowland has offered to loan her some clothes until she can buy her own and I have given her twenty pounds to spend on herself, for the things she needs. I have the marriage licence but it seems that it must be formalised in London, so we are unable to marry for a month or six weeks. Maria is well cared for, you should not worry, and I will ask her to write to you and her father soon.'

He turned to go but my stepmother pulled at his arm.

'Did she change her dress?' He turned back to her, his shoulders tight with tension 'She was wearing your brother's clothes?'

He stiffened, remembering.

'She did. She changed in the Red Barn.' A twitch set up at the side of his mouth and she peered closely at him. 'I took James's clothes in the gig with us so that I could return them to him. She had on her straw bonnet. She looked very fine, Mrs Martin, and was exceedingly happy.' He thought that this would put my stepmother's mind at rest, but she was not finished. She drew closer to him and clutched at his sleeve.

'My boy George saw you.' I thought William's legs would fail him then, that he would fall in a faint before her, but he did not. He was stronger than I thought. 'You were coming away from the Red Barn with a pickaxe.'

He swallowed hard.

'Not I. Your boy was mistaken.' William was not a tall man but he drew himself up to his full height. 'What need have I for pickaxe? I have men who do that kind of manual work for me. It was not me.' He was brazen and I admired him for his courage.

'George was sure it was you. He recognised your coat.'

'It was not. Perhaps he confused me with Tom Akers? Akers was planting trees on the hill around that time, at my direction.'

She hesitated then, doubt sown and seeded.

'Maybe. I will have to ask him again.' She let go of his sleeve and stepped back. 'Be sure to tell Maria to write to her father. He was sorry not to have said farewell to her and a letter would put his mind at rest.' She gave William a long, considering look, then closed the door. He walked out of the gate and up the lane out of sight, before moving towards a wall and slumping against it, breathing hard. The thudding of his heart disturbed the air around me so hard that it was as if my own was beating again. I watched over him as he rested his head against the coarse brick then put my arms around him. It was as if he felt my presence for his breathing calmed. He looked around, puzzled, then shrugged his shoulders, composed himself, straightened his hat and set off for home.

CHAPTER

THIRTY-SIX

I t was only a week later that James Corder died. I was next to William at the bedside, watching in the shadows as his brother's frail body drew its last, rattling breath. I saw his mother and sisters bent over with grief and felt William's sadness. I saw James's spirit leave him and float past me, upwards, heaven-bound. For his was a good soul, not troubled like mine. His passage to God was ensured, whereas mine . . . ?

The rain fell steadily on the day of the funeral and William emerged from Polstead church unfurling an umbrella. His family had gone home after the burial, leaving him alone to pray.

'Why do you have Maria's umbrella?' My stepmother stepped out from behind a dripping tree. 'Why does she not have it with her?'

'Mrs Martin. Is it Maria's? I believe I borrowed it from a neighbour.'

My stepmother would not leave it alone.

'No, it is Maria's. It is the same green as hers and anyway, I recognise the handle.' William put on his eyeglasses and looked at it carefully.

'She did have a similar one. She must have loaned it to me and I forgot to return it.' He looked at her. 'Yes, that was it. I am sorry, I have become forgetful. James's death – it has been hard for us all.' My stepmother looked at him and then nodded.

'I am sorry for your loss, William.' She turned and then paused. 'Be sure to remember me to Maria and ask her to write.'

William nodded.

'I will, I shall see her soon.'

EVERYTHING WAS BECOMING TOO much for William now. His brother's death, coming only ten days after mine, broke him. His mind fragmented. He could no longer think straight for the grief that overwhelmed and tortured him, and he swung from despair to happiness. He kept visiting my parents, even showing them a gold ring he had bought for our wedding, trying to convince them and himself that all was well. And he came to believe it, this story he had woven, convinced himself of its truth, rather than think on the horror that had happened. Then John Corder, his older brother, began to show signs of the same illness that had taken James. It could not have been foreseen that the consumption took him quicker than anyone could have imagined, for it was only two weeks later that John followed his brother to the grave. Now William was the only remaining son and the duties and responsibilities of running the farm fell solely to him. His was a family destroyed by sorrow, a house of death – in only eight weeks three people who were so dear to him were gone. His poor mother was laid low with grief and clung to him again as a rock to the shore, ever deferring to his opinions. She could not leave him alone, stroking his hair, patting his arm, telling him how much he was loved and needed until he could scarce bear it. His sister stayed with her to care for her but William felt that he had lost everything – the dream of a wife and children, the support of his family. Me.

. . .

ALL THAT SUMMER he kept bumping into my stepmother. I had seen her watch his movements – she learned where he would be and when he would be passing the cottage, and she stood in wait for him. She pestered him with questions about me, but he always had an answer. Sometimes he did not see her for days and when he did he told her that I was well and happy in Ipswich, or visiting Great Yarmouth with Miss Rowland. He said that the licence was still delayed but that he was confident of receiving it shortly and then we would be wed. He told her that the reason I had not written was that I had injured my hand and was unable to hold a pen, or that I was too busy. He kept them fed with untruths until they stopped asking. He managed the farm as best he could but he hated it. He was not himself, not the William I had known and loved so dearly. His mind had become fogged and confused so that when he was asked a question he said the first thing that came into his head, whether it was true or not. His moods swept from fear to elation and he exaggerated and told so many lies that he found it hard to remember them all. He kept to his story that I was with Miss Rowland as best he could, but the strain of it all was taking its toll on his health and his cough worsened.

HE COULD NOT ESCAPE the questions. Although my family seemed satisfied, there were those in the village who were nosy and outspoken. Phoebe Stow was one of them. As the village midwife she knew everything and everybody, and one day, when William was walking to the fields, she stopped him.

'Mr Corder. Thank you for returning the spade you borrowed.' I saw William go white and felt the fear bubble inside him. The spade he had used to bury me. I never thought that he may have borrowed it.

'My pleasure, Mrs Stow, thank you for loaning it to me.'

'I was glad to have it back, I had not told my husband, for he does not like to lend his tools, but I knew, as it was you . . .' She smiled at him. 'And how is Maria?' The question hung between them like a corpse.

'She is well, save for a damaged hand. I am not sure how she did it but it has been very sore. She cannot use it very well at the moment and has been unable to write to her father.'

'I'm sorry to hear that.' She drew in closer. 'And I was very sorry to hear about your child. But you will have more, I am sure of it.' She patted his arm, her face concerned. 'I know she was brought low by the births of her other babes but she is a strong girl and I'm sure in no time – '

'She will have no more children, Mrs Stow.' I willed him to say no more.

'Because you are not yet married to her?' She smiled widely, teasing now. 'There is a remedy to that.'

'I can go to her whenever I please.'

'But her mother says you are often apart. Do you not get jealous, her there alone in a busy town? A lovely girl like that would have no end of suitors.' William pulled away from her, his face angry and she looked puzzled. 'I was only teasing you, Mr Corder, I meant no harm. Your arrangements are your own.'

'They are, and no business of yours.' He softened then. 'I know you only meant well. Maria is fine and happy and I thank you for asking after her. I am here frequently because my mother needs me. I am her only son now, and I have the farm to run. I will commend you to Maria when I next see her. I bid you good day.' He touched his hat and strode away, leaving her embarrassed and perplexed, but his very attitude had set up a doubt in her mind.

CHAPTER

THIRTY-SEVEN

That summer was hot and dry and the harvest was good. The men laboured in the fields day after day, horses dragging carts stacked high with sheaves of corn. William worked like a thing possessed, wielding scythe and pitchfork, helping load the wagons. But all the time he was thinking of me and, when the first cart arrived at the Red Barn and the corn was unloaded he was there. He still kept the key on his person, as he had done when we visited together in those long-ago days and he was careful, so careful. The floor was still littered with old chaff, my grave well-hidden, but, even then, he made sure they lay the first bundles over me, piling them high, covering any lingering trace. The light in the barn danced dry with dust and William's cough worsened but he carried on, helping the men until the last remaining stook was gathered in. I watched, as I always had done when I was living, as the men threw their scythes down. Loaves were made from the new harvest and William hosted the harvest supper in celebration. His mother did not attend that year, her grief still too raw, and the villagers, aware of this, made their celebrations more muted. There was many a sore head the following day but not William's, for he still never touched strong drink.

I missed it. The camaraderie, the joy of another harvest safely in. I missed the songs and stories, the food and ale. All the families were there, mine included, and I wanted so much to be with them. But I could not. I had to be content with watching from a distance, floating through the people as they danced and sang, following William. The urge to reach out to him was overwhelming, the desire to draw him away to one of the quiet places we had found the year before, to lie with him and love him again.

But he was changed and I was no more, and those times were lost to us and would never come again.

It was in July that William saw Peter Mathews. Peter had returned to Polstead to visit family and had called on Mrs Corder to express his sincere condolences on the death of her two sons, who had been his friends. He was like that, Peter, always a gentleman, always knowing the right thing to do – perhaps this was one of the reasons William took against him so much, for he was always jealous of him.

It was as Peter was taking his leave of Mrs Corder that he spied William in the hallway and drew him to one side.

'Is it true that you have married Maria, William?' William looked up at him, his head to one side, silent. 'Mrs Martin said it was so, but your mother did not mention the fact. I can only assume that she still knows nothing of your relationship. So you are being secretive once more.' He paused and looked searchingly at William who lowered his gaze. 'I have visited my boy. Mr and Mrs Martin say that they have not heard from his mother since she left with you in May. Where is she? And why is the child not with her?'

William found his voice.

'We thought it best that Thomas Henry stayed with Maria's family until we are more settled. We have not yet been able to marry – there has been a delay in obtaining a licence, but Maria is staying with friends until we are wed.'

Peter peered at him, his face stern.

'I cannot but help think of that missing letter and the five-pound note. I am still not satisfied that you were not more involved.' I could feel William's mind whirring, trying to think of a satisfactory answer. I swirled around him, willing him to tell the truth, for there was no escaping this question.

'Maria explained it. I cashed it at the bank at her request and gave the money over to her. I thought she had given it to her step-mother for the boy's keep.'

Peter looked angry.

'So you say, but I find that hard to believe. Money went missing and you seemed to be behind it. I do not trust you, William, I never have. That money was not yours, it was for the boy. So if it happens again I will go to the constable. Do I make myself clear?' He held out a paper. 'I have a letter here for Maria. You are to ensure she receives it and I expect to hear from you shortly, confirming that you have sent it to her. I will not risk a bastardy order being drawn up saying that I have not paid my dues for my child when I always have.' He poked a long finger into his chest and I felt William flinch. 'Do you understand?'

William nodded and looked up at Peter, who seemed to tower above him.

'I apologise for the earlier confusion, Mathews.' He took the letter from Peter. 'I will send this to Maria and ask her to write to you when she can, but at the moment she has a sore on the back of her hand and is unable to hold a pen. I understand that she is currently staying with a friend in Yarmouth but I do not have the address to hand.'

Peter stepped back and gave him a hard look.

'Very well. I have made myself clear on the consequences if money should ever go astray in the future. This is your final warning, William. If this ever happens again I will not call on you to discuss it but take the matter immediately to the constable. They hang men for theft, as I'm sure you know.'

William pulled at his collar.

'It was a misunderstanding. I will write to Maria today with your letter. You shall hear from me by tomorrow's post. You have my word.'

Peter leaned towards him.

'Your word is worth nothing in my eyes. It seems to me that there is much concealment around this. I care only for the welfare of Maria and the child, you are of no account. I look forward to receiving your letter confirming you have sent it to her.' Peter turned on his heel and then paused in the doorway and looked back over his shoulder. 'It would be a shame to trouble your mother with this matter.' He gave William a meaningful stare and strode away.

William shut the door behind him then sank down on his haunches and put his head in his hands. My heart went out to him.

THE FOLLOWING morning William saw my stepmother as he passed our cottage. She was waiting on the doorstep, arms folded.

'Mr Mathews has seen you, has he? He said he would. Good as his word, that gentleman. Not like some I could mention. What news of Maria?' From the gloom behind her, my father appeared but said nothing.

'We still wait for the license to be signed but she is well, apart from a cough and her damaged hand. She is staying with friends of mine near Yarmouth.'

'She should write to her father. It is his due.'

William looked at my father.

'She is unable to write at the moment, Mr Martin, as I have explained. I have bought new clothes for myself and for her for the wedding, which I hope will be soon. I will be sure and pass on your good wishes when I next see her.' My stepmother sniffed and shut the door.

He closed his eyes briefly against the insult, then moved away, making his way home reluctantly, forming the words he needed to write to Peter in his mind. He spoke with his mother for a while then made his way to the study, where he sat down at the old oak desk and drew pen and ink towards him. I leaned over his shoulder to guide him, breathing the placating words into his ear so the letters flowed from his nib. He begged Peter's forgiveness, threw himself at his feet and made abject apologies. He signed it with an unsteady hand and then put a postscript to say that we were to be married in a month or six weeks' time, after which he would be able to settle his affairs properly.

He did all he could to make matters right and it seemed that Peter forgave him, for, by return of post, a letter arrived from Peter with his best wishes for my recovery and saying how pleased he was that we were to marry. He finished by saying that he wanted to remain friends with all for the sake of William's mother who had suffered such unbearable bereavement. And that seemed to be the end of it. William's relief was palpable but I knew Peter better than he and did not believe he would let matters rest.

I knew he would be watching and wondering.

CHAPTER
THIRTY-EIGHT

The rest of the summer was taken up with the running of the farm but events were taking their toll. William became ill. The cough he had long suffered with grew worse, and he often woke in the night sweating with a high temperature. There were days when his joints ached and his head thumped until he could bear it no longer. It was his mother who called the doctor and he who recommended that William needed complete rest, suggesting that he should go to the south coast for the good of his health. His mother persuaded him to go.

'I could not bear it if you were taken from me, William. You are my sole remaining son and I must see you well. If that means that you must leave me for a few months then so be it.'

'But what of the farm? I cannot leave it now.' He ran his hand through his hair distractedly.

'Surely there is someone worthy who could take it on. What about Mr Pryke? He already knows the running of the farm, he is very capable.' She patted his hand. 'Ask him, we will pay him suitable wages. He can report to me in your absence. It will give me something to do, take my mind off. . .' She dabbed at a tear with a white lace handkerchief. 'Your father's Will means we have enough money to do this. Your health is more important, my boy. If the doctor recommends it, you must go.'

So it was in September William called on my parents to take leave of them, telling them of his plans and saying that as soon as I had returned from Yarmouth we would marry. Pryke took over the running of the farm under Mrs Corder's supervision and it was he who drove William in the Corder gig to Colchester. And when Pryke asked after my health, William said he had not seen me since May.

THE WEATHER WAS warm and fine when William arrived on the Isle of Wight. He spent a month there, walking each day, resting and reading. His mind was easier in those weeks than it had been for a long time and I could see his health improving. But the past would not leave him alone. He felt obliged to reply to my father's letters, telling him of the slow progress of our wedding plans, but maintaining the fiction that I was well and content. And in the dark nights, he cried silently for me, wetting the pillow with his tears. I comforted him as best I could, lying down beside him, cocooning him in my arms, and I know he felt my presence, for a calm would come over him and he would sleep.

There were other people staying in his lodging place and he became friendly with the Moores, a mother, her grown son and daughter, who were also there to take the air. They would meet for dinner each evening and recount their day's adventures and, with their light company and merry laughter, William began to regain his strength, the sea air and brisk walks ridding him of his cough. He was like the old William then, the one I had first loved, and I was happy for him, but full of regrets for what might have been.

But time was running out. The money his mother had given him when he left Polstead was diminishing, so he visited

Southampton, then Portsmouth and then took lodgings in London as he had the matter of James's Will to sort out. In the middle of October, he wrote to my father to tell him that we had married. He said that he was surprised that Father had not replied to the letter I had sent him about our wedding, that it must have been lost in the post. The lies grew as he wrote about how his friend, Mr Rowland, had acted as father to give me away and Miss Rowland had been my bridesmaid. He thought that this would be enough, that the matter was at an end. He believed that telling my family that we were finally married would be enough to placate them and to stop the rumours.

But William was unravelling, no longer thinking clearly. I could see that in the way he thrashed around, trying to explain the unexplainable, laying one untruth on top of another until the pile of lies grew too tall, wobbled and fell. The situation grew worse when my father wrote to him. Father was angry with me for not replying to him and accused me of neglecting Thomas Henry. He said that Peter had stopped maintenance payments due to my now being married, that my stepmother was frantic because of the loss of such a sum and that she wanted someone to write to him.

William was in a blind panic and nothing I could do could calm him. He replied by return, enclosing a sovereign. He repeated that the letter from me must have been lost in the sea voyage from the Isle of Wight and that he did not wish to pursue the matter with the Post Office in case our whereabouts became known. He said there was danger in us returning to Polstead, and he was obsessed with Peter Mathews finding out where we were and asked Father to tell anyone who questioned our whereabouts that we had gone abroad. Finally, he said that Nancy and my stepmother could have my clothes as he would buy me new ones in London. He swung between tears and great waves of happiness but he was sinking, sinking under the pressure of all that had occurred. He could no longer sleep, instead spending the night pacing up and down in his lodgings.

I tried everything I could to stop him, to slow his mind and make him think, but he was growing beyond me now, becoming erratic and manic. My powers were fading as time went on and I feared that his illness would recur, that he would say too much and implicate himself.

But then fate intervened again, for one morning, he ran into Miss Moore.

CHAPTER
THIRTY-NINE

He was waiting to be served in a pastry shop in Fleet Street. It smelt beautiful, that shop, of fresh bread and spun sugar. How I yearned to be able to sink my teeth into one of those pastries, to feel the crust burst on my tongue, the soft sweetness filling my mouth, but I could not. I was gone from such sensations and could only watch as William handed over payment and accepted the parcel of warm cakes from the proprietor. As he turned to go he bumped into a small figure.

'I beg your pardon, Miss.' He doffed his hat and then looked again. 'Miss Moore! I did not expect to see you here. What a small world.'

She smiled at him and her face was transformed.

'Mr Corder. A small world indeed. London is not the Isle of Wight, is it? How are you keeping?' She gave her order to the shop-keeper and William waited to one side as the transaction was completed. She tucked her purchases into a wide basket on her arm and then turned to William. 'Do tell me how you are. Do you live nearby now?'

They stepped outside and he smiled warmly at her. Mary Moore reminded William a little of me. She had dark hair, the same figure, but her eyes were a doe-like brown and, unlike mine, her nature was kind and generous. I felt a flutter of jealousy.

'I am lodging at the Bull Inn in Leadenhall Street. It is quite comfortable, but it is certainly not the Isle of Wight.'

'And is your cough still improving?'

'Well enough since I saw you last, but now, with the London air, I fear . . . Here, let me take that for you.' He reached for her basket and swung it as they walked along the street. 'And how is your dear mother, and your brother?'

She looked up at him shyly.

'They are well, thank you, and I will tell them how I ran into you, they will be pleased to know you are still in London. Will you be here long?'

William hesitated.

'I do not know. I have business to attend to and will not return to Suffolk for now – family matters, you know. An overseer is running the farm quite capably in my absence, and my sister is there to care for my mother. Mother writes to me each week and all seems to be well.'

'So you live alone still? There is no sweetheart here?' She was more forward now, unchaperoned by her mother and brother, and she knew it, for she blushed prettily. William looked at his feet.

'No, I have no one.'

'Perhaps you need a wife, Mr Corder, to take care of you?' I see William start at the question, then clear his throat.

'Miss Moore, there was one who was to be my wife, but it was not to be.'

'She found another?' Mary rested her hand on his arm and he did not pull away.

'No, sadly, she is no longer with us.' Tears filled his eyes. 'Do not ask more of me, I can't bear to speak of it.' I felt grief bear down on him once more.

'I did not mean to pry and certainly did not wish to upset you. I can see that I have been tactless.' Her voice was soft, full of concern. She paused outside a tall building with a small jewellery shop at the entrance. 'This is my brother's shop. Mother and I live above it. Charles dines with us each day.' She looked up at William and smiled. 'I should go in. Mother will be wondering what kept me.' She held out her hand for her basket and William passed it to her. 'Please accept my sincere apologies for any pain I have caused you, I had no wish to stir up bad memories.'

William dabbed at his eyes with a spotless handkerchief.

'You have no need to apologise, Miss Moore. It is in the past now and I must move on. It was delightful to meet you again.'

'And you, Mr Corder.' She paused expectantly, but he did not speak. Face thoughtful, he doffed his hat and walked away as she looked after him. I could feel her disappointment.

It was Mary Moore who set up the idea of marriage in William's head.

THOSE WERE DIFFERENT TIMES. If a woman of good standing did not mix in the right circles she would not be able to meet a suitable man to marry. And Mary Moore was confined by her family, treated like a child, her brother expecting that one day she would take over the care of her mother, as a good daughter should. But Mary was made of stronger stuff and when she saw the advertisement in the Morning Herald she knew.

November 13th - MATRIMONY

A Private gentleman, aged 24, entirely independent, whose disposi-

tion is not to be exceeded, has lately lost the chief of this family by the hand of Providence, which has caused discord among the remainder under circumstances most disagreeable to relate. To any female of respectability, who would study for domestic comfort, and willing to confide her future happiness in one every way qualified to render the marriage state desirable, as the advertiser is in affluence. The lady must have some property which may remain in her possession. Many happy marriages have taken place through means similar to this now resorted to . . .

I had watched over him as William had worded it, carefully and thoughtfully, not wishing to give too much of himself away, but just enough to seem attractive to the right kind of lady. I blew the phrases into his ear, whispered them into his thoughts. Mary Moore's words had turned over and over in his head as he walked home until he convinced himself that a wife was what he needed, someone to ease his pain and uncertainty. Marriage could be the making of him, for he was one who needed to be loved. And he thought that, perhaps, with the love and devotion of a new wife, he would be able to forget about me.

By the last week of November, to his amazement, he had received forty-five replies. Another advertisement in the Sunday Times garnered a further fifty-three letters, all from women seeking to marry one such as he. He was surprised by the response but saw this as a way to wipe the slate clean, to start again, in a new place, with a new wife.

Then he noticed that one of the replies was from Mary Moore and his spirits rose. He had thought Mary was far above him but it seemed that she did not feel the same. She would be good for him, I could see that. She was good-natured, even-tempered – all the things I was not. I had seen how she was with him during all those dinners on the Isle of Wight, how he was with her. She had a sweet smile and an air of stability about her and I knew he could grow to love her, not in the way he had loved me maybe, but with a gentle love that would suit him better. I could only feel happy that, at last, he may find peace.

He picked up his pen and began to write to her. I tamped down the sparks of jealousy as soon as they sprang to life.

CHAPTER
FORTY

I t took them only two days to decide to marry and Mary invited William to tea with her family to tell them of their decision. I watched as he dressed in his best waistcoat, brushed his hat and polished his shoes, all the time whistling happily. There was a lift in his step as he walked the short distance to their house, a smile as he knocked on the door. He looked as he did when he courted me and my heart jumped.

Mary answered it and her face was white.

'My brother has found out that you are to take tea here, he saw the extra plate laid. I told him that it was a friend coming to see me but he was angry not to have been consulted. I asked him to join us but he has refused. Oh, William, I am hoping that when he finds out it is you, he will be more kindly disposed.'

William squeezed her hand.

'I will speak to him. All will be well, you will see.'

She let him into the hall, a small, dark passage lit with a single lamp.

'We are in here.' She held out her hand and he walked into a room stuffed full of ornaments and knick-knacks. A fire was blazing in the grate, making the room so stuffy that William could scarcely breathe. Mrs Moore rose from her chair, one hand on her walking stick.

'Mr Corder, what a pleasure. I had not expected to see you again. We did enjoy your company while we were staying by the sea. I hope it did you as much good as it has me. Please, sit.' She indicated a chair by the fire. 'Now, may I offer you a cup of tea?'

THE CONVERSATION WAS light until Charles Moore came in. He sat down and he and William exchanged polite pleasantries then William cleared his throat loudly.

'I have come to ask for permission to marry your sister, Moore. She is in agreement and we wish to wed as soon as possible.'

The room fell silent.

Charles looked at his mother, then back at William.

'Marry?' He looked at Mary then at William. 'How did you meet with my sister? We thought, after the Isle of Wight, not to see you again. Did you form some attachment there that I was not aware of?'

William sought to placate him.

'We did not. There was nothing clandestine, I assure you. We met by chance in a pastry shop in Leadenhall Street.' He looked across at Mary and smiled. 'She responded to an advertisement that I put in the Morning Herald.'

'Advertisement?'

'For a wife. It is not unusual for men of my station who seek to find the comfort of a soulmate.'

Charles glared at him.

'It is not unusual for men of your station to wish to find the comfort of a mistress, Corder.'

202

William leapt to his feet in agitation as Mrs Moore put her hand to her mouth in horror. Mary looked aghast.

'No, no, that is not my intention. Such a thing never crossed my mind. I wish to make her my wife. I would never, ever, consider suggesting such a thing to a woman as honourable and chaste as Miss Moore.' She smiled at him and took his outstretched hand. 'I wish to marry her, Moore, and she me.'

Charles turned to his sister.

'But what do you know of this man, Mary? Enquiries should be made. What kind of person he is, whether he has told you the truth about his wealth and position? Suffolk is a long way away. We do not know the veracity of what he has told us, or whether there is any whiff of scandal attached to his family name – as your brother it is my duty to protect you.'

Mary rose to her feet and took his arm.

'Charles, William has told me nothing but the truth, I am certain of it. He has lost his father and three brothers in just a few months through tragic circumstances. He lost the one he loved too. He is a man of integrity and position and has been running the family farm as his poor mother's sole remaining son. He now has an overseer to do that and is finally in a position to wed. His duties will not call him back to Suffolk too often.' She clung to him tighter. 'Charles, I assure you he is honest. He has shown me nothing but kindness and you know how well we all got on before. I wish to be his wife, and that is all I can say.'

I could see Charles was moved by this speech, William too, but still he persisted.

'That may be, but it would be remiss of me not to make enquiries. You do not know this man well.'

She drew herself up then, her eyes blazing, and I saw the courage in her.

'I am fully satisfied that he has been honest with me. I am my own mistress and I beg leave to make my own judgements. I am asking you, Charles, to give us your blessing. We are to be wed tomorrow. It is all arranged, and I intend to do this with or without your approval.' Her eyes filled then. 'But I would like your blessing, Charles, I do not wish to take a step like this without your agreement.' She looked at him pleadingly. 'But, with or without it, I intend to marry William tomorrow.

THEY WERE MARRIED by licence at St Andrews, Holborn the next morning. It was a crisp November day as I watched from the trees, my dead heart heavy with sadness. I could not help but think that, if I had been different, if things had not taken the turn they had, then it could have been me standing there. I had ruined my chances of love but did not begrudge William his. He was content and Mary clearly adored him. Charles Moore had accepted their relationship, despite his continued misgivings, for he could not deny the love in his sister's eyes and the kind and considerate way William treated her. Yes, I was happy for William. He deserved better than me, deserved to have a wife who truly loved and cherished him.

They did not stay long in London. Mary had always wanted to run a school for young ladies and, with her money and William's, they were able to find an opportunity in Brentford, an up-and-coming area on the outskirts of London. Grove House whad been owned by Mrs Ingleton whose three daughters remained there, and it soon became successful, for Mary's education and abilities made her the perfect teacher. William helped to support her and Mrs Moore, who had moved with them to be with her daughter and to help with the school. Times were good and William faded more and more from my reach as his relationship with his new wife flourished. But, still, in all this newness and joy, there were dark nights. Nights when William would toss and turn in his sleep, crying out and talking aloud, when I had to go to him and stroke his forehead, for fear that someone would hear him. But those nights became fewer and I slowly withdrew, leaving his care to his wife. And I was at peace with that, pleased that William had at last found contentment. All seemed well.

Until they found my body.

CHAPTER
FORTY-ONE

Everyone said that it was my stepmother who found where I was, for it had come to her in a dream. She became famous for that, people flocked to speak to her, the newspapers were full of her story and she lapped it all up. She had always loved attention and this was more than she could ever have hoped for. But there was no dream. I knew, for I could see inside her thoughts. My disappearance and lack of contact had been the subject of many long conversations between her, my father and Nancy. They went over it again and again, thinking of all the things that could explain it. But it was Nancy, not Ann, who first spoke it, Nancy who drew me back.

They were all sitting around the table, dinner finished, the boys restless, keen to be outside and my sister not looking forward to clearing the pile of dishes that were left. Thomas Henry's face was full of mischief and my heart constricted as I watched him. He was happy, healthy and long gone from me. I hovered in dark corners as I listened to my family speak of me. Nancy's pain had brought me to her and I felt a thought prick her mind, take hold like a thorn, and work its way under her skin until she spoke it out loud.

'What if Maria never left Polstead?' My father and stepmother looked at her. 'We know she went to the Red Barn with William. What if she never left?'

I drew closer, putting out a hand to touch Nancy's arm. She shivered.

My stepmother leaned forward.

'You mean that she came to harm there? That William harmed her?' Nancy looked at her, her face stricken, her thoughts tumbling. It was then that George piped up.

'I saw Mr Corder with a pickaxe, I told you.'

'You did, son.'

'And he did not leave as soon as he told us.' I could see he was close to tears. 'I saw him. I did, but no one believed me.'

His mother looked sternly at him.

'He told me that it was Tom Akers you saw, planting trees.'

George's voice rose, his face reddening.

'It was not Tom. I know Tom. It was him – and you still don't believe me.'

He burst into floods of tears as Father leaned across to him.

'That is enough, George. You did tell us, that is true, but we asked Mr Corder and he explained it all away.'

'He's a liar!' George screwed his fists into his eyes, trying to control himself.

'Silence! You must not call anyone a liar, it is not the Christian thing to do. I brought you up better than that.' Father's voice was harsh.

My stepmother reached out and patted George's shoulder, pulling him to her. She held on to him as her face became thoughtful.

'But Thomas, what if Nancy is right? What if the person George saw *was* William? We have not seen or heard from Maria herself for nigh on eleven months now, despite all William's excuses. There has been no letter – ' My father looked haggard. 'What if she came to harm in the Red Barn – what if she is still there?'

'You are talking about the Corders here, Ann. They run this village and without their employment, many of us would starve. You can't go around accusing one of them, especially after what happened to the brothers. Think of poor Mrs Corder, how she would feel if such rumours reached her ears. No, there must be another explanation. Maria is happy and married and we must accept the truth, that she is a wilful daughter who does not care enough about her family to write to them.' My stepmother opened her mouth to say more but Father held up his hand. 'I will have no more talk of this matter. We will write to Corder again and insist he brings Maria for a visit or at least tell her she must write to us and put our minds at rest. There will be a simple explanation. That is an end to it. Nancy, clear these dishes.'

But my stepmother would not let it go. At every opportunity she berated my father, insisting he do more to find me, but he brushed her away. So she thought of the idea of a dream, how he could not ignore that. She only told one person about it, Phoebe Stow, but that was enough. Soon, all of Polstead were talking about Ann Martin's dreams and my father had no option. He took up his mole spike, went to Mr Pryke to ask for his help, and together they walked to the Red Barn.

CHAPTER
FORTY-TWO

I had thought never to visit that place again, for the memories were fierce and painful. But I went with the two men, following close until Pryke turned his head as if sensing me. I drew back a little then, watched as they walked on in silence, heard the clump of their boots, the snick of the key in the lock, the creak of the tall door as it opened, letting the light in. Dust and chaff danced in the sunlight as the two men stood there, gazing around.

'I am only doing this out of respect for you, Mr Martin, and Mrs Corder must not learn of it.'

My father nodded.

'Of course, and I am grateful.'

'I know you have not heard from your daughter for many months, but I have to say that I cannot believe that young Mr Corder would cause any harm to come to her. From what I saw he was very fond of her.'

'Not fond enough to marry her here, as he said he would.'

'That was because of his mother. You know how terrified he was of upsetting her. She doted too much on the boy after his brothers were so cruelly taken, and she is still worried at his absence. I know, I see her each week to report on how the farm is doing. That woman will not believe a single wrongdoing from William, and that's a fact.' His words hung in the empty barn, the light shimmering patterns on the hard earth floor, their boots scuffing the chaff which rose high to the arched roof. Pryke paused, looking around him, then dropped his voice. 'There was some fuss about money recently. Someone went into the bank in Manningtree to cash a cheque. The bank did so, gave him the notes, but then they contacted Mrs Corder, for one of the staff recognised the man as William. Turns out the cheque was a forgery. God alone knows why he did it, you get transportation for forgery, but Mrs Corder was able to hush it all up so that the magistrate did not come to hear of it. You did not hear that tale from me, mind.'

'But what was he doing in Manningtree? Why did he not call on us if he was so close?' My father rubbed his head with his hand. 'There is much about this business that does not make sense.'

'I hear your Missus has had dreams about Maria?'

'So she says. She has been on at me for weeks, telling me to check the barn.' He sighed heavily. 'I wouldn't have troubled you else, but she will not let it lie.' He turned and looked around. The barn lay silent in the spring sunshine, only the soft sound of bird-song blowing in through the open door on the cool April air. 'Best get on with it then.'

Pryke removed his jacket.

'Where do you want to start? It's a big place.'

They looked around, considering. The corn had been threshed out and only the litter remained, the barn floor waiting for the next harvest, so they set to clearing it with the rakes that were kept there for the purpose. It was not a quick job. Pryke and my father laboured all that morning, scraping back the husks until they reached the alcove to the right of the great door, where the first

212

sheaves had been laid last harvest. The tines clattered against stones in the ground as they raked the debris away.

'Does this look to you like it might have been disturbed? What do you think?' It was the place where the earth had been trodden down and my heart stopped. My father wiped his brow and grunted, then hefted his mole spike and thrust it down into the ground several times. He lifted it out and was about to turn away when Pryke grabbed his arm.

'Look, there – '

A thick wetness, foul smelling and dark, covered the point of the mole spike. The two men covered their noses with their sleeves as they peered at the spike, and then my father's knees buckled. Pryke held him up as they both stared and stared.

'What is it?'

'It may be nothing, a dead rat perhaps?'

'But how did it come to be buried?' My father's voice was small and pleading, and in that moment I realised that he had loved me, despite his hardness toward me in the past.

'Leave it now, Thomas, come away. This is not something we should deal with. I'll lock the barn tight. We need help.' Pryke took my father's arm and led him outside. The barn door crashed hollow behind them and the key clunked.

Pryke found a man called Botwell, and they and my father came back armed with pickaxes and sharp spades. They rolled up their sleeves in silence as they set to and dug. They had told no one else about their suspicions, not wanting to look fools if it were nothing. But a foot and a half down they stopped dead.

'There is something here, that's for sure.' said Pryke. 'It's no rat.' They pulled the earth away carefully to reveal the sacking and the white glimmer of bone. He turned to my father. 'It looks like a foot . . .' His words faded as the three men stood and stared at the horror they had unearthed. 'We must raise the alarm, notify the authorities.' Pryke pulled himself together. 'We will leave this as it is and notify the constable and Surgeon Lawton. They will tell us how they wish to proceed.' He took Father's arm. 'Come, Thomas, this is all we can do for now. And we do not yet know who it is.' I watched my father lift his gaze and saw all hope die in his eyes. He knew.

They covered me with a layer of straw for modesty's sake, then left me in the barn that night, while Constable Baalham sent to Bury for the coroner.

I STAYED THERE, watching over my earthy remains, until, the following morning, just as the sun began to rise, I heard the thrum of footsteps outside, the clatter of the vast doors opening wide and saw a group of men coming in, two carrying an old door.

One man stepped forward and took charge. Small but upright and wearing a black coat, he directed proceedings with an air of authority and confidence.

'I am Mr Wayman, the district coroner. These men – ' he waved a hand behind him. ' – are my jurymen, here to glean the facts of the case.'

He nodded to my father and Pryke. 'Let us see what you have found.' His jury of local men stood in formation behind him as he covered his nose with a handkerchief and bent down towards my remains. 'Hmmm, it's a body alright. Mr Pryke, Mr Martin, please begin to uncover it. Do it with great care as we need to preserve any evidence.'

Pryke tugged his cap

'Will do, Sir.'

The two men bent to their task as Surgeon Lawton moved to their side.

'You must remove the last of the soil very carefully. We must

214

not damage the remains.' He turned to my father, who looked grey and ill. 'Mr Martin, are you sure you are well enough to assist Mr Pryke? You must have had a great shock.'

'I am well enough, Sir, and I must see if it's . . .'

'Very well, you may proceed, but cautiously.' The coroner stood back.

The men set about with rakes, pulling at the earth gently, then bending to use their hands as my corpse was slowly revealed.

'There are stays – a woman then.' Pryke looked at my father, concerned, but Father continued to drag the earth away with his bare hands, his face blank. Material from my clothes came up next, tangled in the tines of the rake, and then, finally, they revealed my face. The surgeon held out his hand and the men stopped, breathing heavily from effort and shock.

'We must raise her out of the hole. I cannot examine her here.' Slowly, carefully, they took my body from the earth and laid it on the door they had brought with them. 'Will you please carry her into the daylight.' They lifted me up and took me outside the Red Barn then placed the door reverently on the ground.

The men stood back and looked in horror at what they had uncovered.

CHAPTER
FORTY-THREE

My legs were drawn up and my head rested on my shoulder at a peculiar angle. My body was very decomposed and the stench was foul. You could not see it was me, there was nothing left of how I had been. I did not look as if I had ever had a life, that I had breathed and laughed and loved. You could only make out the shape of my stays, a petticoat and shift, suspended in a dark liquid sludge, like the bottom of a pond. I was lying on my right side with my arm across my breast and, as the men watched in horror, my fleshless hand detached itself from the wrist and slid down, finding the door with a dull thump. Pryke went white, then green and, pushing his hand to his mouth, he ran to the side of the barn and, in the silent spring air, we could hear the noise of violent retching. My father stood, motionless, all strength sucked from him by the discovery.

Mr Wayman cleared his throat and took charge again.

'Mr Lawton, is the body identifiable? Can you say if it is likely to be Maria Martin?'

The surgeon knelt on the packed earth.

'The body is badly decomposed, it is liquid in places. There appears to be some blood here, see, on the face.' Mr Lawson bent to his work with grim efficiency. 'There is a neckerchief, green I think. Mr Martin, does this belong to your daughter?' He hesitated. 'Can you identify the remains?'

My father peered over his shoulder, then put his hand to his mouth.

'I could not say for sure, Sir. The head and face are so . . .' He looked away briefly, then turned back. 'I couldn't swear to the body but the face, the mouth – they may be Maria's' My father groaned then and fell at the surgeon's side, his legs giving way. Mr Lawson helped him to his feet and took his arm. 'Mr Martin, it would be better if you went home. This is not a sight for any parent to see.'

The surgeon looked concerned at the horror etched on my father's face and turned to the coroner. As he did so the jurymen clustered around my body and one drew out his knife and pushed it through the case of my ribs. It slid in with no effort, as if into soft butter, and he withdrew it quickly, turning to the man beside him.

'Rotted right away, she has. Nothing left of her.' He wiped his knife on his overcoat as a second man knelt and reached for the fabric around her neck. The surgeon turned back and saw what they were doing.

'Stop! Please do not interfere with the body, gentlemen. Evidence must not be moved or damaged.' The two men stood back, chastened, as the surgeon turned again to Mr Wayman. 'Surely Mr Martin could be excused now, Sir? He is fairly sure that the body is that of his daughter and it seems inhuman to expect him to witness my further examination of the corpse. He has suffered the greatest of shocks.'

'I agree.' The coroner turned to my father and patted him on the shoulder. 'Mr Martin, you may go home. The coming days will be very hard for you and your family now that we seem to have found your daughter, and you have had enough upset today.'

My father looked at him blankly.

'I must stay with her. Until she is buried. It is not right that she is left alone.'

Mr Lawton stood up.

'That will not be soon, Mr Martin, I have to examine your daughter's remains most carefully. But I will look after her and treat her with respect, you can be sure of that. You should go, speak to her mother.' Father nodded, looked at the rotted remains once more and I felt sorrow weighing him down. I wanted to put my arms around him to comfort him, but he had never encouraged such behaviour, never once held me when I was young and now it was too late. He took a final look at what was left of me and I watched him hollow into an old man as he turned and walked slowly away.

The tension in the group eased a little when he had gone and the surgeon bent again to his work, the jurymen drawing closer.

'Her face is in a very bad state. It appears she may have been placed in a sack – see, here?' He looked at Mr Wayman. 'We need to take her indoors so that I can carry out a proper examination.'

The coroner nodded and pushed his handkerchief tight to his face as four of the men tied their scarves and neckerchiefs over their noses and mouths and picked up the door. Slowly, solemnly, with long steps and grey faces, they carried me away.

At the Cock Inn the following day Mr Wayman convened a formal coroners court. My body was still lying on the door, supported now by tables, and the items of clothing that they had uncovered were laid out for all to see. The small sum of my life; my stays, a petticoat, my shift, black silk stockings and garters and my shoes. My beautiful straw bonnet, all but rotted, the black trim just visible. My mother's earrings, blackened and bent. There was my lawn handkerchief and part of the sleeve of my blue coat. I could not believe that this was me, could not tear my eyes from what I had turned into.

The news of the finding of my body had spread and the inn was full to bursting, with many more villagers waiting outside as Surgeon Lawton relayed his findings.

'I removed pieces of sacking. There was the appearance of coagulated blood upon the cheek.' I could no longer bear to listen. Instead, I focused on the wind rattling the windows, the tap of a door not properly fastened. Anything to avoid hearing and seeing what I had become.

My father and stepmother were called as witnesses, then Nancy. The surgeon had laid a cloth over my remains to spare their feelings. Father told how he had found my body after going to the Red Barn to search for any of my things that may have been left there. He produced letters from William and said that they had received no word directly from me since May of last year. Then he told about my lying-in in Sudbury, how William and I came home with the babe. He told how the child had died and how we took him back to Sudbury for burial. He looked at the items laid out on the table and said he thought that they were mine. Then my step-mother was called. She described in detail my clothes, my bonnet and hair combs, she identified them as belonging to me and said that I was wearing them, and a green neckerchief, when I left for the last time.

'Tied it around her neck myself, I did. Poor Maria.' I remem-bered how she had left me to dress, how I had tied the neckerchief myself. She was lying. Then she leaned forward, peering closely at the table. 'Those earrings. They are hers. All she had left from her late mother.' She lifted her handkerchief to her eyes and dabbed them dramatically.

'Do you need a moment to compose yourself, Mrs Martin?' She looked up at the coroner.

'No, Sir, I will go on.' It was then that her lies truly began. She told the jury William had threatened me with being taken up by the constable for bastardy. And she told them of her dreams.

'I have very frequently dreamed about Maria and twice before Christmas, I dreamed that Maria was murdered and buried in the Red Barn.'

Nancy stepped forward then. She looked so small and young in that dark room and my heart went out to her.

'I believe this to be the body of my sister, Maria Martin.' She stifled a sob as she stepped back and my stepmother put her arm around her shoulders.

The coroner looked around him.

'Gentlemen, we have heard the witnesses and I believe a crime has been committed. Therefore I intend to adjourn this inquest until the culprit is brought before me to answer my questions. The jury will then decide if he should be sent for trial. I understand that the Boxford parish constable is here?'

A middle-aged man stepped forward, portly and red-faced.

'Yes, Sir'

'Ayers, isn't it?' The man nodded. 'You will go forthwith to London. I will issue you with orders on how to proceed there, and provide money for your expenses.' The coroner looked around him, then back at Ayres. 'Find Corder.'

CHAPTER

FORTY-FOUR

Ayres had begun his search by speaking to Mrs Corder, who told him her son was now in London, having been at the coast for some time for his health. On arrival in London, Constable Ayers went straight away to the Police Office at Lambeth Street to inform them of the discovery of my body and the coroner's order and requested assistance. A young Police Officer, James Lea, was appointed to help and the two began their search for William. It was not straightforward. They were sent from one address to the other until they had word that he was married and living at a boarding school in Brentford. They convened at the Red Lion there, where it was decided that Ayres should stay behind, as William knew him, while Lea went out to search. But the first day drew a blank and he returned to the inn. The two officers were discussing how to proceed over their evening meal when the innkeeper knocked on the door of their room.

'Begging your pardon, Sirs, but I believe you are looking for someone?'

Lea nodded.

'We are. A man wanted for a crime back in Suffolk. Name of Corder.'

'I don't know of him myself, but there's a man downstairs may have some news for you.' The two constables followed the landlord to the bar where he nodded towards an old man who sat in the corner, pulling at a mug of ale and smacking his lips. 'Nathanial there – he's a barrowman, see. Says he took some furniture to a school on Ealing Lane, the one that belongs to Miss Ingleton, or used to. Nat knows what's going on around here, keeps his ear to the ground. It may be worth speaking to him.' The innkeeper looked at them expectantly.

Ayers handed over a few coins. 'Buy one for yourself, won't you?' The innkeeper smiled and pocketed the money, turning to the cask of ale, as the two constables moved toward the old man.

'You are Nathanial?'

He looked them up and down with rheumy eyes.

'Who's asking?'

'Constables. You took a barrow load to a nearby school I hear?'

The old man nodded.

''bout four months ago, yes. Saw the load to the door. I can tell you where it was. It'll cost you another ale though.' He pushed his mug towards the men and Lea, with a sigh, got up to fill it as Ayers listened to the directions.

When Lea returned he handed the mug over to the barrowman who took it with a nod, then sat back in his chair and looked at Ayres.

'We can't just turn up there, y'know. He knows you and who knows what state of mind he may be in. He may attempt to flee. He may be violent.'

The landlord had been wiping down the table, his ear cocked to the conversation.

'My wife knows a man whose daughter is at that school. They live nearby, she could introduce you?'

Ayers sighed deeply and reached into his pocket for more coins. 'Tomorrow morning?'

'Aye, Sir, the wife will take you.'

Early the next morning the landlord's wife walked with them to a large building a few streets away.

'The man lives here, Sirs, it is his daughter who attends the school as a day scholar.'

A tall man answered their knock.

'Ah, yes, I was expecting you. *Elizabeth . . .*' A plain child, dressed in a clean pinafore, came and stood beside him.

Lea bent down to look at her.

'There is nothing to be afraid of, you have done nothing wrong. It's just that we are looking for someone, Elizabeth. A man by the name of Corder. Do you know that name?'

She looked at Lea, trembling, as her father pushed her forward.

'Tell the constable, Lizzie. Tell him the truth now.'

She looked up at her father and then at Ayers and Lea.

'Mr Corder, Sir? Yes, I have seen him.'

'That is good. And what does this Mr Corder look like?'

The girl thought for a moment.

'He is a short gentleman. He is always kind to me, him and Mrs Corder. He wears eyeglasses.' She thought again then looked up at Lea. 'He is there about twelve o'clock as a rule.'

And with that they had him.

LEA WENT EARLY. A maidservant opened to his knock and invited him inside to wait. It was a few minutes before William came out to greet him. I was in the corner of the hallway in the shadows, watching in fear, unable to warn him, as he came forward and smiled at Lea.

'May I help you?'

He looked so calm, so assured. He had no idea what was coming.

'Mr Corder? William Corder?'

'I am he.'

Lea looked at the maidservant who hovered in a doorway, then back at William.

'Could we go somewhere a little more private, Sir? I have a matter of some importance to speak to you about.'

'I was about to have my breakfast.' Even then, William did not realise.

'William, dearest? Is anything the matter?'

A small woman came into the hall, her face surprised, and I recognised Mary Moore. She looked happy if puzzled and my heart went out to her for I knew what she was about to face.

'It is nothing to worry about, my dear. This gentleman wants to speak to me, that is all. About his daughter joining our happy school here?' He turned again to Lea. 'That is what this is about, is it not?'

'Is there another room, Sir? What I have to say is best said privately.' I saw William's face blanch, felt his heart quicken.

I could do nothing but watch.

CHAPTER
FORTY-FIVE

'This way.' William showed Lea into the drawing room then, with a quick look back at his wife, he closed the door. "Now, what is this matter of importance? My breakfast – I was timing the eggs you see.' He looked away. 'They will be ruined now.'

'I am a police officer from London and I have been sent to apprehend you on a very serious charge. You are to consider yourself my prisoner.'

William's face was blank but his heart was pounding fit to burst from his chest. I hovered close to him now, I felt everything.

'Very well, but on what charge?' He cleared his throat and ran his hand through his hair in the gesture I knew so well.

'It is relating to a young woman who I believe was known to you. Maria Martin? She has been missing for some eleven months. Well, now a body has been found and I am to take you to be questioned about her death.'

I don't know why he said it. His mind was not working properly, his thoughts tangled and unstable. That must have been the reason, but it did him no good later.

'I know of no Maria Martin. You must have the wrong man.'

Lea looked at him, amazed.

'Maria Martin. A young woman from Polstead, where you lived. A young woman you were known to have associated with.'

'No, you have the wrong man.'

Oh, William.

'I am certain I do not, Mr Corder. There are many witnesses to your association with the deceased, including members of her own family.'

I could feel William's agitation rising, for his hands had begun to shake and his eyes flitted from side to side. Lea could see it too,

'I must . . . may I speak with my wife in private? ' Lea shook his head.

'I'm sorry, Sir, that won't be possible.'

William looked at him.

'May I finish my breakfast and speak to her?' His eyes had filled with tears and Lea suddenly felt sorry for him.

'Very well. Go and finish your breakfast. I must come with you but I will allow you a little time with your wife before I escort you out. If she asks, tell her what you wish to help to soften the blow. I will wait here.'

'I will not flee if that is what you fear. Thank you for your kindness.'

The dining room was abuzz. There were three governesses as well as Mary sitting at the long table. Lea stood guarding the door, his hands behind his back as William sat down and buttered some cold toast but his mouth was dry and he put it down again. He turned to his wife.

'Mary, I must speak to you. Come into the drawing room.' He held out his hand and she rose from the table and took it. Hers was thin, cold and trembling.

'William? Please, what is happening? I am frightened.' He took her into the drawing room and, shutting the door, settled her carefully on a chair. Lea stood, stern, behind him. 'Who is this man?' She gazed at Lea, her brown eyes frightened.

He looked away from her and cleared his throat.

'Mr Corder, I must search you.' He reached into William's pockets and patted down his body. 'Do you have any weapons on you?' William shook his head. Mary sat, frozen, too stunned even to cry.

Finally, William found his voice.

'Mary, I must go with this man. He is an officer of the law and has some questions for me. Would you be good enough to get me my coat and hat? His voice was gentle with her, soothing, but her fear was palpable as she did as he asked, returning to help him on with his coat. They moved into the hall and she watched as he straightened his collar. She held out his hat to him, her hand shaking. Then all turned at a clatter of footsteps on the stairs.

I HAD NOT KNOWN that Charles Moore lived with them in Brentford. I had thought he remained at his jewellery shop in London. But there he was, large as life, and it was he that took charge.

'Who are you? What is going on?'

Lea pulled himself upright and looked him in the eye.

'James Lea, Sir, an officer of the police, from Lambeth Street. I am here to arrest Mr Corder.' He glanced at William. 'I do not wish to say more in front of Mrs Corder here for fear of causing further upset – '

Charles moved closer and stood next to his sister, putting a protective hand on her shoulder.

'I insist you tell us on what charge you are arresting him.' He looked at William, who failed to meet his eye. 'Well?'

Lea cleared his throat.

'I am sent to arrest William Corder on a charge of murder.' The very air stilled.

'Murder? William?' Charles looked at him derisively. 'He would not have the courage. Look at him – he couldn't kill a mouse. Who is he said to have murdered?

'A young woman in Suffolk, Maria Martin. All the evidence . . .'

'All the evidence? This man married my sister only a few months ago. I have come to know him and from my dealings with him and from what my sister has said, I know him to be a kind, tender and indulgent husband. He could not have killed anyone.'

Mary's face was white and peaked as she moved forward and clutched at William's coat sleeve.

'William, when this officer called, well, my first thought was that you may already be married to another. One reads such things and we met so quickly, married within the week and I have always wondered what it was you saw in me. I could understand if that had been the case, but murder? I do not believe it.' She turned to Lea. 'I do not believe it.'

'Madam, I must do my duty.' He reached into his jacket and produced a pair of handcuffs. 'Your husband will be taken to the Red Lion where myself and the constable from Polstead will decide what is to be done next. I will return shortly – his room will need to be searched. No one must go in there until I have done so.'

Mary's legs finally gave out beneath her and she slid to the floor, all her strength gone. Her brother bent to help her up and my heart went out to her, for I knew then that she truly loved William. Lea secured the handcuffs and took William's hat from her shaking hand. 'He will be taken care of, Mrs Corder. He will not be badly treated. But a young woman has met with a foul death and we must get to the truth of the matter.'

Charles Moore stood next to his sister and put his arm around her, holding her close as pale faces peered around the dining room door and the maidservant stood open-mouthed in the hall.

'Let the officer do his job, Mary, they will get to the bottom of this, find out what has happened, and your husband will be back with you soon.'

Mary looked gratefully at him, then moved towards William. She reached for his chained hands and placed a tender kiss on his cheek.

'I will make arrangements here. I will come and see you whenever they let me. Have faith.'

I looked at William. He was shaking, struck dumb. He had truly believed himself free of the taint of my death and now, just when he had found happiness, it had come back to haunt him. I never imagined it would end like this, for all he had done was to cover up my deed. It was my wildness, my foolishness, that had caused this, and I had never considered those I would leave behind. I stood close to William and reached out my hand to stroke his cheek. My hand slid straight through him, he felt nothing, so I leaned in close. Mary Corder was sobbing hard, her brother berating the constable. There was noise and confusion all around but it was as if the cord pulled tighter between us, drawing us close once more.

'*William, don't be afraid.*' He lifted his head and looked around him then. He had heard me.

FORTY-SIX

Lea could not contain himself as he escorted a shackled William to the Red Lion.

'The body of this young woman that they wish to ask you about. What do you know of the matter?'

William said nothing, striding beside the officer, trying to keep up. But then something stirred in him and he looked up at the officer.

'When was . . .when was she found?'

Lea paused and looked at him.

'On Saturday morning last.'

'Whereabouts was the body?'

'In the Red Barn. On your land.'

The officer watched William closely, looking for a response, a flicker of emotion, and, silently, I begged him to deny any knowledge of it, for, if they could not connect him to the body, they would have to release him. But William stayed quiet and the two continued on their way in silence.

When they reached the inn Lea pushed open the door and nodded for William to go ahead. He stepped inside. It was clear word had spread that something was happening, for the inn was noisy and full, but as soon as they saw William the drinkers paused, put down their mugs, and looked at the handcuffs in shock and excitement. The room fell silent. Lea nodded at the landlord and then led William upstairs to their room, where Ayres was waiting, his hands behind his back. William blanched at the sight of him.

'I have him, Mr Ayers. I spoke briefly to him when I took him but he denies knowing the victim. Are you sure we have the right person?'

'I know him of old, Lea, I have seen his antics in our village. He is the one we want, there is no doubt.' Lea moved towards William and took a key from his pocket. He fitted it into the lock of the handcuffs and William rubbed at his wrists as they came free. Ayers nodded to a chair and William sat as the Polstead constable looked him up and down, then turned to Lea.

'You'd best go back there now, search his rooms.'

Lea looked grave.

'While I am gone I think he should be handcuffed to you, Mr Ayers, for if he should flee – ' The older man nodded and held out his wrist and the handcuffs clicked shut. Lea fastened the other cuff to William who sighed deeply.

'Is this necessary?'

'It is. We cannot risk you escaping.' Ayers looked at Lea. 'Do your duty, lad, you know what to look for. I will look after this one.' As the door closed softly, Ayers turned to his prisoner. 'Mr Corder. This is a sorry state of affairs, is it not? Not so cocky now, are you? You may not have admitted anything to young Lea, but you know me – so why not tell me what you did to poor Maria, and make things easier on yourself?'

It was said firmly, politely, but he was not asking this for William's good, I could see it in his eyes. He wanted to be the one to extract a confession, to bathe in the glory that this would bring.

Aye, he wanted his moment in the light, to be recognised as more than some village constable with little wit or talent. He wanted notoriety and prestige, to be the man who broke William Corder. It was there in the glitter of his eyes, clear for all to see. But William said nothing, just looked downcast and as tired as I had ever seen him.

Ayers pulled up another chair and sat down beside him, resting his sturdy arms on his legs as he leaned forward, friendly now, his voice softer. 'Come now, William, we both know of your history with Maria Martin. Why not clear your conscience, tell me what happened? I know what life is like in Polstead, how rumours start. Why not tell me the truth, while it is just you and me? Before Lea comes back.' He patted William's shoulder as if they were the best of friends. 'What do you say? Come on now, son.'

THERE WAS a long silence and I could see William was tempted, for he was an honest man at heart. I knew him like no other, he was part of me and I part of him. But he could not cope with adversity and confrontation. That's why he said what he did to me at the end when my moods had been more than he could deal with. All he had ever wanted was a peaceful life, to have someone who loved and looked up to him. He had always had this ideal in his head of what life should be like, was always fantasising about what could be. But he was tormented now, he needed to speak just to ease his anguish, so I drew close and put my lips to his ear.

'Deny it all. You did not kill me.' I pressed my lips in a kiss and drew back. Ayers was still talking, still trying to get an answer, but he stopped dead as William looked up.

'I do not know Maria Martin. I have no acquaintance with her. I have done nothing wrong.'

Ayers' face went red and tight.

'Very well, if that's the way you are playing it. But we have enough evidence already to send you to trial, so are you sure you do not want to . . .'

William looked straight at him then.

'I do not know Maria Martin. I am sorry for any ill that befell her but I had nothing to do with it.'

Ayers sat back in his chair with a deep sigh.

'Then we must wait for Constable Lea, and see what evidence he comes up with."

I willed William to silence as I pulled away from him and went in search of the constable.

CHAPTER
FORTY-SEVEN

L ea was thorough. He was proud of his job and his uniform, proud of being part of a new force for justice and right. When he got back to the school it was Charles Moore who answered his knock and who was now following him around as Lea searched the property.

'Is there any need to search my sister's room and the sitting room? She is extremely upset, as you can imagine. Her mother is with her now, offering comfort and I would rather they were not disturbed.'

'Very well, Sir, but if you could show me Mr Corder's room that would be most helpful. I take it that it was separate from your sister's?'

'They adjoined.'

Just then, Mary Corder came out of the sitting room. She was pale and shaking but so dignified – I could see why William was attracted to her. She had an inner strength that I had never had. She drew herself up to her full height and looked up at her brother.

'I will show the officer my husband's rooms, Charles. Go to our mother, she is in need of your support.'

Charles looked down at her.

'Are you sure?' His eyes were soft with compassion.

'I am.' She patted his arm and turned to Lea. 'Shall we?'

I watched them, floating above them in dark corners as Mary showed Lea to a good-sized bedroom, furnished with a carved and draped bed, a colourful carpet and thick curtains. The fireplace was empty but, even so, the room was cosy and private. I could imagine William being content here.

'My husband used this room as his office as well. I have my own desk elsewhere.'

Lea tipped his hat.

'I understand, Madam. I do not wish to cause you any more distress than is necessary. This is a difficult situation for all concerned.'

Mary looked at him.

'You have a job to do, Officer, and I am sure this matter will be cleared up to everyone's satisfaction. There will have been a mistake. It is impossible that William would hurt anyone, let alone kill them.' She stood back in the doorway, proud and fierce, as Lea began to search. Only her hands trembled, hidden under the lace at her cuffs.

WHY WERE you so foolish as to keep things with you? For Lea found them all. The pistols, hanging in a black velvet bag in his dressing room; the small sword which he had sharpened in preparation for our wedding, which he intended us to use to cut our bride cake. Locked in his writing desk, copies of his advertisements for a bride were carefully cut from the newspapers. And in his trunk, packed away with his fine linen and clothes . . . oh, William, why the books? They were the type of books that gentlemen keep privately, away from the eyes of their wives and sweethearts. 'Fanny Hill', banned, with such illustrations to make you faint in shock. And another, worse, bound in fine Moroccan leather, that even Lea snapped shut quickly, his face blooming with embarrassment.

The constable had a leather bag with him. In it, he put the pistols, the letter and the books. He took up the powder flask, bullet mould and bullets. He was precise and efficient. But I was sure there was still hope – for these items alone did not mean that William killed me. They were not proof enough.

CHAPTER
FORTY-EIGHT

Charles Moore visited William that evening, the two constables allowing him to dine with them. The conversation was muted but William ate heartily.

'You spoiled my breakfast this morning, gentlemen.'

All eyes were raised to him but William seemed oblivious, tucking into his meal as if it were to be his last. Charles said little, just looked sorrowful and confused as the silence lengthened.

Mary was permitted to visit him before they took him away the next morning. She was solemn but tried to be light of spirit for William's sake. I could not watch their farewell, my heart would not take it. I had thrown away the chance to say my own farewell a year ago in the barn but, even now, I could not bear to see him look tenderly upon another.

He was transported to London at first, where Mary again visited him, having followed him there, and from there the officers were ordered to take him to Polstead. I sat with him on his journey – he was a changed man. No longer silent and distracted, he had become bright and full of bravado. But his mood was brittle, taut.

'What is to happen to me now?'

Lea looked at Ayres and then turned to William.

'You are to be taken before the coroner and his jury. They will hear the evidence and decide whether you should be formally charged with the murder of Maria Martin. If you are, you will be taken to the gaol at Bury St Edmunds to await trial and then it will be up to the judge and jury there to decide your fate.'

'And if the coroner's jury says I have no charge to answer?' In his corner, Ayers snorted. 'What happens to me then.'

'Then you would be free to return home to your wife.'

'Then all will be well. Mary will be glad to welcome me home.' He smiled at Lea and Ayers leaned towards him.

'We found some books, Corder.'

William laughed.

'I feared you might. Well, a man cannot be tried for that, else the courts would be full to overflowing.' I willed him to be quiet, tried to warn him that it was a trap as the conversation became lewd, but I was far from his thoughts then and could not reach him. However, the other passengers heard, sat atop the coach, and their disgust and horror were later held against him. He was foolish to speak so flippantly and coarsely, yes, but frightened too, and who is to say how any one of us would react if accused of such a crime?

It was nine o'clock at night when the coach reached Colchester. The streets seemed unusually crowded for that hour and the coach was forced to slow to walking pace as it reached the George Inn, where they had written ahead to arrange accommodation for the night. As the coach came to a halt Ayres pulled back the curtain and tutted but his eyes gleamed.

'Looks like you have a reception committee, Mr Corder. News seems to have got out.'

William leaned past him. Immediately there was a jeering from the crowd and he pulled back hurriedly, pushing himself hard against the seat so as not to be seen.

'Drop the curtain, Mr Ayers, for pity's sake. Are they here just to gawp at me?'

'Looks that way. There's all kinds of people out there.' Ayres dropped the curtain and William relaxed a little. 'Hadn't bargained for this though.' He looked at Lea. 'We'd better cover his head when we take him out, there's quite a crush.' The men pulled William's coat up over his head, forcing his handcuffed wrists high, as Lea opened the door. There was an immediate roar from the crowd, a press of people jostling and hurling insults.

'Quick, get him inside.' Lea could barely make himself heard over the commotion. I drifted above it all as they pushed William forward towards the inn door. It opened and a short beefy man stood there, wiping his hands on his apron.

'Come in, gentlemen, here, this way.' He showed the men into a small room behind the bar. 'I have prepared this room for you.'

Lea looked around.

'It is not going to be secure enough. What do you think, Ayers?'

Ayers grunted.

'We need somewhere back from the road. Landlord, do you have another room? I'd hate you to get your windows broken by a mob trying to get in.'

The landlord's eyes widened.

'I didn't expect there to be this much disturbance. There is another room which will be more secure and it's just as comfortable.' He showed them up the wooden stairs to a larger room, away from the street, which was quieter, although the jeers and shouts of the crowd could still be heard. The three men looked at each other as William sank onto a chair, pulling his coat back and wiping his brow as best he could.

Ayres removed the handcuffs.

'I don't think you'll be trying to escape, will you lad? That crowd would tear you to pieces in minutes.' He turned to Lea. 'I'm not happy about staying here. This place isn't secure enough. You'd best go to the gaol and ask if we can lodge him there for the night. I'll look after our prisoner here.'

'If you're sure. I shouldn't be long.'

'It'll be safe enough tonight, but come the morning word will have got out about who we have here, and I don't like to think of what might happen then. We have a duty to look after our prisoner, keep him safe. Go on, off you go, try leaving by the back door and keep your head down lest you're seen. You can't miss the Castle, the watchman there will see you to the governor.'

'I will be as quick as I can. Best put those handcuffs back on him.' William sighed and held out his wrists as Lea put on his hat, took one last look around the room then clattered down the stairs. As the back door slammed, a cold gust of air swept through the room. On the chair William fell forwards, head in hands and I drifted in a corner, watching over him.

CHAPTER
FORTY-NINE

The room fell silent after Lea had gone, save for the chanting and jeers of the crowd outside. Ayers was tense, his brow furrowed as he sat next to his prisoner.

William said nothing for a long while then looked up as if a thought had struck him.

'Mr Ayers, may I write to my mother? She will know nothing of this and I would not want her to hear of it from anyone but myself.'

Ayers thought for a moment.

'It is not some ploy to free yourself? For I will not remove these handcuffs for anything.'

'No, of course not. And anyway, as you said, I would hardly get far with that mob, baying for my blood.'

Ayers thought about it.

'It's not an unreasonable request, Mr Corder. Very well, I will send downstairs for some ink and paper. But you will remain handcuffed, is that clear? And if you try anything . . .'

'I will not, you have my word.'

Ayers blew out his cheeks at this and looked shrewdly at him.

'Not worth much though, your word, is it, son?' William looked down, ashamed. 'But you may write your letter.' He stood and went to the door, shouting for the landlord.

'Ink and paper if you please. The prisoner wishes to make his confession.' He laughed at his own wit and then sat back at the table, waiting in silence until the landlord came puffing up the stairs.

'Is there anything else, Sir? The inn is full and we can scarce pour the ale fast enough.'

'No that will be all, thank you, until my colleague comes back. What time do you close your doors?'

The landlord scratched his head.

'Midnight as a rule, but earlier if I can tonight. As soon as it quietens down I will give them their marching orders. Under the circumstances, it might be best.'

'I agree.' Ayers nodded. 'Best to get the place locked up as soon as you can.' The landlord set an ink pot, pen and paper on the table and nodded as he closed the door behind him and clattered back down the stairs. From the bar below came a roar. 'They'll be wanting an update on how you are faring. Popular man, aren't you?' Ayres chuckled and sat William at the table, settling himself opposite. 'Well, write away, son. I will have to read it before it is sent, you understand?' William nodded and looked at the blank sheet before him. He picked up the pen and dipped it, then put it down again, rubbing his eyes with his hand. 'For your mother is it? This will all come as a shock to her I have no doubt.' He looked at William and his eyes seemed to soften a little. 'Best just to start at the beginning, son.'

He meant well. But where was the beginning? William had kept his mother in the dark about us and had never even told her of our lost child, our plans to marry. He had not spoken to her of my death, nor of his advertising for a wife. She did not know of his marriage to Mary Moore. I wished then that he had not been so secretive. He had wanted to protect his mother but now? A shock

246

such as this, coming after the loss of her husband and sons? I did not know how she would be able to bear it.

William put on his eyeglasses, dipped the pen in the ink pot and, scratching nib against paper, began to write.

CONSTABLE LEA WAS NOT BACK AS QUICKLY as Ayers expected. It was over an hour before he returned and anger was clear in his face. Ayers ordered a mug of ale from the landlord and sat him down.

'What happened? Will he take him?'

Lea took a long drag of ale and put down the mug.

'No, he will not. He demanded a warrant showing that Corder be committed to Colchester Gaol. Obviously, we do not have such a document.'

'But the Polstead coroner . . .'

' . . . overstepped his authority according to the governor. He should have given us a warrant.' Ayres blew out his cheeks in frustration. 'Anyway, I obtained the name of the magistrate here and went to see him.'

'Well done, lad.'

'I explained the situation and said that Corder was in fear for his life if he stayed in the inn and the mob outside became unruly. The magistrate summoned the governor to explain himself. That governor laid it on thick. He said that he must have a warrant, that the offence was committed outside the jurisdiction of Colchester Castle and then said he had no one available to watch the prisoner and was concerned that Corder might lay violent hands on himself.' It was clear he was worried about his own back if that should happen, for I suppose he would be held accountable, but even so.' Lea drained the rest of his ale and rubbed at his mouth.

'So where does that leave us, apart from in the shit as usual!' Ayers was angry now. 'I suppose we have no option but to keep him here, although I don't like it, I don't like it one bit.'

Lea sighed.

'Neither do I but we have no alternative. It's always the men at the top with their rules and regulations, stopping the ones lower down from doing their job. And it will be our necks on the line if anything were to happen to a prisoner in our charge.'

'Let me speak again to the landlord. He must have somewhere else, even further away from the street.' Ayers picked up the empty mug and went downstairs.

Lea looked at William.

'We are doing our best for you, Sir.' William nodded but said nothing.

Then, a mumbling of voices, a chinking of keys, and Ayers returned. 'Apparently, there is an attic room, unused now, which he thinks will be more secure.' He held up a large key. 'Come on, Corder, up you get.'

I drifted after them as the three men mounted a narrow dusty staircase and entered a tiny room. There was a bed in the centre with a washstand and jug. 'It looks like they've used this for servants.' Ayers looked around him, appraisingly. 'If we take it in turns to sleep while the other keeps watch, and we handcuff him to the one who's sleeping as well as the bedpost here, he should be secure enough. We can keep the door locked – the landlord is closing up now anyway, so the inn will be shuttered and barred. You take the first watch.'

He kicked off his boots and wrestled his bulk on the bed.

'Come on, Corder, you lie here.' He indicated the space next to him and William lay down beside him cautiously. 'Come on now, I won't bite.'

Lea picked up the restraints and locked one cuff around William's left arm, then fastened the other to the metal bedpost. He clipped the second to William's right wrist and fastened it to Ayers.

'You'll have to sleep as best you can. We'll change over at

midnight.' Ayers nodded in agreement and shut his eyes. Lea sighed heavily and locked the door, then settled himself in a chair facing it. The sounds of the crowd had died away now and the town was quietening for the night.

I watched as Lea tried then failed to keep his eyes open. Ayers was already snoring loudly but next to him, William lay awake, eyes wild and wide. I knelt by the side of the bed and rested my hand on his chest, willing him to hear me.

'*Sleep now. I am with you.*' His eyes searched the room as if looking for me but I am not sure he heard me and it was a long time before he, too, slept.

CHAPTER
FIFTY

I t seemed word had spread, for early that morning the good and the great of Colchester began to arrive at the George Inn, asking to see the prisoner. Sir William Rowley, various magistrates and other local gentlemen were shown to his room to speak to him. Ayers and Lea kept him handcuffed and William said little, seemingly deep in thought. But when the room cleared towards mid-morning he turned to Lea and smiled.

'You could have made a pretty penny this day if you'd charged them to visit me.'

Lea smiled.

'Maybe, Sir, but that would not be right for an officer of the law, would it?' William opened his mouth to reply but just then there was a knock on the door and the landlord entered.

'Begging your pardon, Sirs, but there is a clergyman down-stairs, says he knows the prisoner's family. Demands to see him.' He jutted his chin at William. 'Shall I see him up?'

Ayers looked at William who nodded.

'Why not, we have nothing else to do. We aren't moving you from here until midnight for fear of crowds gathering again.'

The landlord leaned down the stairs and called out then turned to William.

'Your next visitor.' A tall figure entered, his white hair a deep contrast to his black robes and William sat up in surprise.

'Reverend Seaman.'

The minister looked down at him and held a hand over his head in blessing.

'I had to come, Corder. Your poor family are mortified at what has occurred, the blow has struck them hard.'

'How is my mother?' A look of shame came over him. 'I never intended to cause her any hurt. I have written to her, did she receive my letter?'

'She did and is barely able to leave her bed for distress. Your sisters tend to her but they are also severely affected by these events. I come to offer my services on their behalf and I have brought you this.' From beneath his coat, he took out a small volume.

Lea started and stood quickly, moving towards the minister.

'What is this, Sir?' He looked at the book and then turned to Ayers. 'It is a hymn book. May the prisoner have it?'

Ayers nodded.

'Check it first to make sure there is nothing hidden within.' Lea fluttered the pages, turned the book upside down and shook it then handed it to William, who turned it over and over in his hands, opened it and brought the pages to his nose, taking a deep breath in.

'Thank you, Reverend Seaman, it is a fine book, handsomely bound.' He smiled and closed his eyes. 'It reminds me of better days.'

The Reverend sat down opposite him and steepled his long fingers.

'William – I may call you that?' William nodded. 'I have come to ask you to unburden yourself to me. Declare your sins, be shriven.' William's face was impassive so he carried on. 'How did you come to be in this situation? You can tell me. Your poor, distraught mother, your sisters – they do not understand what has happened.'

William glanced at Ayers and Lea.

'Hardly a place to confess, Reverend, for all my actions are watched, as you see. But I do declare that I am a sinner.' The two police officers sat forward, like dogs scenting a fox and William looked at them. 'We are all sinners in the eyes of the Lord, so if I am to confess my sins, so should we all.'

'But if you were to confess and repent, then Christ would show mercy. And if you are guilty of the foul crime of which you stand accused, when you come to finally stand before your Maker, He will pardon you your sins.' William looked hard at him and frowned. 'And if you are found innocent of the charge . . .' the minister continued as, behind him, Ayers snorted. '. . . if you are found innocent, then your repentance now would serve to render you a better man and enable you to live out your life in virtue and honour.' He drew a deep breath and dropped his head, clasping his hands before him as William rose from his seat.

'Reverend Seaman, I thank you for your concern and for the volume you have given me. I am grateful to you for coming to see me.'

'But what of your mother, Corder, what of her feelings?'

William stiffened.

'I have no wish to cause my mother undue hurt. Confessing now would not help her, nor would professing my innocence. I admit I am a great sinner, but no more than the next man. I have nothing more to say. Good morning, Sir.' He held out his hand and the Reverend shook it.

'If you are sure?'

'I am sure. Thank you, Reverend.'

The minister bowed his head and turned on his heel. Back in the room, William slumped back into his chair, deep in thought.

It was not many minutes before the landlord came puffing up the stairs again.

'Another visitor for you. You are a popular lad today.' He wheezed a laugh.

'The prisoner is to see no one else.' Lea stood tall. 'This is not a side-show.'

'And I wouldn't have struggled up those stairs again if it had been just anyone, Sir.' The landlord glared at him. 'But this one says he knows the prisoner personally.'

'Does this person have a name?'

'He does indeed, and I asked it.' The landlord looked resentfully at Lea. 'A Mr Moore. Charles Moore.'

Lea turned to Ayers.

'The brother-in-law is here?'

Ayers nodded, his eyes sharp.

'It appears so. Send him up, man.' Behind him, William's face blanched. 'Let's see if this visitor has any more luck than the last.' He turned to Lea. 'If we obtain a confession, then it would go well for us.'

The stairs rumbled once more and Charles Moore entered. He nodded once at the officers then drew up a chair and sat down. He studied William for a full minute then rubbed his face with a gloved hand.

'My sister – your wife – her pain and upset is immense. This accusation is unbelievable.'

William looked down at his hands, his distress palpable.

'I would not have caused her this upset for all the world.' He looked up at Charles. 'Your sister has always been kind and loving towards me and any pain she feels is my pain also. It was never my intent to . . .'

Charles rose sharply from his chair, which rocked on its back legs, and the two officers sprang to their feet. He held out his arms to them in submission. 'I do not intend to harm your prisoner, you have my word. I just want answers.' He turned to face William. 'How could you send letters to your parents telling them that you were living happily with Maria Martin when you were married and living with my sister – without my blessing, might I add? How could you do it, man? She thought for a moment that when the officer came to arrest you, it might be for bigamy and she was even prepared to forgive you for that, fool that she is, but murder?' His face was red now, and he was clenching his hands as if to keep himself from lashing out.

William trembled before him.

'I cannot answer your questions. Your sister is most dear to me and never intended to hurt her in any way.'

Lea stepped between them and put his hand against Charles' chest.

'I think it best if you desist, Sir. I can quite understand your anger, but it is improper and indelicate to question the prisoner like this. He is likely to stand trial, and that is the time to have your say.'

Charles was calming now.

'I apologise, Officer, you are quite right. It's just that my poor Mary –'

'I can only begin to imagine what your sister must be going through, Sir, but you must see that the law will protect her and determine the truth of the matter.' William was slumped now in his chair, distressed by the attack, and my heart went out to him. Lea opened the door. 'I thank you for coming, Mr Moore. I'm sure any trial will provide you with some satisfaction, whatever the outcome.' Charles nodded and turned on his heel without a backward look.

William looked after him pitifully.

'Tell Mary I think of her. Give her my best regards, Charles.'

But Charles had gone.

CHAPTER
FIFTY-ONE

William seemed much changed by the encounter. He paced the room, watched closely by the officers, frequently wiping his face with his handkerchief, not speaking, just staring at the ground.

'Why not sit down now, Corder? You've been pacing for an hour or more.' Ayers glanced at Lea, his voice sharp and firm. 'You are wearing yourself out, and us, just watching you. Come now, there are books here, a bible. Sit down, man. Rest.'

William did as he was told, falling heavily into the chair and opening the hymn book the Reverend Seaman had brought him. He reached into his pocket for his eyeglasses and then began to turn the pages but I knew he was not reading. I could feel his mind racing, his thoughts muddled and jarred, and soon he rose to his feet once more. I pushed a memory of Polstead out to him, hoping to calm him; I gave him memories of the walk across the fields, the wind soughing in the trees. The plash and muddle of ducks on the pond, the swoop of swallows in the summer as they flew to the eaves of cottages that sat snug in the landscape. But still, he could not settle, it made the officers nervous and wary and when the landlord brought the news that a post-chaise had been arranged to convey the prisoner onward, they breathed a sigh of relief. There was a sudden bustle of activity, voices sharpened and belongings were collected together.

'Is it all clear outside? No crowds?'

The landlord nodded.

'It may be well to leave as soon as you can, gentlemen, before word gets out that you are on the move. I wish you a safe journey.' He paused and looked at William, proffering his hand. William looked at him curiously then took it. 'And a safe journey to you, Mr Corder, be it to heaven or hell. To think that I have shaken the hand of the famous murderer. That should stand me in drinks for weeks to come. God acts in mysterious ways, does He not?' The landlord cackled and stood aside, watching as the two officers handcuffed William securely between them. They stepped out of the room and pushed him down the stairs to the waiting chaise. As they did so the town clock struck midnight and William looked around him, breathing in the fresh air deeply.

'Why am I being moved at this hour?'

Ayers grunted.

'It was thought best that you were taken when folk had gone to their beds, so there is no excitement. You saw the crowds here, and word has spread even more now. It was thought better not to inflame people further by seeing you removed, for who knows what they may have done. You are famous, man – or should I say infamous.' He smirked. 'No, it was felt better all round to do it at this time of night. You'll have plenty of time to sleep where you're going anyway.'

Lea looked at him.

'He's not been tried yet, Mr Ayers. There is no need for that.'

Ayers pulled his face close and Lea stepped back.

'There's every need. He's a murdering bastard and the court will hang him in due course. And in the meantime, he leaves his wife and his poor mother to pay the price of his actions, not to mention the victim's family.' He turned to William. 'And that's another reason we go by night. We are taking you to Polstead and, if it's done in the dark, your mother won't have the pain and ignominy of seeing her precious son brought back to her village in irons. For you are to pass the door of your house. We are to take you to the Cock Inn for the inquest.'

FIFTY-TWO

I watched William fall into a fitful sleep as the carriage rocked over the rutted roads. He was chained to the two officers, who remained upright and alert, wary of any passersby, any other carriages. But there was no one, not a soul around and it was just before two in the morning that the chaise rattled down the lane into Polstead. William woke and looked blearily around him, still thick with sleep, then as the chaise turned up the hill he gasped and put his hands to his face. The sudden movement startled his escorts.

'What are you doing?' Ayers pulled on the chain linking them and William's hands were forcibly dragged away from his face. 'Keep still, man, we are nearly there.'

Lea looked out of the window.

'That his house?'

Ayers nodded.

'It is, and his poor mother lies there, too distraught to sleep so I hear.' William was sobbing now, banging his head against the leather-clad side of the chaise.

'My poor mother. She has had so much to bear.'

261

Lea leant towards him.

'How do you mean, Mr Corder?' On the other side of him, Ayers tutted. 'Tell me what you mean.'

William looked at him, raising his hands to wipe his face. He tried to reach for a handkerchief but Ayers forcibly pulled his hands away so he had to make do with the back of his hand.

'My father died. Christmas before last. It was a big shock, for he had not been ill. After that, Thomas, my older brother, took over the running of the farm but then, he too died.'

Ayers leant forward.

'Aye, and a shock to the village that was. Winter of last year. Fell through the ice on the pond, he did, trying to cross it. Thought it would bear his weight but . . . February it was.'

William looked sharply at him.

'It was the thirtieth of January. It was his birthday. He was only twenty-six. Twenty-six.'

Lea looked at William, shocked.

'That is a tragedy.'

'But that was not the end of it. That May my brother James died of consumption. Twenty years old. Then, six weeks later, my last brother, John, was taken. That was consumption too. We have a weakness of the chest. I have it also. So you see my mother has had intolerable grief to bear.'

Ayers looked at him and I knew what he was going to say. And he did.

'Pity you didn't consider your poor bereaved mother when you murdered that girl, then! You could have saved her much pain if you'd just been the son she needed. You were supposed to take over the running of the farm, weren't you?' William nodded. 'But no, you played at it for a few months then off you went, leaving her and your sisters alone to fend for themselves.'

'No, that is not how it was. I stayed to see the harvest in, but the doctor said I needed sea air for a time, for my chest was bad. They were all concerned that I would follow my brothers.'

Ayers grunted.

'May have been better if you had. You would have saved your mother the suffering of seeing you put on trial as a murderer. And you haven't mentioned the child.' Ayers was fishing for information now, seeking more words with which they could damn him. William looked at him, his face blank. 'There were rumours that poor girl had borne your child and now it is said you did away with it.' I willed William to keep quiet, not to say anything, and I think he heard my plea. Someone does, for Lea looks out of the window again.

'We have arrived.'

THE LANDLORD of the Cock Inn was not in the best of moods when the chaise pulled up outside. He eventually opened the door to Lea's hammering and stood, candle in hand, in his nightshirt.

'I thought you would be arriving in the morning. No one sent a message to say you would be this late. The maid has put the fires out and I was abed.'

Lea nods an apology.

'It was decided to move the prisoner during the night to avoid any crowds. And we wanted to save Mrs Corder the further pain of seeing her son brought here in daylight in chains.'

The landlord rubbed his chin, the bristles rasping.

'Aye, that poor woman. Well, you are here now.' He turned back to the dark room. 'Sarah. Stir yourself, girl, get the fire lit in here, there's visitors aplenty. Will you take a mug of ale, a bite to eat?' He looked at William who seemed to have grown taller, now he was in familiar surroundings. 'Mr Corder. I am sorry to see you here under such dreadful circumstances.'

'Mr Gordon, I thank you for your kind words. A mug of ale

would be most welcome – if that is permitted me?' William looked at Lea and Ayers who nodded in agreement. 'And a little cheese and bread if you have it?

Ayers yanked on the chain that still attached him to William.

'You're not here on a friendly visit, Corder, remember that. We are in charge and what we say goes. So, yes, some food and ale would be most welcome, but, landlord, any future questions are to be directed to me or Lea here. This man is a prisoner, charged with wilful murder, no longer your neighbour. I'd be pleased if you'd remember that.'

The landlord nodded, his face serious.

'Indeed. Sit yourselves and your prisoner down there.' He indicated a long bench next to the fire, from which smoke was beginning to curl. 'Sarah will bring your refreshment. There is a room prepared for you above here; you should be safe enough there.'

'And all arrangements are in place for the inquest tomorrow?' Lea looked around him at the small room with its low ceiling. 'Will there be room for all?'

'Everything is organised, Sir. As I understand it, all the parties have been informed and have confirmed that they will attend. But as to space, we will have to see. The village has been bustling these last days, since word of the arrest of Mr – the prisoner here. Strangers, all sorts. Mr Wayman is the coroner in these parts, he is to take charge of proceedings and he will say who comes in and who does not. He's already prepared for the unusually high interest in this case.' There was a rattle behind him and he stepped aside to let the maidservant into the room. 'Now, look, here is Sarah with your food and ale. I will be on hand to show you to your room when you are ready. Is there anything else you need?'

Ayer's eyes slid towards the mugs of ale.

'No, that will be all for now.'

Lea reached for the keys in his pocket, undid the shackles and William rubbed his wrists as they came free. 'I will lock the door behind you, landlord, so that this one cannot think of escaping. The outer door is barred fast I hope?'

'It is, aye.' The landlord passed over a long battered key and stepped away as Lea moved swiftly and turned the key in the lock. Ayers rattled the windows, making sure they were secure.

'Right, let's make haste with this.' He picked up a mug and swigged from it with a loud gulping sound, then belched heartily. Lea picked up a nub of bread and some cheese and held it out to William, who took it silently and tore it into small pieces, pushing them, one at a time, into his mouth, swallowing each one with a sip of ale. When they were done, Ayers unlocked the door and shouted for the landlord, who came scurrying out of the darkness.

'We should be off to our room, landlord.'

'It is this way, gentlemen. I have assumed you will all share?'

'You assumed right, Mr Gordon. We can't take any chances. This one could become as slippery as an eel now he is back on home ground.'

They walked up the stairs in a line, William in the middle, both officers with cudgels drawn. When they reached the top of the stairs William hesitated, just for a second, until Ayres prodded him hard in the back. The room was warm and airy and Ayers positioned himself on a chair by the window, whilst Lea sat with his back against the door. William was left, handcuffed now to the bed, tossing and turning, sleep evading him. I lay down beside him as he lay on his side, and curled my body into his, holding him still against me.

'*I am here with you.*' And, deep into the night, my words reached him. His eyes opened and he rolled over and looked at the ceiling.

And he whispered my name.

CHAPTER

FIFTY-THREE

News of the case had reached the London newspapers, causing a flurry of reporters to travel to Polstead, joining with the crowds that had grown overnight, and by the time the inquest opened the next morning the tiny village was overwhelmed.

William had dressed in his best jacket and tidied himself up ready to attend but, as the noise from downstairs grew in volume, he became hesitant and fearful.

Ayers looked at Lea in concern.

'I'll go down and see what is going on. I know these people, they are easily fired up.' He was gone but a moment, then hurried back, locking the bedroom door behind him. His face was flushed and flustered. 'It's the press. Inn's full of them.' He pulled a handkerchief from his pocket and wiped his face. 'The coroner has told them that they can stay but they are not to take any notes. Caused quite the fuss, I can tell you, arguments back and forth. Anyway, your solicitor begs leave to attend you, Corder. I'll see him up.'

A burly man plodded up the stairs and stood in the doorway, a file of papers under one arm. Beneath his bald head, small blue eyes looked shrewdly at William, assessing him. William shrivelled a little under his gaze but when the man spoke his voice was polite, his manner business-like and brisk.

'William Corder? I am Humphreys, your solicitor, here to act for you in this matter. I don't need to tell you that the charge against you is the most serious a man can face and there are a number of witnesses who are here to testify against you.'

'I am ready to face them, Sir.' William pulled at his cuffs and straightened his collar, his face expectant.

'There we have a problem. I have spoken to the coroner and asked that you be present while he interviews the witnesses but he has refused.'

William's face dropped.

'But surely that is my right? How can I prove I did not do this thing if I cannot ask questions of those who may speak against me?'

Humphreys sighed.

'That is exactly the argument I made on your behalf, but the coroner is adamant. I have cited cases from the law books to show a precedent. I have asked him how you are expected to show you are not guilty if you are not able to put questions, with my assistance, to the witnesses.' He rubbed his face in frustration. 'I asked him how you were supposed to meet such a serious accusation if you had no knowledge of the evidence being placed against you.'

'And still he refused?' William's voice was pleading now, his confidence gone.

'Still he refused. I had no option but to concede defeat. He *has* agreed that all depositions will be read out in your presence. It was the best I could do, he would not be moved on the matter. He will not allow you to be present when the witnesses are heard.' He looked at William, who had slumped back onto his chair. 'All is not yet lost, Corder. I will read the witness statements to you and we can advance our case from there. And I am not sure that you would receive a fair hearing anyway, there are so many people downstairs, and the atmosphere is hostile. I doubt you could ask any questions of the witnesses without interruption.' William's head was in his hands. 'So there we have it. I must return to the inquest and at least I will be able to listen to each witness and ensure that the depositions are all in order and correct.' He stooped and patted William's shoulder. 'Take heart, man, I will do my best for you.'

William nodded, his face still obscured.

Humphreys turned back down the stairs and Lea locked the door behind him. From outside a baying could be heard, getting louder.

Ayers looked out of the window, then pulled the curtains, cloaking the room in half-light.

'Best they don't spy you up here. We don't want a riot and there's enough of them out there.'

From the room below, a loud knocking and silence fell, inside and out. William was unmoving, holding his head between clenched fists. There was nothing I could do for him there. So I gathered myself and slipped down between the floorboards to the room beneath.

I HAD NOT THOUGHT about how it would be.

The first witness called was my half-brother, George. He was called to the stand before the coroner, who looked at him sternly. He had grown since I last saw him, and he looked so solemn.

'Tell me your name and what you know of this matter.' The coroner's voice was kindly, but his gaze was sharp.

'I am called George Martin. Maria was my sister, well, half-sister. Her father is mine also. I was ten years old on the day she went away.' He straightened, his confidence growing. 'On that afternoon I saw Mr Corder go from the Red Barn carrying a pickaxe on his shoulder. He went across two fields. He was going in the direction of his house.'

'And how did you know it was Mr Corder? Were you close by?'

'I was a fair way from him but I saw his face very plainly.'

Oh, George, did you really see him? My little brother was always malleable. Are you being truthful here? But the coroner seemed to be happy with his evidence and waved him away. George pushed through to the side of the room and clasped someone's hand. Ann, my stepmother, determination radiating from her every pore. My heart jumped to my throat.

'I call on Phoebe Stow.' Our neighbour, midwife and village gossip. I should have known she would be in the midst of this.

She stood before the coroner, her head high, but her hands were twisting the stuff of her dress. She was nervous. He waved a hand for her to speak.

'I live in the cottage nearest to the Red Barn. One day last year, before I'd had a chance to clear away the dinner things, William Corder came to my house.' She looked around her. 'He asked if I could lend him a spade. I said that there was one of my husband's, that it was old and good for little, but he said it would do. So I fetched it and I was going to ask him what he wanted it for and how was Maria, but he told me he was in a hurry and could not stop to talk. Well, I was a bit put out, what with me loaning him . . .'

The coroner put up a hand to stop her.

'Did he have an air of worry about him? Did you notice anything unusual in his manner?'

'No, nothing, otherwise . . .'

'And when did this exchange take place?'

She thought for a moment.

'I am not certain. I had been expecting a child. I was confined on the twenty-ninth of April and was churched four weeks later as is the custom, and it happened in the interval.'

'Was the spade returned?'

'Yes, but I do not remember when it was.'

'Very well, Mrs Stow, thank you.' The coroner looked out into the crowd. 'I now call Francis Stow.'

Phoebe's husband moved to the front. He was always a dour man and William and I had often wondered how such a man had become husband to a chatterbox like Phoebe. Now he looked grey and afraid, twisting his cap between his hands, over and over.

'You are husband to the last witness?'

Francis mumbled into his chest.

'Speak up, man, this court must hear you clearly.'

He looked up and cleared his throat.

'Yes, Sir.'

'Your wife has told us of a spade.'

'Yes, Sir, she said she had loaned it but I did not miss it. It was old, no use.'

'And how do you know William Corder, the accused?'

'I worked for him, Sir. Last summer I helped with the harvest. I filled the very bay in the Red Barn where that poor girl was found. Corder was there supervising. He told me a constable had come for me.'

'A constable? Why?'

Francis looked up, smiling.

'It was by way of a jest, see. He was fond of jesting with the men, was Mr Corder. One time, he said he would give me a pound note if I would cut his throat for him. He was laughing as he said it, that's how I knew it was a jest. Towns, the foreman heard him – asked how he could run on so. Aye, he liked to laugh, did that one.'

Francis gazed into the distance, as if deep in thought and the coroner dismissed him.

Lea was next, called down from his duties guarding William. He told how he apprehended William in Brentford, concisely and accurately as I had come to expect from him. There was a short break and then the inquest reconvened. I was heartened. No one had provided any proof. This evidence was not enough.

CHAPTER
FIFTY-FOUR

The person called next was my stepmother. I stared at her, willing her to feel my presence.

'Mrs Martin, you were the stepmother to the deceased?'

'I was like a mother to her, your Honour.' She looked straight at him, unhesitating, making the most of her time in the limelight.

'And your son, George, he told you about seeing the prisoner with a pickaxe on the day Maria disappeared?'

'He did, and I asked Mr Corder about it the day after, but he denied it was him.'

'Now, you must prepare yourself, Mrs Martin, for I have something distressing to show you. Are you able to identify this item for me?' The coroner nodded to his clerk who placed a small stained draw-string bag onto the table before him, damp and mildewed. Ann gazed at it for a moment and then burst into tears, flapping her hand before her face.

'Mrs Martin?'

She composed herself, reaching into her pocket for a handkerchief, bringing it to her mouth, and then she pointed to the bag.

'It was my daughters, this was poor Maria's reticule. I saw her put it into her bag on the very day she went away.

'You are certain?'

'I am, my Lord, it is hers.'

'And did you hear any cross words between your daughter and Corder at that time?'

She paused for a moment, tipping her head to one side in a way I knew she thought was endearing. I hated her in that moment.

'No words, not like that. There was nothing angry. But Maria was very low and in poor spirits, and she could be snappish, I know that much. And who could have caused that but Corder? He had pistols that day too.'

'Pistols?' The coroner nodded the the clerk who reached into a bag. 'Like these?'

She peered at them.

'The very same, Sir. I had seen them before, as he often carried them. He had them with him when he called for Maria on the day she left.'

'Very well.' The coroner scribbled on the paper before him. 'Now, Mrs Martin, please take a closer look at these items on the second table. Can you identify any of them? Are they familiar to you? Take your time.' The clerk removed the cloth covering them. A smell of must, damp and earthy, and something else, worse, leached from the items and into the room as hands moved to noses. My stepmother moved closer to the table clutching her handkerchief dramatically.

'This is her neckerchief.' She sobbed audibly. 'And her bonnet, and the shift – the stitches – I know her handiwork. The shoes too, they are hers.' She moved to the stays, tattered and black with dirt and looked for a long time. 'Yes, these are Maria's. See, the busk?' She pointed to the stiffened piece at the front of the stays. 'I saw her put this ashen one in on the day she left. New it was then. Now look at it.' She buried her face in her handkerchief and then looked at the coroner with tear-filled eyes. 'Is that all, Sir? I cannot bear to look any longer.'

The coroner looked sympathetically at her.

'Thank you, Mrs Martin, I can see how distressed you are. You have been of great help and I should not need to trouble you again.' My stepmother nodded and moved slowly to the back of the room, standing next to my father who patted her hand. She lifted her head and smiled wanly at him, then looked back at the proceedings, her eyes now dry.

Towns, the foreman of the Corder farm was the next to be called. He confirmed that he was with William when they were bringing in the last harvest and had been told by him to fill the front bay with wheat. He said that the litter found on the floor had been there since it was cleared of corn the year before.

'And when would that have been done, Mr Towns?'

The foreman screwed his face up in concentration.

'We cleared it before Stoke Fair, Sir, which begins on the sixteenth of May.'

I wondered at the relevance of his words. The front bay had always been filled first, and everyone knew the day of Stoke Fair. That was not proof of wrongdoing, merely custom.

Lucy Baalham's evidence was more damning.

The coroner smiled at her.

'You are the daughter of John Baalham, constable, are you not?' She nodded. 'And you are employed by Mrs Corder as a maidservant? Please tell us what you saw.'

She was wide-eyed and breathless as she told how, after Stoke Fair, she had been cleaning William's room when the lid of his trunk fell off by accident and she happened to see a pair of lady's kid gloves and Denmark satin boots. Accident, my foot. She was always a nosey piece, William had told me his mother only employed her because she was distant family. No, she had been poking her nose into something that did not concern her, that's for sure. But the gloves and boots were mine. I had left them behind one morning and William said he would return them.

Next to speak was a man I did not recognise.

'You are the cutler from Hadleigh?' What did this man have to do with William?

'I am, Sir, Robert Offord, at your service.'

'And what have you to say on this matter?'

The man straightened his shoulders and looked around him, then back at the coroner.

'About this time last year the accused, William Corder, came into my shop. He had a small sword, scimitar-shaped, about twelve inches long. It was an attractive piece, with an ivory handle and mounted with brass. I thought he had come to sell it, and I would have bought it from him gladly, but he wanted it sharpened. For a cousin who was going to be married, he said, wanted it good and sharp so he could sit at the table and carve with it.' I smiled at this. William, so secretive even then. He had wanted it for our wedding, that was all.

'And did you sharpen it for him?'

'Oh, yes, Sir, and polished it, and he came and paid for it that evening and took it away with him. Very pleased with it he was.'

'Thank you, Mr Offord, you are dismissed.' The coroner turned to the room. 'I now call the surgeon, John Lawton.'

CHAPTER
FIFTY-FIVE

The room erupted as the surgeon pushed his way through the crowds to stand before the coroner, who called for silence.

'You are John Lawton?'

He nodded.

'I am, Sir. I live at Boxford and was called to examine the body of the deceased when it was first found.'

'Please continue.' The room was silent now, save for the breathing and coughing of old men. All eyes were fixed on the surgeon, mouths open, faces flushed with anticipation.

'I was present when the body was viewed by the gentlemen of the jury and yourself, and I made as detailed an examination as I could. The body had not yet been disturbed when I saw it, just the earth covering it scraped away. I had it fully exposed, removed from the ground, and placed on a door. It was much decomposed from having lain in the ground for so long.' He cleared his throat. 'The deceased was covered with some pieces of sack which I removed. She was lying on her right side, with the head forced down towards the shoulder. There was the appearance of dried blood on the cheek and on her clothes and handkerchief. A green neckerchief was around her neck.' There was an intake of breath in the room. This is what they had come to hear. Then silence, so quiet you could hear a pin drop. I leaned in to listen. The surgeon took a deep breath and looked around him. All eyes were on him and he straightened his collar, suddenly nervous.

'And what of the rest of the body?' The crowd craned forward.

'It did not appear as if the deceased had been wearing a gown. There was a shift, stays, stockings and shoes. Items I found on the body were given to John Baalham, the constable. The internal bone of the orbit of the right eye was fractured as if a sharp object had been thrust into it. The bone dividing the two nostrils was displaced and, on the right side, the bones were materially injured. There was a wound to the neck. The brain was in such a fluid state –' In the room a woman began to sob. ' – that I was unable to see whether it had sustained any injury or not.' He paused and cleared his throat. 'I examined the chest and the abdomen and found no injury anywhere within the body, but there were two small portions of bone in the throat which may have passed there from the nose or the orbit of the eye, or fallen down through decay. The left hand separated from the wrist as she was lifted and was lying on the body. The other handkerchief and the shift had blood on them, considerable amounts of blood. In my view, the neckerchief was pulled tight enough to have caused death.' There were gasps from the crowd, murmurings, but all fell silent as the surgeon continued. 'The neck of the deceased appeared very much compressed.'

'So, in your opinion, how did she meet her death?' The temperature in the room was rising and beads of sweat had appeared on the brow of the coroner. He wiped at them with a pristine white handkerchief.

'The deceased's death proceeded from violence. A jab to the eye with a knife or other object would certainly have caused this injury, but it was impossible to discover what damage had been done, due to the decomposition of the body. A sharp instrument such as a pistol ball, may have penetrated the brain which would cause a mortal injury but as I have said, the brain was too decomposed to be able to tell. It is my opinion that the most likely explanation for the injuries is that the pistol ball, found at the scene, entered the neck in the vicinity of the jugular vein and proceeded in an oblique direction to the opposite side of the head, which would have produced the fracture to the orbit of the eye. This may or may not have resulted in death. Alternatively, the neckerchief may have caused strangulation. I removed this and examined it minutely and I consider that it could not have been pulled that tight by any natural means. These are my opinions; I believe the deceased met her unfortunate end either from a pistol shot to the neck or strangulation by the neckerchief, but due to the decomposition of the remains I am unable to say which was the actual cause of death.'

I thought of the pistol and how it had jerked when I fired it, of William dragging me to the grave he had dug for me by my green neckerchief. My father, prodding deep with his mole spike, trying to find his lost daughter. I thought of Pryke and Botwell, digging and breaking the ground with their spades and pickaxes. But the words were turning it into something different, something untrue.

William's solicitor, Mr Humphreys, stood then.

'Sir, as all the witnesses have been examined and you now have the evidence, will you permit my client to come into the room to hear it read?'

The coroner looked at him then at the clerk.

'I will. Bring in William Corder.'

CHAPTER

FIFTY-SIX

They ushered William in. I slipped to his side as he came down the stairs from the upper room, handcuffed firmly to Lea. I could feel exhaustion and agitation leaching from him and he shivered, despite being wrapped in a large cloak. The heat in the room now was intense but William did not seem to feel it. He could barely support himself and the coroner noticed this, asking for a chair to be brought for him.

William slumped into it and looked around him at familiar faces and I felt his confusion. He had grown up in this village. His family had provided employment for these people. His mother had given them charity and support when the lean times had come; his sisters were known for their good works. But now they all stared at him as if he were a stranger. Phoebe Stow and her husband Francis, Lucy Baalham and William Towns too, all owed their livelihoods to his family, and all knew him well. Then he spied Ann and my father at the back of the room, George holding tight to his mother. Was he to be damned by a child?

His thoughts were like water through a mill-race now, swirling and crashing, twisting and foaming. I could feel it all, but I could not reach him to offer comfort. His agitation was too great and his body too exhausted.

THE CORONER BEGAN TO SPEAK. He read all the evidence against William in a dull monotone while William slipped into inattention, the words passing over his head like the motes of dust caught in the breeze from the door. But when it came to the surgeon's evidence he blanched and swayed on his seat and Lea put out a hand to steady him.

Mr Humphreys spoke up.

'Sir, my client is overwhelmed. These details, about a woman he once loved and planned to marry . . .'

'Shame!' The woman's voice carried over the heads of the crowd. 'He should be made to listen to what he did.'

'Madam, that is enough. I will not have this hearing disrupted.' The coroner looked towards the back of the room but could not see who had caused the disturbance. He turned to Mr Humphreys. 'Is your client unwell?'

Humphreys bent to whisper to William then straightened.

'He is extremely distressed, Sir, and begs leave to return to his room. I have advised him that this would be best.'

A growling in the room now as people looked at each other in anger.

The coroner sensed the changing mood of the crowd.

'Very well.' He turned to William.

'William Corder, you are charged with the wilful murder of Maria Martin.' The room grew silent at his words. No one moved. 'I shall be very happy to hear anything you have to say and listen to any evidence you can provide to prove your innocence.'

William leaned towards Mr Humphreys, whispering softly, all the while gathering his composure, then he rose and bowed to the coroner. I thought he would speak then, tell them that this was all a mistake; that he had not killed me and his only crime was to cover up my body. I thought he would tell the inquest how I took my own life and, knowing that this was a mortal sin, he chose to cover it up so that I may rest in peace. That he did it all for the good of my soul. I thought he would say all this and try to save himself. But he did not. He merely turned to Lea, nodded, and followed him back up the stairs to the room.

He had not said a word.

THE CROWD WAS IN UPROAR. They pushed and shouted, full of anger and hate. The coroner called for silence but he was ignored until Ayers, who had been standing to one side listening to the proceedings, stepped forward and banged his stave down hard on the coroner's table. The commotion stopped as soon as it had started.

The coroner stood.

'Be silent. This is a court of law, not a fairground. Anyone else disrupting these proceedings will be forcibly removed.' He had their attention now. 'Members of the jury.' He turned to the jurymen who were huddled against the wall, looking fearful for their safety. 'Members of the jury, you have heard the evidence presented to this hearing. That murder has been committed there is no doubt. Your job is to decide, not by what instrument or method the deceased came by her end, but whether you consider that there has been sufficient evidence to convince you that the accused was the murderer and should be sent for trial at the next Assize. Do you wish me to read the evidence again?'

The jury conferred briefly then the foreman stood up.

'No, Sir, we have heard enough. We beg leave to retire to consider our verdict.' The coroner nodded and the men shuffled out into a side room. I could barely breathe, I felt near to fainting. But I had to stay.

I thought the jury would take longer but it was scarcely half an hour before they returned.

The coroner looked stern.

'You have reached your verdict? You are all agreed?'

'We have, Sir.'

'And?'

The foreman shuffled, looking pleased with himself and my heart sank.

'We return a verdict of wilful murder against William Corder.'

FIFTY-SEVEN

The room erupted as the coroner again called for order, but he was ignored. He turned to his clerk, raising his voice to be heard above the mob.

'Issue a warrant, direct it to Mr Orridge, the governor of Bury gaol. Request that he receives the prisoner into his custody and keep him safe until he is brought to trial at the next Assize.' He looked at the room. Chairs were overturned and people milled and jostled each other, all shouting to be heard. He glanced out of the window. There was a mob outside, waving clubs and staves, baying for blood. The whole of Polstead and more were there. People were pouring into the inn now, the room next door to the inquest filled to bursting point and, as the ale began to flow, so the noise increased. Coarse voices began to sing, the shouts grew louder, the laughter long and ribald.

The coroner turned again to his clerk who was gathering up his papers.

'Do they have no respect for his poor mother? She lives only a short distance away, she must be able to hear this racket. This is a solemn proceeding, you'd think they would treat it with some dignity.

The clerk shrugged.

'The case is becoming famous, Sir, and folk have always liked to see the downfall of those higher than them. The Corders are well known in this village and many are astounded that a member of such a respected family should become a murderer. No, none can fall further than he has done and it is the way of country folk to celebrate such a thing, I'm afraid. Nothing will change that.'

'You are right. I fear this will only get worse as the news spreads. I wonder what Corder makes of all this, sat upstairs.' He raised his eyes to the ceiling. 'God help him.'

I STOOD next to William as he was told of the verdict. It was Ayers that did it, in his normal, brusque manner.

'There is little surprise there.' William's voice was resigned, thin and reedy. 'I had thought it would come to that.'

'They were quick though, were they not, the jurymen?' Lea looked at Ayers. 'Only half an hour?'

'Aye, quick it was, but all the evidence was there. And anyway, the trial will get to the truth of the matter. All they did downstairs was to see if he – ' he nodded towards William, ' – was the culprit.'

William's head dropped to his chest.

'What will happen to me now?'

Ayers straightened.

'The coroner has issued a warrant. You will stand trial at the next Assize. You are to be taken to the gaol at Bury St Edmunds.'

There was a tap on the door and Lea opened it to see the landlord standing with a tray holding portions of a meat pie. Steam rose off it and swirled in the air.

'Thought you gentlemen might want something to eat before your journey.' He peered around Lea's shoulders at William. 'Mr

Corder, is there anything else you want, Sir?' He cleared his throat. 'I've always had the greatest of respect for your family and I am sorry to see you come to this, what with your recent losses and all.' William rubbed at his face hard, not far from tears, and I moved towards him and put my hand on his shoulder. I think he felt me then, for he rallied a little.

'I'd very much like a glass of rum if you please. If it is allowed?' He looked up at Ayers who nodded and the landlord bustled away, to return moments later with a glass half full of brown liquid. William put it to his lips and took a large gulp, relaxing a little as the rum seared his throat.

The landlord looked at the constables.

'Begging your pardon, officers, but there are people below who would like a brief word with Mr Corder here.'

'People? What people?' Lea was puzzled but Ayers took charge.

'Want to say their farewells, do they? Well, that won't go amiss I daresay. Send them up, only two at a time, mind, just in case someone tries something.'

The landlord nodded then went out onto the landing and shouted down.

'You can come up. Two at a time only and you mayn't stay long.' There was a clatter of boots on the stairs and I recognised two of the jurymen, come to say farewell. They were followed by Pryke, the bailiff, who had been with my father when they found my body. He took William's hand and shook it firmly.

'Have courage, Sir.' He dropped his voice. 'I cannot believe you guilty of this. You have my support and blessings and I ask your forgiveness if anything I must say at your trial in any way detracts from your innocence.'

'How is my poor mother, Pryke? Have you seen her?' William's eyes filled with tears and his voice wavered.

Pryke rubbed his chin and I heard the rasp of bristles.

'I've not seen her myself, Sir, but the maidservant said that she

is not too good. She has taken to her bed and is refusing to eat.'
William's eyes filled with tears and Pryke patted his hand. 'But she
is convinced of your innocence, she tells everyone that you cannot
have carried out such an outrageous act. She says the gypsies that
were here for the Fair must have done it. She will rally, you have
seen how she was after the death of your father and brothers, she
is made of strong stuff. We will look after her, don't you worry, me
and the other staff. And your sisters are constantly at her side.' He
stood back and gazed at William. 'God, be with you, Sir.'

Towns, the foreman, was the last to come. He seemed to have aged
in the past weeks and moved slowly. Ayers found a chair for him
opposite William and he sat down heavily.

'Mr Towns, it is good of you to come. I know how much my late
father thought of you and I have valued your help all these years.'

Towns reached forward and took his hand.

'Oh, Master William, I am sorry to see you in such trouble. You
must read the Holy Scriptures, for they will comfort and support
you in the coming days. Read them well, Master, let them be your
guide and solace.' His face creased with grief. 'I hope you will be
returned to our midst very soon, for the village will not be the
same place without you.' He stood unsteadily and moved towards
the door, then turned. 'I am sorry that I was forced to be a witness
against you, for you were always a good master to me.'

'Thank you, Towns, for your kindness. I will do as you say.' The
old man raised his hand in farewell and the room fell silent. All
that could be heard was the baying of the crowd and Town's
unsteady footsteps creaking down the stairs.

CHAPTER
FIFTY-EIGHT

They had dug my grave while the inquest was in progress and now the soil, full of stones, was piled alongside a yawning void. The smell of earth reminded me of my mother's garden and the pleasure I once took in tending it.

I looked down in sorrow as they placed what was left of my earthly body in a good oak coffin and fastened the lid down tight. At six that evening, the church bell began to toll and the village began to assemble. A group of men carried the coffin to the church-yard and I watched from the branches of an elm, my heart aching, as my father and stepmother followed behind with the boys. Nancy was there too, her face buried in her handkerchief, and I tried to reach out to her, to console her, but she was far away from me now, too wrapped up in her grief and regret.

I looked then at Thomas Henry. He had grown so much in the year I had been gone and now he hardly seemed like a part of me. I remember how he once smiled and chuckled at me, the weight of him in my arms and my heart went out to him. I reached out a hand and gently smoothed his cheek and he smiled as if he felt me.

They buried me next to my mother and little Matilda. Reverend

Whitmore read the service with a brisk solemnity, then, with a path opening between the crowd, the coffin was carried to the grave and carefully lowered in. There were tears from some of them, my stepmother leading the grieving, and her sobs mingled with the rustling of the wind through the sycamores that stood guard over my resting place.

I watched as my body was laid to rest, enveloped in twilight, seeing the faces I once knew now tear-stained and sad. I remembered the girl that I had been when I was amongst them when I was younger, carefree and not brought low by loss and grieving. How quickly life can change. But I would be at peace, for I had been given a Christian burial. I had so feared being buried at the crossroads in a suicide's grave, unblessed and unshriven. Suicide was a sin, its stain passing down the generations, but William's actions saved me from that. He had done his best to cover my sin. So I could rest, but not yet. I had to be sure he was freed from the taint of murder. He still needed me.

Below me, the crowd slowly dispersed. When they had all but gone the surgeon, John Lawton turned to John Baalham, who was watching the filling of the grave.

'Constable Baalham, you will need to retain this as evidence for the trial.' He handed over a soiled leather bag. 'I will leave this with you for safekeeping.'

'What is it, Sir?'

The constable opened the bag and recoiled in horror.

It was my head.

CHAPTER
FIFTY-NINE

The rattle of a post-chaise and a loud cheer outside the inn brought the officers to attention. Lea looked out of the leaded window into the dusk.

'Yes, it's ours. Come on Mr Corder, we'll gather your things. You'll need to be handcuffed between us, there's quite a mob out there.'

William nodded and held out his wrists while Lea fastened the irons around them, and then the three men moved towards the stairs, descending in a line. The landlord stood at the bottom, ready at the door and he nodded to William.

'Good luck, Mr Corder, Sir.' William opened his mouth to reply but, at that moment, the door was opened, a huge roar filled the air and his words were whisked away.

'Good God, where have they all come from?' Ayers drew his stave. The crowd was packed tight around the inn, everyone pushing to try and get a glimpse of the prisoner. I swooped upwards and over their heads, horrified that the people of Polstead, the village where he had been born and grew up, should turn against him like this. But as I looked closer at their faces I realised that the majority were not local, that they had come from far and wide to be part of this and that they were not friendly.

'There he is!'

'Murdering bastard, I hope you get what you deserve!'

'What of poor Maria?'

The two policemen pushed their way through the melee, staves flying, with William struggling for balance between them, his head lowered, his face white. They bundled him up the steps and into the chaise, closing the door firmly. Ayers banged on the roof, the driver shouted and the horses struggled to move forward through the crush. There were shouts, screams, a thumping of fists on the carriage doors as slowly the crowd was forced to part. The chaise proceeded down the hill, a group still following behind it, baying for his blood. It was as it reached his mother's house that William finally looked out of the window and gave a great shudder of anguish.

'Oh, Mother. My poor mother. I hope she cannot see this.' He closed his eyes and sat back in his seat.

THEY TRAVELLED ON, through Boxford and on to Lavenham, and in every village, jeering crowds gathered in the night to watch his passing with horrified excitement. William had been quiet, drawn in on himself but as the time passed he began to look around and pay more attention. Lea and Ayers sat in silence until William spoke up.

'Do you think there is any truth in dreams?'

'What's that?' Ayers shuffled in his seat.

'Dreams. Do you think there is anything in them?'

Lea sat forward, interested.

'Why, do you, Mr Corder?'

William nodded slowly.

'I do wonder if there is, for on the Friday night before you came for me I had two frightful dreams. I dreamt that my dead brothers and sister passed before me, dressed in white shrouds. I thought that it meant something bad was going to happen. Even when I woke up, I was still troubled by it. I told my wife about it, for it was still vivid.'

'And what did she say?'

William rubbed at his chin and looked at Lea.

'She said that to dream of the dead was a sign that I would hear of the living and that I should not worry.'

Ayers snorted.

'Well, she was wrong in that, now, wasn't she?'

'And what of your other dream?' Lea leaned towards William, but he was deep in thought again, so the officer sat back on the hard seat, moving his shoulders to ease them. After a while, William spoke again.

'There were lies told in those depositions.'

Ayers sighed theatrically.

'Were there now?' His voice was aimed to silence William but it did not.

'Ann Martin. She lied about the pistols. She said I took them when I went for Maria on the day she left, but that was untrue.'

'So you are saying you didn't have pistols?'

'I did have them, but not on that day. I had taken a loaded gun to the Martin's house previously, to show young George, but not that day. Not then.'

'Is that so?'

'She lied about questioning me on the Sunday too, about the pickaxe. She never asked me anything.'

Ayers smiled grimly.

'Well, the trial will get to the truth of the matter I expect. Examine all the statements, and hear all the witnesses. That's what it's for. That's why they are going to all this trouble over you. To prove you did it.'

'But I did not. I loved her, I would not harm her. They will try to trip me up with their clever words.' He looked about him, fear writ large on his face. 'I do not have a gentleman's education. I am not as learned as they are.' He dropped his head to his chest. 'If I had, I might have done as well as any young man hereabouts, for I had many advantages in my favour.'

'Which you wasted, did you not?' Ayers said, irritated, and Lea leaned forward and patted his arm.

'We must not to argue with the prisoner, Mr Ayers. Let him speak if he wishes.' He nodded meaningfully at Ayers who pursed his lips and sat back in his seat. 'Do continue, Mr Corder.' But William had fallen silent and sat with eyes closed. Lea looked at him. He could not tell if he was asleep or just deep in thought.

CHAPTER
SIXTY

As the post-chaise rattled its way closer to Bury, the silence became tense. It was William who broke it. I was curled in beside him and knew he had not been asleep, for the enormity of what was happening was beginning to crowd his mind.

'There are two things I very much want.' Lea looked at him, eyebrows raised. 'I want a bible and a prayer book. Do you think they would allow that where I am going?'

Lea nodded.

'I am sure they will supply these, and any other religious works you may require. The prison chaplain will be on hand for you as well.'

'I have another request.'

'Yes?'

'This world is nothing to me now but I wish that my wife could be with me in the gaol, for she is a good and pious woman and would be of more comfort to me than any minister of the gospel.'

Lea looked at his hands, unsure what to say and I could feel the doubt flicker through his mind. It was a few minutes before he spoke.

'The Bury governor is Mr Orridge. I am told he is very fair and humane and I am sure he will provide all that he can whilst ensuring your safe custody and following the prison regulations.'

William looked at him thoughtfully.

'You are a very careful man, Mr Lea, and you have been most considerate.' In the corner, Ayers snorted. 'I am glad this matter is nearing a close for I have not had one happy day since it happened.' I leant my head towards him, for I thought he had found happiness with Mary, but then, with a stab of realisation, I knew that he was telling the truth. He cared for Mary but he did not love her – I had been his one true love all along.

My heart sang. I smoothed his cheek with my fingers and, just for a moment, I felt his head soften against them. 'I am glad that there will be a long space between my committal and my trial. So that I may prepare for death.'

Lea stiffened and looked hard at William.

'Do not say such things, Mr Corder, you are not tried yet. The jury may find you innocent. The statements were not conclusive, there were flaws – '

Ayers straightened up in the cramped space.

'That is enough, Lea. If the prisoner wants to unburden himself to us now, then he is at liberty to do so. It is not for the likes of us to say what is and is not right or truthful. You are not a juryman, you are an officer of the law. Remember your place.'

Lea sat back, chastened, whilst William looked between the two.

'I am not unburdening myself, I am merely stating what I intend to do until my trial. I will employ my time in reading and writing and I hope that I shall be kept from the companionship of other prisoners, for I do not wish to learn any more wickedness. It is sin that has been my ruin.' I willed him not to say more, to take care not to incriminate himself, and he seemed to hear me for he paused and looked out of the window, watching the night. But his mind was rushing so far and fast that words had to come. 'I suppose there will be others in Bury Gaol who are to die, as well as myself?'

Lea looked at him.

'Mr Corder, it would be best for all concerned if you spoke no more of this.'

Ayers growled from his corner.

'Let him speak if he wants to, what he has said already could be considered as an admission of guilt.'

William looked around wildly.

'I have not confessed! I did not kill Maria Martin. You are twisting my words. I just needed to speak to someone.' His voice tailed off and, from my shadowed corner, I put my arms around him.

Be still, William, say no more. Be calm. His body was shaking so much under my touch that I knew he did not hear me. The threads that bound me to him were wearing thin now and I feared they would not hold.

'Ayers or I may be called to prove our conversations at your trial. It is best if you say no more, Mr Corder.' William looked at him. Lea's face was kindly, concerned, and I wondered at his fairness in such circumstances. Perhaps he, too, thought William innocent? Perhaps there was still hope?

CHAPTER
SIXTY-ONE

The late April night had fallen quickly, the darkness thick. The town clock was striking eleven when the chaise drew up in the silent street outside the Bury gaol. They were waiting for him. There was a loud clatter which echoed away as the large oak doors were thrown open and Lea, Ayers and William stepped down from the chaise and into a vast gloomy entrance-way, lit by oil lamps. I felt William's fear now, real and sharp and he pulled back a little, his handcuffs biting into his wrists.

'Now, now, Mr Corder, we don't want any trouble.' Ayers pulled William close, hissing in his ear. 'We have got you this far without event.' He looked up as a tall man approached, striding with authority towards them, dressed in a good wool coat with a high collar, a thick head of hair carefully arranged around a calm but stern face. 'Governor's here now, Corder, don't ruin it.'

The governor came to a halt before them, a phalanx of prison guards behind him.

Lea stood to attention and handed the governor the warrant.

'William Corder, delivered to your care, Sir.' The governor glanced at it, then turned to William and looked him up and down.

'Corder, I am Mr Orridge, governor of Bury Gaol. I will take charge of you from here onwards. You may make any requests you have to me and I will do my best to attend them.'

Lea cleared his throat.

'The prisoner has asked for a bible and prayer book, Sir.'

'Those will be provided.'

'And he has asked for the presence of his wife.'

'That cannot be allowed.' He turned to William. 'Given the seriousness of the accusations against you, Corder, visitors will be strictly limited. Those are the rules of the gaol and cannot be departed from.' William shuffled his feet and sighed deeply as the governor turned to Lea.

'Please remove the prisoner's handcuffs. We will ensure his security from here.' As Lea moved forward and turned the key to unfasten them, Orridge nodded to two of the guards. They stepped forward and William held out his wrists, bruised and reddened. The governor shook his head.

'You are to be fettered, Corder, like any other prisoner held for murder.' He looked at the guards. 'Carry on.' They moved forward and with grim efficiency fastened the cold iron around his ankles. The chain clanked and rattled as William shuffled, trying to make himself more comfortable. 'You will find them heavy to begin with, especially being a small man, but you will get used to them in time. You will have no preferential treatment here because of your respectability. All in this gaol are criminals in the eye of the law.'

Ayers backed away now, his job done, but Lea stepped towards William.

'I will take my leave of you now, Mr Corder.' He held out a hand and William hesitantly took it.

'I am grateful to you, Mr Lea, for the kind way in which you have performed your duty.' He reached into his pocket. 'I'd be grateful if you would accept this.' He drew out an embroidered silk purse and placed it gently in Lea's hand. 'My wife's workmanship.

Take it as a token of remembrance. I am only sorry that I have not still got my watch, as I would have liked you to have it. I am grateful to you.' His voice wavered a little as Lea took the gift, then stepped forward and patted William's shoulder.

'May God be with you, Mr Corder.' He smiled at William then turned on his heel and followed Ayers out into the street. Behind him, the great doors banged closed and a cold silence fell, broken only by the clatter of chains.

TIME SEEMED to stand still for William in those weeks before his trial. I stayed with him, settling into the corners of his cell, lying beside him, trying to reach him. For the first night and day, he was given the bible and prayer book he had requested, but he was kept in a cell on his own with no human contact, save that of the warder. He tried to read but he could not focus, could not absorb the words, and I felt his mind begin to slip further. Once he called out for me and I went to him, stroking his hair and soothing him until he lay back on the coarse mattress. The weariness of the past day's events caught up with him and he fell into a fitful sleep until he was woken by his cough, which was worsening. The following morning, being a Sunday, he was called to church where the sermon was on how God's laws had been so grievously offended. It seemed that this had been deliberately directed at him and it affected him greatly. His mind was full of his sins now, and of those he had sinned against. He was tormented and asked again for his wife to be allowed to visit for an hour or so each day, but Orridge refused.

'You are allowed no visitors, Corder, those are the rules for prisoners such as yourself. I have told you this before. I cannot make an exception. You may write to your wife as often as you wish, but only her, no other.'

'But what of my mother? Can I not write to my own mother?'

Orridge looked down at his shoes.

'I am sorry but it is against the regulations. You can write to your wife only. I will ensure you are supplied with pen and paper.'

I stood at William's shoulder while he composed his letters. I wanted to see if he wrote of me. But when he began to pour out his thoughts to Mary I found that I could not watch after all. Those letters were between him and her and not for my eyes, so I settled in the darkest corner of the cell, waiting.

Soon news began to reach him, via the warder who brought him his food each day.

'You are becoming something of a notoriety, Sir.' the warder said one morning as he placed a bowl of porridge on the table. 'The newspapers are full of it, even the London ones. The gentlemen of the press have picked it up there too. I know all about you now.'

'They write of me? What do they say?'

The warder licked his lips and bent close to William.

'Did you really have an assignation with a gypsy? Made her your mistress? Ask her to curse that poor dead girl?'

William looked at him aghast.

'Gypsy?'

The warder leaned in further.

'That is the very least of it, Sir. They are telling of how you murdered poor Maria in cold blood so that you could run away with another.'

'Enough!' William covered his ears with his hands. 'It is all untrue, all of it. How can people possibly think that of me?'

'But they do, Sir. It is in the news sheets and people believe what they read.'

I shrank back into a dark space, pressing myself against the dank wall. I had never imagined that my actions would lead to this. For all his faults, I would not have caused hurt to William. My deed, done in the heat of my anguish, was taking on a life of its own now, like a ball of earth and ordure rolling downhill, gathering more filth as it went.

As the warder left, locking the door behind him, William moved to the table and sat down, putting his head in his hands. Then he picked up his pen, pulled a sheet of paper towards him, and began to write. I had sworn I would not look but now I could not help myself. I drew close to him and peered over his shoulder.

Bury Gaol, May 3rd

My dear wife,

Let me entreat you that you do not give ear to the false reports that are abroad, for they will only add to your distress. You are aware that such news as this quickly spreads with much false rumour . . .'

I stepped back into the shadows.

CHAPTER
SIXTY-TWO

It seemed Mr Orridge had a change of heart.

'I am inclined to allow you short visits from your wife, Corder. You have been a model prisoner in the three weeks you have been here and Mrs Corder has contacted me many times asking to see you. It seems she has left her home and taken lodgings in Bury to be near you.' William's heart jumped. I felt it against my breast as I held him to me.

'I am most grateful, Mr Orridge. She will be a great comfort to me and I have missed her company sorely.'

'She will be relieved to see you, I have no doubt. These newspaper reports that are going around have painted you as black as pitch.'

'I wrote to her and asked her not to read them. I know those who write such things have to earn a living but no one would like to have all their faults laid out for the world to see. When may Mary come to see me?'

'I will allow her to visit this afternoon. You will not be left alone while she is here and the visit must be short.'

'It is more than I expected, thank you, Sir.'

. . .

WILLIAM SPENT the next few hours pacing the cell. He could not eat his midday meal, such was his agitation, and he sat down and then stood up over and over until he heard the sound of footsteps on the stone step outside. The door opened and there she was.

'Mary! Oh, my dearest Mary, how I have missed you.' He held out his arms and she fell into them, stifling a sob.

'My poor husband.' She stepped back and looked at him. 'Are you well? How have they been treating you? You look thinner.' I watched them closely for a few minutes, looking for signs of passion, but there were none. He did not love her as he had loved me and my heart sang.

William took her gently by the arm and led her to the table, pulling out a chair for her, then sat opposite. They clasped hands and gazed at each other as Mary cleared her throat.

'There is some news, but I am not sure how you will take it. Mr Humphreys, who was your solicitor at the inquest . . .'

'I remember him.'

'I'm afraid he has declined to represent you at your trial.' William's mouth dropped open and Mary rushed to continue. 'But all is not lost. Charles and I, we have engaged a barrister, a Mr Broderick, to represent you.'

'A barrister? At what cost, Mary? And why did Humphreys decline my case?' His voice was rising now, his panic clear. Mary squeezed his hands and looked hard at him.

'William, we had no option. You need good representation, this is a very serious matter and we need to prove your innocence. Mr Broderick comes highly recommended and Charles has already paid his fee. Once you are freed and back with us we can find a way to repay him, I am sure.'

'How much?'

Mary hesitated before she looked him in the eye.

'One hundred and forty guineas. Plus his expenses.' William sat back hard in his chair, pulling his hands away, his face pale. 'William, they – my solicitor, your friends, your family – all want you to say that Maria's death was suicide.'

'It was.' William's voice was so small it went unheard and I moved to his side.

'Mr Humphreys strongly disagreed with this view. He thought the charge of murder against you would stand and that you should admit manslaughter and face transportation, rather than –' She faltered for a moment then regained her composure. 'Because of this disagreement, he felt it better that he should not represent you. So we found Mr Broderick, who seems to think that there is a very good chance of your regaining your freedom.'

'Oh, Mary, is that possible? Since being here I have not dared hope.'

Mary took hold of his hands again, shaking them gently for emphasis.

'There is always hope, William. I have given up everything to follow you and I will not rest until you are freed. I will write to you on the days I cannot visit, and you must write to me also. But be careful of what you put onto paper for the governor reads all correspondence.'

By the door, the warder shuffled his feet and cleared his throat.

'Time to go, Madam.' She looked at him and then stood, carefully straightening her skirts. She looked different somehow, but given the immense strain she was under I could only admire her assurance.

She held out her arms.

'Husband.'

William clasped her tightly.

'Be strong, Mary, and come again soon.' She kissed him tenderly and then moved away, the warder opened the cell door, and with a swirl of skirts she was gone.

CHAPTER
SIXTY-THREE

I should have known when I saw her stand up to leave. The difference in her, a softened roundness, the way she straightened her skirts so carefully. But it was not until later that I realised, for I had been in that position myself. Mary Corder was with child. She was old to carry a child, over thirty, and she and William had only been married a few short months before he was seized. But God moves in mysterious ways and it seems theirs was a full relationship. How I envied her.

She did not tell him at her next visit, for she was not yet certain. She was shown into the cell and sat down carefully opposite him as William smiled at her.

'Mary. I am so glad to see you.' He sat down and reached for her hands.

'William, I need to go to London and visit my mother. She is still seeking a tenant for the school and she would be overjoyed to see me, for she is most concerned for your welfare and mine.'

'Dearest, I will hate to be apart from you again, but you should go. And while you are there you must obtain copies of my brother's Will and also my father's for me. I need to know that you will be left comfortable in the event of . . . I must put my affairs in order.' He looked at her to make sure she understood. 'I need to sign over my inheritances to you so that you are able to pay my legal fees and have enough for your comfort. Will you do this for me?' Mary nodded, her head lowered. 'Your mother will be a great comfort to you while we are apart, you must not fret.'

She smiled wanly at him.

'I will be gone only for a matter of days, a week at the most.'

William squeezed her hands gently

'Then you must go. I will be quite well here in the meantime and it will do you good to get away from this place.' He looked into her face quizzically. 'Are you quite well, Mary? You seem distracted.'

She gazed back at him and I could see she was minded to tell him her news. But she swallowed, quelling the thought.

'I am not myself, William. And I feel I should have written to your poor mother. What must she think of me?' She looked around her and the warder, propping up the wall by the door, straightened. 'I wish things were different, that is all.' She turned again to her husband. 'I do not regret one moment of our lives together, I just wish we had more time, more to look forward to. I hope you do not repent of our marriage, William, for I do not. I am your friend, you know that, and I will not forsake you in your time of need.'

He looked at her with tenderness and my heart lurched as I remembered how he had once looked at me that way. Those memories were fading now and I yearned to get them back.

He raised her fingers to his lips and kissed them gently.

'I will see you when you return from London. God be with you, Mary.' She leaned forward, resting her forehead against his until the warder cleared his throat.

'Time to go, Mrs Corder.'

She was gone for a week. She wrote to William to say she had obtained the Wills and spoken to a solicitor and that her mother was well, but nothing more.

WHEN SHE CAME BACK she brought him cherries. She took a cloth from a small basket and pushed it towards William. I saw them, dark and gleaming, lying in the bottom and, in a flash, I remembered it all – the smell and freshness of them, the firmness and sharpness of each one as I had bitten into it. The memories flooded back and overwhelmed me and I ached for what had been, for the love I had lost. The very air was thick and sticky with my longing.

'I thought you might like these. They are Polstead Blacks, fresh from the market.'

'Thank you, that is kind of you.' But William did not take one, just gazed at them as Mary related the news from London. He was not listening to her. He was remembering. His mind was back at the day of the Cherry Fair, holding me in his arms, drinking me in as I took the cherries from his fingers.

'William' He started and Mary paused and looked at him. 'There is another thing. I am not sure how – ' She took a deep breath. 'While I was in London, I saw a doctor.'

His face whitened and he held her hands tightly.

'Are you unwell? Tell me, are you ill?'

'No, not ill.' She looked him full in the face. 'William, I am with child.'

He did not move, nor change his expression and I saw the worry in her eyes. Then, gradually, a wide smile split his face.

'Oh, Mary, my love, that is wonderful news. A child – it is more than I deserve.'

'The doctor there said I must rest, that I must refrain from emotional scenes and not take too much exercise in case I damage the child. He said that thirty-one is old to bear a first child.' She shook her head sadly. 'He did not know to whom I am married. He could not know of the immense suffering and worry I feel, the continual trickle of dread down my spine. And I have been so afraid you would be angry.'

William looked at her and leaned across, kissing her tenderly.

'I am not angry, the news has brought me happiness in this dark place. You must do as the doctor says as best you can. Your health and that of the child are at stake. And when – when is your confinement?'

'The doctor thinks November.'

'And are you well?'

'Apart from a little sickness, yes.' She looked down and put her hand over her stomach protectively. 'It is early yet, the babe has barely quickened. Are you truly pleased?'

He smiled warmly at her.

'I am, and once I am freed we can plan our life together with our child. It will be wonderful.'

She paused and looked up at him.

'There is another thing.'

Mary hesitated.

'I took the liberty of writing to your sister.'

'And what was her reply? It must have been a shock to her, hearing from you, and under such difficult circumstances.'

'She was friendly, and that meant a lot to me. She said she would send some provisions. But your mother – '

'Is she unwell?'

'No, it is not that. William, your mother has refused to allow you to pass your inheritance on to me or for any of it to be used for your defence. She says that you have made your bed and now you must lie in it.' William's mouth opened in shock. 'She does not believe that paying for counsel is a wise choice, given the cost and the evidence against you. Oh, dearest, I did not know what to say. I thought her to be tender-hearted, but this – now I do not know what to think'

William sighed heavily.

'I will write to her, explain the situation. She must help me, she is my mother.' He looked at Mary's anguished face. 'All will be well. She will come round, I will see to it. And now she is to have a grandchild.' His face had brightened now he had a plan. 'I will write to her. She will not forsake me. I am her only living son. She will not desert me.'

He troubled over that letter for hours, writing a few words then crossing them out or throwing down his pen in frustration. He threw himself on her mercy, begging her forgiveness for his many sins. He told her of the coming child and how he wished her to acknowledge it, and Mary. His mind was racing with the words he needed to say, events churning over and over in his mind. He invoked his dead father and spoke of how the visit of Mr Towns and other neighbours when he was held at the Cock Inn had so affected him and strengthened him, how he was reading his bible daily and repenting of his past transgressions. He poured his heart out in that letter. And his words must have struck a chord in her for his sister wrote to him saying that she and his mother wanted to visit.

SIXTY-FOUR

He told Mary the news at her next visit.

'I must be strong for them. I must not give them any cause for concern. Mother must have thought about what she said before and realised that you and our child must be provided for. I have told them that they must wait a week before undertaking the journey as I am expecting my legal advisor to call on me here, but I don't know yet on which day he will come.' He stood up and moved around the room with an excited energy. 'Oh, Mary, I feel in good health and much better in spirits than I have since I was brought here. Your news changes everything; it has lifted me more than I can say. This charge hangs over me like a sword, waiting to fall on my neck and my heart bleeds, but to have Mother visit – she must have changed her mind.'

Mary sat quietly. I had seen William like this many times before, his spirits suddenly raised, although I knew also that he could come crashing down at the slightest discord. But this seemed new to her and she did not know how to deal with it. She did not know him as well as I did. The cord between us may be stretched and thinning but it was still there. He was still mine.

Mary did not come the next time. She wrote to him but gave no reason for her absence, merely expressing her regrets, and speaking again of his kindness, tenderness and indulgence towards her. She did not tell him how afraid she was that she might lose him, and how she could not bear to think about it. For there was to be a child and her troubles were great. Instead, she said how anxious she was to know how his religious study was progressing, believing that if he truly repented of his sins, he would be pardoned. On the twenty-second of June, William's twenty-fourth birthday, she sent him a copy of Blair's Sermons. She had inscribed in it.

'Mary Corder presents this book to her husband, William Corder, on his birthday as proof of her esteem and hopes that he may live to enjoy many happy returns of it.'

She had convinced herself that he would be free. For anything else would be unthinkable.

MY BODY HAD lain quiet in Polstead churchyard for weeks but suddenly there was a rumour that some of the evidence was faulty and that the cause of my death was in question. It was John Baalham, the constable, who wrote to William to tell him what was about to occur and the shock of what he said drew me back to Polstead.

Mr Wayman, the coroner, was tucked away in a back room of the Cock Inn holding forth.

'Gentlemen, it seems there is some doubt about the cause of death.' The three surgeons present nodded solemnly. 'There is now talk of a stab wound. This could change the course of the case if it is found to be so. We need to examine the remains again.' I looked around for Mr Lawton, the surgeon who had first examined my body after I was found in the Red Barn, but he was not there. His assistant, Bewick, spoke up.

'Mr Lawton has refused to attend or give his agreement to such a course of action. He considers he made a thorough examination of the deceased at the time and remains firm in his conviction that the deceased died from a pistol shot to the neck or strangulation. He has instructed me to tell you that the putrefaction was great and that he considers there would be even less evidence now that the body has been buried for a further six weeks. He thinks there is no need for a second examination and that the family of the poor girl have suffered enough.'

Wayman stroked his chin thoughtfully.

'That is indeed a shame, for his contribution would have been invaluable. But I have been informed that there are cuts in the chemise and stays that have been caused by a knife or blade. And, remember, a sharpened sword was found in Corder's possession. I say we exhume.'

Bewick leaned forward.

'But was the sword found not scimitar-shaped? This would not cause the same type of wound as a knife, for the blade is curved.'

The second surgeon leaned forward.

'In my opinion, it would be best to examine the body again.'

'Thank you, Mr Chaplin.'

'I agree.'

'Thank you, Mr Nairn. And you are willing to undertake the task?'

'I am. It is in the best interest of justice that all evidence is provided at the trial. Mr Lawton was thorough, I am sure.' He nodded at Bewick. 'But it is possible he missed something. After all, the liquids seeping from the body may have masked . . .'

Bewick puffed himself up indignantly.

'Mr Lawton is an experienced surgeon. He missed nothing!'

'But he had not had experience of dissecting a body so long in the ground.'

'And Nairn has?' Bewick was furious now.

'Mr Nairn is the more experienced surgeon, which is why I have chosen him to carry out this sad task.' Wayman's voice was smooth as silk, persuasive.

I thought of how I was found, the care taken by Mr Lawton. And I remembered the jurymen as my body lay on that door. How, when the surgeon was turned away, one had leaned forward out of curiosity and pierced my side with his knife.

'So we are agreed that the body should be disinterred? That we will examine the deceased specifically to look for a wound to the left-hand side of the body and that Mr Nairn will carry out the task?' Bewick looked as if he would like to object but he kept his silence under the gaze of the coroner and the two other surgeons. Wayman looked around him in satisfaction. 'Then we are agreed. Arrangements have been made for the body to be exhumed in the early hours of tomorrow morning. This will avoid any interference by members of the public. We have all seen the sensation this trial has caused. We are under scrutiny here, gentlemen, we must not fail in our task to find out the truth.' There were nods of approval. 'Then I say we eat now, enjoy a glass of wine and wait until Baalham the constable comes to say all is prepared. He stood and called for the landlord as I waited, full of horror, in the dark.

A few hours later John Baalham entered the room, his face white and pinched.

'The grave is uncovered ready, Mr Wayman.'

The coroner rose to his feet.

'Well, gentlemen, shall we?'

CHAPTER
SIXTY-FIVE

The coroner and surgeons followed the constable out in a slow, solemn procession, making their way down the hill and up to the churchyard. I followed, slipping from tree to tree like the ghost I was.

The sexton and another man were wiping the sweat from their brows with grimy sleeves as the party arrived. Mr Wayman nodded to them and the sexton stepped forward and dropped lithely down into the hole as his assistant leaned in from the top. Together they hauled up my coffin, placing it unceremoniously on the stony earth then the sexton bent over to unfasten the lid. As he pulled it clear it slipped and fell to the ground with a clatter that rang loud in the summer darkness. The men winced but moved in closer, lamps held high, then groaned as one, covering their noses with handkerchiefs brought for the purpose, as they unfolded the shroud from my body. Mr Nairn leaned forward and looked closely, a lamp held high.

'Where is the head?'

Baalham stepped forward.

'Removed by Mr Lawton, Sir, after the inquest. It was evidence of a pistol shot. I have it in my care' He stepped away and looked anywhere but at the scene before him.

The men gazed at my body for a long time, then Nairn dropped to his haunches and began to probe the soft sludginess with his fingers. I could see as well as they that the putrefaction was so great there was nothing left. No detail could be made out of the mess that was me. But he leaned in closer.

'There does appear to be an aperture here. How wide would you say that was, Mr Wayman?'

The coroner knelt beside him and looked closely at where he was pointing.

'I'd say that was about two, two and a quarter inches wide. The sword that was found is the same size.'

Nairn sat back on his heels, looking pale and drawn, breathing heavily into his handkerchief.

'The slits in the stays and shift appear to correspond with it. Do you agree?'

Mr Wayman leaned back.

'I do. So, in your professional opinion, could these wounds have been caused by the sword found in the prisoner's belongings?' The two exchanged a meaningful glance.

'It could well be, Mr Wayman.' said Nairn.

'But we must have evidence to back up your findings. There must be no doubt.'

Nairn nodded and pulled his surgeon's bag towards him, unrolled a cloth and drew out a thin, fine knife, which gleamed in the torchlight. He leaned forward into my corpse and with a few swift movements he cut out my heart. 'I will preserve this in spirits as an exhibit for the trial. Look, there is a small perforation here.' He pointed at the grisly object in his left hand. 'That would also align with the damage to the items of clothing.' He paused, looking down at my remains. 'I had best remove these two ribs as well, for they may also be needed in evidence.' He bent to his grim task as the other men watched in silence.

I looked down in horror. They had assumed William's guilt from the outset. They were never going to believe that he had not murdered me and now they had made the proof. As they bundled my last remains back into the coffin and sealed the lid I could only watch, drifting restlessly in the branches of the great sycamores that overlooked my grave, rustling their leaves in protest.

THE PUBLIC OUTCRY about the case grew daily. Newspaper articles, plays and songs flooded the country and William's name was on everyone's lips. He was the only subject of conversation, from the lowest of taverns to the highest gentleman's clubs of London. People scoured the weekly journals, seeking the next piece of gossip about the case. And there was plenty of that, especially when my stepmother spoke to journalists and told them that she had dreamt of my grave in the Red Barn. Oh, yes, she became an overnight celebrity, glorying in her new-found fame. It seemed that the whole of England knew about the evil squire who had seduced and brutally murdered the young innocent maid. Worst of all was the preacher, who came to Polstead from London, young and fervent, and stood under the Gospel Oak by the church, declaiming William from his makeshift pulpit. Several thousand people heard that sermon, heard William described as my murderer, and they all believed the word of this man of God. It was reported in the newspapers and hundreds read it and came to believe it. There was even a *camera obscura* set up in a tent only a few streets from where William awaited his trial, and many coins changed hands as people queued to see the images displayed there.

I wanted to scream and shout out at them, at their folly, their narrowness of mind, but my voice was long gone. And I thought

William had forgotten me. I knew he did not truly love Mary but now there was to be a child, and his thoughts were no longer of me. It had all brought me low, made me silent.

I stayed with William in his cell while his mother and sister visited, crying over him, patting him like a sick animal that only they could save. Mary visited each week, dignified, her condition disguised by careful arrangement of her stays and cloak, quoting the scriptures and uplifting texts. They gnawed away at him, these women of William's. They were all convinced of his innocence, that there had been some horrible mistake, and they began to convince him too. His mother spoke of when he would be returned to her, the meal she would prepare to celebrate his liberty, little considering that, if he were freed, it was his wife to whom he would return, not her. She still refused to acknowledge Mary, never mentioning her name and turning her head away when he spoke of her. He was in despair over it, for he had hoped that Mary might feel the support of his family.

And so the weeks passed, with William, every day, becoming more certain of his freedom. His barrister, Mr Broderick, thought he had a good case, that the charge of murder would fail due to lack of evidence, but what he and William did not know was that evidence of my stabbing had been prepared. His counsel was not aware that the prosecution had my head, my heart and ribs, and that the marks on them were going to convince a jury that William had brought about my death.

CHAPTER
SIXTY-SIX

The trial was set for Thursday the seventh of August. As the day grew closer the warder came frequently with food and news. It seemed that Bury St Edmunds was full to bursting, there was no bed to be had in the many inns, and people had taken to going from house to house to try and find accommodation. The taverns and public houses were doing a roaring trade, and pie and bread vendors were selling out almost as soon as they had reached their street corners. And, as the day crept nearer, so the warder's excitement grew.

'The town has never seen such crowds, Mr Corder, and all down to you. You've brought prosperity to this place and many are grateful to you for it. They all want to attend your trial though, but there's no hope of that, not with those numbers.'

I watched the warder from my corner, his face gleeful, bright with gossip, full of energy and life, as once I had been. And I watched William become convinced he would be freed. I felt little myself now, for my energy was sapped, my soul exhausted, and I was tired unto death. But he was my love and I had to stay with him until the end, whatever that end may be. Despite that, I could not raise myself to go to him and comfort him as I had once done but had to content myself with offering soft words from where I lay, slumped in the shadows of his cell.

When the warder came with the midday meal there was more news.

'They are going to ban women from the trial, for their own safety, so I've heard. Too many people, they fear the ladies will be crushed in the melee.'

William looked up.

'The time has come then?' He looked confused and the warder's brow furrowed.

'Not until tomorrow, Mr Corder. They will fetch you tomorrow morning, do you not recall? Mr Orridge told you himself only yesterday. I have been asked to bring your breakfast early so that you are ready when the gaol cart arrives for you.'

William sighed deeply.

'Of course. Time stretches here, it distorts somehow. I had lost track of the days. A momentary lapse only, I shall be ready to face my accusers tomorrow, have no fear.'

THEY CAME for him at eight o'clock the next morning, two guards armed with staves, Mr Orridge standing watch. William stood, wiping the remains of his breakfast from his mouth. Mary had brought him new clothes to wear, and he was dressed in a fine frock coat with a velvet collar, black waistcoat, blue trousers, and silk stockings and pumps. Around his neck, he wore a white neckerchief.

'You must look confident, William, dress to show your importance. You are not one of the ordinary rabble, you must hold yourself like the gentleman you are.'

William had smiled at her and taken the parcel.

'You are right, Mary, after all, I am there to prove my innocence.'

But now the day of the trial had dawned he was not so sure. I felt uncertainty flood through him.

'Is this coat not too fine, Mr Orridge?'

The governor smiled.

'No, Corder, it is not. Your wife feels you should dress like a gentleman and that is what you look like. Come now, it is time to go.'

The guards left his shackles on and put handcuffs around his wrists as he stood still. I was proud of him in that moment, the way he held himself as if he had nothing to lose. We could hear a growing sound from outside, a baying as if of many hounds. It rang unnatural around the cell.

'What's that noise?'

Mr Orridge stepped into the room and checked that the handcuffs were secure.

'That is your reception committee, Corder. Brace yourself, this is not going to be easy.'

I heard them clatter down the stairs, the sound of William's chains clanking like a cracked bell as he took each step slowly. Silence, then a great roar as the outer doors opened and the mob saw him. There was shouting, oaths and cursing and I imagined Mr Orridge and the guards trying to hack their way through the crowds to get him into the cart. Then, with a rattle of wheels, the shouting died away and he was gone. I wanted so much to go with him but I could not follow. The last of my strength was ebbing away.

CHAPTER
SIXTY-SEVEN

The summer had been hot and dry but on that first day of the trial, the heavens opened; a dreadful thunderstorm raged until the afternoon. It was a portent. I lay in William's cell, listening to the rain and the shouts of the people who seemed undaunted by the downpour. I was heavy with exhaustion, all emotions drained from me. I could not raise myself to be with William, nor did I want to. For I knew how it would go, I had seen the evidence they had now and dread lay deep in me.

They brought him back at seven that evening. I heard the baying of the crowd first, then the rattle of cartwheels, the ring of voices as the guards waited for him inside the gates. As he was brought through the cell door he could barely stand and a guard had to support him on one side. They took off his handcuffs and stood aside as Mr Orridge came through the door.

'Sit there, Corder, I will have some food brought up to you. You'd like a meal, I'm sure?' William nodded, too tired to speak. His hands were shaking.

The warder rushed in with a mug of ale and William drained it gratefully. He returned moments later with a plate laden with pie and potatoes.

'Here, Mr Corder, this will make you feel better.' He passed William a knife and fork and watched as William began to eat, tentatively at first, then, as his hunger took over, more quickly, barely pausing between mouthfuls.

The warder looked at Mr Orridge.

'I hear it was chaos, Sir?'

'That it was. Some members of the crowd put a ladder against an adjacent building so that they could sit on the rooftop to get a view of the prisoner. Ladies fighting for a glimpse too. Appalling scenes. Some men even managed to get above the ceiling of the courtroom and lie on the joists to peer over the cornice. I had them removed smartish, I feared for the ceiling with all that weight on it. I had to station an officer there in case it happened again.' The warder stared at him, wide-eyed. 'The mob were everywhere. We took the prisoner through the back door of the court in the end, for the crowd was too dense at the front, but there were masses of people there too. Standing on the ledges of the windows to see in, piled into the graveyard next door. Some even stood on the head-stones to try and get a glimpse. And it wasn't just the hoi-polloi. Gentlemen and ladies, and of quality, some of them. I've never seen such a disgraceful show.' He turned to look at William who was sweeping his plate with a piece of bread. 'Now I've seen you settled, Corder, I'll leave you to it. I understand that your legal advisers are coming in this evening?'

William wiped his mouth and nodded.

'Thank you Mr Orridge, yes they are. We are to go through my statement.'

'Very well, I will bring them to you as soon as they arrive.' He nodded and left, taking the guards with him.

. . .

THE WARDER WATCHED THEM GO, listening as they went down the stairs, then drew up a chair and sat opposite William, his face expectant.

'How was it, Mr Corder, Sir? Was it as bad as you feared?'

William looked at him, blinked slowly and sighed.

'My wife had told me to stand tall, to keep any expression from my face and I did that, all through the evidence. Those people – I thought they were my friends.' His voice tailed off and he looked towards the barred window. 'They all spoke against me. The untruths they told, and from supposedly God-fearing people as well. There were one or two who spoke up for me.' He drew a quavering breath. 'But I kept my composure, as my wife told me, I took it all. But then they called the surgeons who said that they had found a wound on Maria that I had made with a sword. They brought in my sword. But I never stabbed her, I did not. What they said – it was lies, all of it.'

The warder patted his hand.

'There, there, Mr Corder, don't fret. Your legal man will be here soon, he will see you right.' He stood up to leave, the chair grating behind him, but as he did so William grasped his arm.

'That was not all, Warder. They brought in her head.'

The warder looked at him in horror.

'*What?*'

'Her skull, yes. Her lovely face – all gone, rotted away, just teeth and shattered bone. They had her heart, her ribs –'

He shuddered.

The warder looked around him.

'Let me get you some more ale, Sir, or a tot of rum. That will help settle you. It must have been a terrible shock.'

'I never expected to see her like that. Her teeth were gleaming white.' A great sob shuddered through him. 'Maria – she was so beautiful. I loved her so much.'

He put his hand to his head and the warder patted his shoulder.

'Let me fetch that rum, Sir.' He hurried away and the room fell silent, then William began to cough. The sound rang sharp and hard in the cell and he put his handkerchief to his mouth as his chest heaved with effort. He staggered a little and I summoned all the strength I had left in me and moved to his side as he sank to the bed and took the handkerchief from his lips. Together we gazed in horror at the red flowers of blood splattering the white cotton. I pulled his head to my bosom, stroking his hair and felt a shudder run through him as he closed his eyes.

'Maria. Oh, Maria. Help me.'

His body shook then softened and he moved into me, resting his head against my neck. He knew I was there. He spoke to me.

CHAPTER
SIXTY-EIGHT

I held William in my arms for a long time, pushing all my strength into him, until his legal team arrived, when I slipped back into my shadows. Mr Broderick was brisk and business-like as they sat around the table but I did not listen to them, just let the words drift over me, for all my energy was used up. William said little but he kept glancing to where I lay. He felt my presence, I knew it, I'd heard him speak my name and that was enough for me. But as the men droned on I could feel his spirits falling, his hopes dashing against the rocks of their words. He was to speak in his own defence the next day and he had prepared a speech but Broderick went through it over and over, crossing words out, muttering under his breath, before pronouncing himself satisfied.

'It is the law of this country that I, as your Counsel, am not allowed to speak for you. The law states that you have to speak in your own defence. I can call witnesses for you and examine them on your behalf and I will do this after you have spoken. When I have done so the judge will proceed with the summing up.' He paused and shuffled his papers then looked at William. 'It is vital that you speak up for yourself, Corder, and speak well. You must say it was an accident, that you acted in self-defence. Admit your intimacy with the girl, say that the child died. You are a gentleman, you were caught up by a pretty face, the jury will have some sympathy with that, I am sure. Tell them how she flew into a wild passion in the barn and took up your pistol. There was a struggle, the pistol went off and you tried to hide her body through fear. You did not run away but stayed in Polstead, only leaving when the doctor said you should go to the sea for your health. You must emphasise that these were not the actions of a guilty man, more one afraid of the consequences of a girl's thoughtless act.' All the time William nodded but I was not sure he was hearing it all.

The barrister stood and straightened his coat.

'Get some sleep now, Corder, you need to be at your sharpest tomorrow.' He gathered up his papers and nodded to his clerk. 'We will leave you to it. I'll see you in the morning.' All of a sudden his facade dropped and he reached out and patted William's shoulder. 'I will do the best I can for you. All is not lost, not yet.' He stepped away to the door and the warder opened it, then closed it firmly behind him. The lock grated, the warder's eye appeared briefly in the peephole, and the cell fell silent.

WILLIAM STOOD up hesitantly and removed his jacket and waistcoat. He lay down on the bed with a deep sigh and I crawled towards him, barely able to lift myself to lie beside him.

'*William. I am here.*' He turned his head and looked straight into my eyes. They were blank at first but then the veil fell from them and he saw me. Truly saw me.

'Maria?' I stroked the hair from his forehead. 'Is it you?'

'*I am so sorry – for everything.*' He gazed at me, smiling gently as he used to, until his eyelids began to droop in exhaustion. I kissed his forehead softly as he fell asleep in my arms.

He rose early the next day, seemingly refreshed, but I knew his spirits were low. He ate his breakfast in silence, not even acknowledging the warder, then he took up his papers and read through them, now and again jotting some word in the margin.

They came for him again at eight and the noise of the crowd was louder than ever, all baying and screaming for his blood. The cart rattled away and I lay back down in the corner and awaited his return.

I had expected him gone all day as before, but by mid-afternoon, the voice of the crowd rose and the sound of the cart rattled the air, and my heart sank.

HE WAS a different man when he entered the cell – I scarcely recognised him. All the light had gone out of him and I knew instantly what the verdict had been. He slumped into a chair, numb, as the warder removed the handcuffs and stood back to let Mr Orridge into the cell. Over the governor's arm was a set of grey prison clothes.

'I'm sorry, Corder, but you are to wear these now.' William looked up at him, eyes blank. 'It is the law. You'll be able to change into your other clothes again for – ' He nodded to the warder who unfastened the shackles around his ankles. 'Now, get into these and I'll take your clothes to a safe place.' William moved slowly as if his limbs had been turned to lead, saying nothing. The governor folded each item carefully as he removed them, then took up the bundle and made for the cell door. 'Would you like a meal? I can arrange that for you.' William shook his head. 'Ale then, or something stronger? A tot of brandy? That should set you up.'

'Brandy, please. I feel . . .'

'You have had a shock, it's natural to feel the way you do.'

William looked at the governor.

'Do other men feel the same? When they learn they are to die?

And after – they said my body is to be dissected – I cannot bear to think of it.'

In the corner, I shuddered in horror as the words dropped into the room like stones. Mr Orridge clasped the clothes close to his chest, his face sorrowful.

'I have never known a man – nor woman neither – who did not feel the shock of such a sentence. You are not alone, Corder, such feelings are to be expected. But the law is the law and it says that those found guilty of murder are to have their bodies dissected or hung in chains. It seems harsh to you now, but you will be beyond pain by then. Try not to dwell on it.' He looked at William and his face was kindly. 'I will send the warder back with the brandy. In the meantime, I advise you to try to get some rest.'

William sat down heavily on the bed and gazed at him.

'You have been most civil, Mr Orridge. I had not expected such kindness from a prison governor. I expected my treatment to be harsh.' He paused, thoughtful. 'Even your warder here has been courteous and caring.'

The warder smiled sadly at him.

'That is good of you, Mr Corder, Sir. And may I say you have been an exemplary prisoner. No trouble at all.'

William smiled wanly.

'And I shall be even less trouble in two days.' The warder looked down at his boots and William turned to the governor.

'Please, may I see my wife? I implore you, I must see her. I need to explain to her . . .'

'I will send for her, but I'm afraid that you will only be allowed to see her for a short time and only in the presence of a guard or myself. The law, y'see.' William nodded then lay down and turned on his side to face the wall. The two men left quietly, save for the clunk of the door and I shuffled towards his still figure, lay down beside him, moulding my body to his, and held him tight until dawn.

CHAPTER

SIXTY-NINE

They did not leave him in peace to contemplate his death. During the two days before his execution he was watched at all times by guards. Mary came, encouraging him to pray, and the prison chaplain, Reverend Stocking, came time and time again with Mr Orridge, exhorting him to confess to my murder. But William refused, denying it all over and over again until the pressure became too much; his mind roiled with confusion and he barely knew where he was. They took him to the chapel where words were spoken for his immortal soul and I watched him when he returned as he threw himself onto his bed, sobbing uncontrollably. He was much changed. Throughout his ordeal, he had been cheerful and confident but all that had deserted him now. His cheeks were collapsed and his eyes were red and swollen with weeping. His breathing was fast and shallow, his cough far worse, and he trembled continually. But still they would not leave him alone. Reverend Stocking harangued him endlessly, imploring him to confess until he was worn down to the quick.

'I want to see my wife. I must see her one last time.'

The Reverend looked at him, his hands still clasped in prayer.

'I dare say that could be arranged.' He glanced at Mr Orridge who nodded. 'If you were to confess.'

I stiffened at this blackmail, willing William not to do as they asked, but Mr Orridge stepped in.

'Your wife may visit for a short time this afternoon, Mr Corder, to make her last farewells.' He glanced back at the minister, frowning. 'It is normal practice. We are not inhuman.'

She came. Mary entered the cell dressed in black, her face hidden by a veil which she lifted as soon as she saw her husband. Her stomach was rounded now, her condition plain for all to see.

'William, dearest. How are you?' He pulled out a chair for her and she sat down carefully, resting her hand protectively over her unborn child. He looked questioningly at the veil thrown back from her hat and she put a shaking hand to it. 'I was advised to wear this so that my face would not be recognised. There is a crowd assembling in the town and the mood is dangerous. I did not wish to draw attention to myself.' She looked at him through eyes swollen with crying. 'But what of you?'

'I am well enough. But they will not leave me alone.' Mary looked questioningly at Mr Orridge, the guards standing inside the door. He cleared his throat.

'Mrs Corder, it is to ensure his safety. The men are here in case your husband takes it into his head to harm himself.'

She drew herself up proudly.

'My husband would not harm himself. He knows it for the mortal sin it is. He is a gentle soul. He is incapable.' She turned back to William, suddenly overcome with sobbing, and he moved to her side and held her. 'You must pray, William, pray to God for clemency. I know you have sinned, we all have, but to repent now will bring you to God's mercy.' They held each other closely, their tears mingling, until Mr Orridge cleared his throat.

'Mrs Corder, it is time.' She kept hold of William and Orridge laid his hand gently on her shoulder. 'Madam, if you would come with me now?' It took all her strength to step away from him. I felt it, the great wrench as she left him, watched as she staggered and nearly fell. Mr Orridge helped her out of the cell as William stood, unmoving, watched by the guards. I moved to him and took hold of his hand but I could not reach him.

THE REVEREND STOCKING CAME AGAIN, and the prayers he said seemed to soothe William a little.

'You have seen your wife, Corder?' William nodded. 'I have heard it said that parting from one's loved ones is far worse than that which you will experience tomorrow.'

William looked up.

'Do you think so, Reverend?'

'So they say. I understand your wife is a religious person?'

'She is, far more than I.'

'And she exhorts you to repent?' William nodded. 'She is right in what she says. God forgives all sinners if they are truly sorry. *He that covereth his sins shall not prosper, but whoso confesseth shall have mercy.*'

'I think my heart is hardened, Reverend, I doubt whether one as guilty as I could obtain mercy.'

The Reverend looked hard at him.

'Then confess your guilt, admit you murdered Maria Martin. That is the path to God's mercy.'

William's mind was racing, his terror growing, and I could feel him weakening, for the fear of everlasting torment was burrowing into his mind like a maggot. His eyes were glazed and he seemed not to know who was in the room.

'Confess? Is that what I must do?' He raised his eyes to the Reverend, who held up a hand as if in benediction, then snapped his fingers sharply. William, startled, looked back to see one of the guards leaving the room, returning quickly with Mr Orridge in tow.

The Reverend's voice was slow and sinuous.

'Mr Orridge, I think the prisoner is repenting of his great sins and is ready to confess.'

'Is that so, Mr Corder? Do you wish to confess to the murder of Maria Martin? We have only a few short hours before you meet your Maker. Come, man, confess, ease your conscience.'

I saw the moment he took the decision. His face twitched as the last of his control disappeared – he was broken now, alone and fearful, harried by the chaplain and the governor. So at half past eleven on the night before he was to die, his mind gone, he confessed to my murder.

EVEN THEN THEY would not leave him to sleep. It was after midnight when Mr Orridge had finished. He had summoned the Under-Sheriff to witness William's confession, and he and Reverend Stocking looked on as Orridge stopped writing.

'I need to read your confession back to you, Mr Corder, so that these men may witness it. You must state that it is true.' William could barely understand, but he nodded his head.

Mr Orridge cleared his throat.

'*I acknowledge being guilty of the death of poor Maria Martin by shooting her with a pistol. The particulars are as follows: When we left her father's house we began quarrelling about the burial of the child, she apprehending that the place wherein it was deposited would be found out. The quarrel continued for about three-quarters of an hour, upon this and other subjects. A scuffle ensued and during the scuffle, and at the time I think she had hold of me, I took the pistol from the side pocket of my velveteen jacket and fired . . .*'

I could listen no more. Mr Orridge read out the details of how William had buried me, how he dragged me by my neckerchief to the shallow grave he had dug. But, even at the last, he denied stabbing me. He told them the truth except that it was I who fired the pistol. He said it was him. It was wrong, but this confession seemed to relieve him of a huge burden and for that I was grateful.

He did not sleep that final night. He lay on his back thinking of Polstead, of his mother and family. Of his lost brothers, of friends, of his wife, and the babe yet to be born. But most of all the thought of me, of our love. He remembered those few weeks in Sudbury, awaiting the birth of our child, when we had been truly happy, and all that had happened after. The path on the way to the barn, across the fields then through the wood. I clasped his hand as he remembered our dead son, of the ripples on the pond as we had laid him to rest. And he thought of the Red Barn, the place where we had loved and lain together and made so many plans for our future – the place where I had died. He remembered it all.

CHAPTER
SEVENTY

He was brave that morning. The warder served him breakfast and he ate a little. Mr Orridge brought him his clothes and helped him change out of the prison suit and into them.

'Am I to be taken by cart to the scaffold, Mr Orridge?'

The governor cleared his throat.

'No. Bearing in mind the number of people who came to the trial I have decided that it would not be safe. And, looking at the crowds that have gathered outside already, it was the right course of action. We would never have got you through all those hordes. No, a door has been cut in the wall of the prison and the scaffold built next to it. All you will have to do is to step through that doorway. I will be there to guide you. It will be easier for you, quicker.'

William looked at his feet, now cased in his leather pumps.

'Do I have the time to write a brief letter to my wife? She will be broken-hearted.'

I did not read the letter. I could not go to him. I could only slump in the corner, my energy spent, listening to the scratching of nib on paper. Then, the sound of footsteps outside.

'It is time, Corder.'

I looked at the terror in his eyes and reached towards him but I was too weak and fell to the ground in a faint When I came to he was gone.

I COULD NOT LEAVE him at the last. From somewhere I gathered strength, and lifted myself, trembling and weak, up and out of that room, up into the sky. I soared above for a moment, looking at the blue above me, dotted with clouds of the purest white. I looked down.

There were thousands of them. People everywhere, from the very poorest sort to those in silks and carriages, thousands upon thousands of people. Every inch of the grassy slope outside the prison was covered with bodies standing, craning for a view. In the distance was a barrier, its railings heavily guarded, and, beyond this, a high wooden platform. I stared numbly, waiting for the shouts and jeers that had defined the trial, but this time the crowd was quiet, subdued.

Then, as if conjured, the wall of the prison seemed to come away. The crowd surged forward, voices rising in anticipation and I soared over their heads, to the railings. A man stepped onto the scaffold with a cap and a rope in his hands; below him, guards with staves at the ready turned out to face the crowd, alert and expectant. Then, a flash of colour at the doorway and William stood there.

I expected shouting, jeering, coarse words, but at the sight of him the men all removed their hats and a silence fell, thick as butter. I could see that William's upper arms were already bound to his sides, his hands tied in front of him. He trembled unceasingly. I watched the hangman step forward and put the cap over William's head and I saw his head move as Mr Orridge leaned in to speak to him. The governor turned to the hangman.

'Turn up the cap. The prisoner wishes to speak.'

The hangman did as he was asked and I moved so close I could smell the stale drink on his breath. I stood before William and looked at him, sending him courage. He was shaking uncontrollably and terror fired from his eyes, their centres black with fear. He steadied himself and cleared his throat.

'I am guilty. My sentence is just. He wavered, looked as if he would fall and a guard stood alongside him and supported him. 'I deserve my fate. May God have mercy on my soul.'

But his voice did not carry, the crowd could not hear him and they began to shout in anger. Mr Orridge stepped up to the railings and raised his voice, shouting as loudly as he could.

'The prisoner acknowledges his sentence to be just.'

The hangman tied the rope to the beam, pulled the cap back over William's face and placed the noose around his neck and the crowd, as one, drew a breath. I was next to him now, so close I could see the black fabric of the cap moving fast, in and out with his breathing. The guard was holding him up for he was near to collapse. I stood at his other side and searched for every ounce of strength I had left and put my face to his.

'*My only true love. Do not be afraid.*' The minister began intoning the prayer, the hangman moved forward and put his knife to the rope holding the platform, there was a sawing and clattering. It gave way and William dropped.

There was complete silence. His body swung and contorted in the summer air as he fought for breath. I gasped in horror as he raised his hands several times in anguish, unable to move his pinioned arms to help himself until, finally, the hangman moved swiftly forward and, clasping William's waist, pulled him sharply downwards, using own his weight to end his suffering.

After a few minutes hanging there, I saw a white light, pale and shimmering like water, pulling away from his earthly body and out towards the sky.

'William. I am here.'

The light moved towards me and I saw his face shyly smiling at me.

'Maria.'

He held out his hand and I clasped it and pulled him to me, our lights melding and blending until, at last, we soared as one.

EPILOGUE

I watched as they cut him down after half an hour and took his earthly remains to the Shire Hall. His clothes were removed and a surgeon opened his chest. He lay exposed like that all day whilst thousands of people filed past to see him.

They shaved his head and took plaster death masks from it. Then they took his body away to be dissected.

And me?

The stone that had marked my grave was chipped away over time by the ghoulish and the sensation-seekers until nothing remained to show my resting place.

I am no more.

You cannot find me.

All trace of me has gone, save for the wind in the trees, the ripples on the pond, and this, my story.

Think kindly of me.

I am Maria.

I am dead.

HISTORICAL NOTES

The story of Maria Martin and William Corder has been the subject of thousands of words and hundreds of entertainments, from peep and puppet shows to plays, cartoons and ballads. But in all the words written about the case, one person seems to have become lost. You can read all about William, his family, and his motivation; and plenty has been written about the Martins (especially Ann) and their background, but no one talks about the victim in all this – Maria. She is mostly portrayed as either the simple village girl, seduced by the wicked squire, or as little more than a prostitute, no better than she ought to be and therefore not worthy of consideration. Even her surname was changed. From the trial until now it is commonly spelt as 'Marten', but the birth, marriage and death records show that the family name was Martin, so that is what I have called her here.

The case continues to fascinate and horrify and, even now, nearly two hundred years later, conjecture and rumours abound. For no one knows what really happened. This book is a work of fiction, but based on as many truths as I could find. I wanted this to be

Maria's story, told from her point of view as a complex and intelligent young woman who made mistakes but ultimately just wanted to be loved and cherished. I hope I have done her justice.

Maria Martin was last seen in May 1827. Her body was discovered in April 1828 and William Corder was put on trial for her murder that August. He was hanged on 11 August 1828 at Bury St Edmunds gaol and his body was dissected, as was the law in those days. His headless skeleton eventually ended up in the Royal College of Surgeons' Huntarian Museum, used as a teaching device until a distant relative of Corder's, Linda Nessworthy, ran a successful campaign to have his remains cremated and laid to rest.

It has been suggested that William first met Mary Moore and her family on the Isle of Wight where he went for his health, under doctor's advice. He moved to London after his sojourn on the South Coast and advertised for a wife. He received over one hundred replies from interested women, including Mary. He married her on 27 November 1827, two days after she answered his advertisement. She was 31, and William was just 23.

Mary would not have known she was pregnant when William was arrested, and paying for his defence bankrupted her. After his execution, William's mother took her in and William and Mary's child, a boy she named John, was born on 16 November 1828, some three months after William's execution. John was said to have been born with a withered hand. Things were not to work out for Mary and she and her child moved out of the Corder house. In January 1835 she took William's family to court to obtain the share of his father's estate that was left to William, and which was due to her as his widow. The court case was complicated and drawn out, frustrated largely by the intransigence of William's mother and in 1837 the Bury & Norwich Post ran an appeal for help for

Mary, describing her as being *'reduced to a state of great destitution'*. When William's mother died four years later, Mary and John, now twelve, were left penniless. Some years later friends appealed in a local newspaper for funds to support her – she had been making ends meet by sewing, but was no longer able to do this because of infirmity and deafness. Mary died in 1857, aged just 61. William and Mary's son, John, became a bookseller in Colchester but died in the Essex Lunatic Asylum in 1892, aged 63.

Maria's son, Thomas Henry, continued to be cared for by her father Thomas and stepmother Ann and, in later years, worked as an agricultural labourer. The family stayed in the same cottage until 1854 when Maria's father died, aged 84. Her stepmother died four years later and Thomas Henry inherited the rented cottage. He married Isabella Woods in Polstead in 1861. They had no children. Thomas Henry died in 1887.

The Red Barn was gradually broken into pieces by souvenir hunters and was burned to the ground in 1842. Today, no trace of it remains. The site where it once stood is now part of a private house and grounds.

But William can still be found. For, at the time of writing, in the Moyse's Hall Museum in Bury St Edmunds, there are the pistols said to be his. There is a plaster death mask and a portion of his scalp, taken from his dissected body, with one ear still attached. Next to it is a small brown book. The book, an account of the Red Barn 'murder', would not normally attract much comment but for its cover.

It is bound in the skin of his back.

ACKNOWLEDGEMENTS

As always, an enormous thank you to my husband Brian for his encouragement, help and support, and for his continued belief in me.

My books would not have been the same without the cover designs by Sandy Horsley, so a very big thank you, once again, for another fabulous work of art.

Thanks as always to Charlotte at Southwold Library, who always goes the extra mile and has been so supportive of my books and to Melissa West for reading and commenting on the draft version of this book, and for her help and enthusiasm. A big shout out to Mary Torjussen, editor extraordinaire, for her encouragement and support for my book and invaluable editorial advice. I am also very grateful to Kate Bendelow, Crime Scene Investigator, for all her help and patience with my questions about the decomposition of bodies. Last but not least, another big thank you to Phil and Sonja at Small Island Digital for my wonderful website and all the tech advice!

I am so grateful to everyone who has read my books, talked about and recommended them to others, and to those who have taken the time to email me about them or write a review on Amazon and Goodreads. Thank you all! Thanks also to all those local bookshops who stock my books, especially to Steph and staff at Southwold Books, Abbie and staff at The Halesworth Bookshop, and Andrew and staff at Dial Lane Books in Ipswich, Their enthusiasm, encouragement and support have meant so much to this unknown writer.

I first read about the case of Maria Martin and William Corder when I was fifteen. It fascinated me then and I always wanted to look into it more. Now I have had the chance. As usual, my question has always been '*what if?*' and, in this book, I have tried to put a new slant on an old crime, but, as always, from the point of view of the victim. I have read all the books I could about the case, and the theories about what actually happened often seem to venture into the absurd. I am therefore indebted to Peter Maggs and his book '*Murder in the Red Barn*', (publ. Mirli Books, 2015). This is an excellent and detailed summary of the events of 1827 and 28. I highly recommend it if you'd like an in-depth account of the various theories about the case that have surfaced over the years and the events themselves. Thanks also go to Alex McWhirter at Moyse's Hall Museum for his help with the Corder archive.

I also managed to get a copy of '*An authentic and faithful history of the mysterious murder of Maria Marten, with a full development of all the extraordinary circumstances which led to the discovery of her body in the Red barn; to which is added the trial of William Corder. Taken at large in short hand specially (sic) for this work, with an account of his execution, dissection, &c.*' published in 1828 by James Curtis and republished in 1948. Curtis's account is overly dramatic, waspish, verbose (as can be seen by the title!) and highly religious but it is of its time and a fascinating, if biased, first-hand account.

I started on this journey when I visited the Moyse's Hall Museum in Bury St Edmunds. I went primarily to see their witchcraft exhibition but instead, found myself looking at a display of artefacts from the trial of William Corder. His death mask drew me, as did the small brown book beside it. Bound in the skin of his back? I just had to write about it!

About the Author

L M West lives in Suffolk with her husband. In 2020, during the first lockdown, she decided to have a go at writing a book. It was something she had always dreamed of doing and, at sixty-six, she thought she'd better get on with it! 'The Red Barn' is her fourth novel.

When she is not writing she paints, gardens, walks and reads.

For more information head over to www.lmwestwriter.co.uk

ALSO BY LM WEST

An act of revenge. An accusation of witchcraft. A reckoning.
Southwold, Suffolk, 1645. Ann has fled from her past but when her childhood tormentor finds her in a busy street, she realises that the past she thought long buried has come back to haunt her. When rumours of witchcraft begin she knows he will stop at nothing to destroy her . . .

ALSO BY L M WEST

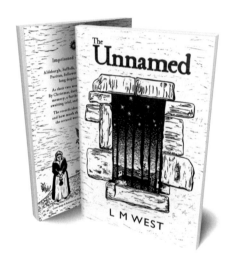

Aldeburgh, Suffolk, 1645. Mary Howldine, innkeeper, Puritan, follower of rules. Joan Wade, widow, long-despised, seized for witchcraft. As their two worlds collide the terror grows. By Christmas, during the hardest winter in living memory, a further six women are imprisoned, awaiting trial, and Mary's beliefs begin to waver. The records identify the many men involved and how much they were paid, but only two of the accused are named. This is their story.

ALSO BY LM WEST

Dunwich, Suffolk, 1615. The King's Men are performing a tale of witchcraft and ambition, murder and death. Firm friends Priscilla, Elizabeth and Aubrey, fourteen years old, watch in excitement and horror as the story unfolds. That day never leaves them.
Thirty years later they are seized, accused of witchcraft by a man who will stop at nothing to destroy them.
History has left us their confessions. This is the story of their lives.